BLOOD
AND
GUILE

Other Fiction by William Hoffman

NOVELS
The Trumpet Unblown
Days in the Yellow Leaf
A Place for My Head
The Dark Mountains
Yancey's War
A Walk to the River
A Death of Dreams
The Land That Drank the Rain
Godfires
Furors Die
Tidewater Blood

SHORT-STORY COLLECTIONS
Virginia Reels
By Land, by Sea
Follow Me Home
Doors

BLOOD AND GUILE

William Hoffman

HarperCollins*Publishers*

FIRST EDITION

Designed by Joseph Rutt

Library of Congress Cataloging-in-Publication Data

Hoffman, William
    Blood and guile : a novel / by William Hoffman.
        p. cm.
    ISBN 0-06-019794-3
        1. Male friendship—Fiction. 2. West Virginia—Fiction. I. Title.

PS3558.O34638 B58 2000
813'.54—dc21   00-055028

96 97 98 99 00 ❖/RRD 10 9 8 7 6 5 4 3 2 1

For Ben McCulloch and Bill Moore
Friends in Deed

The present works of present man—
A wild and dreamlike trade of blood and guile

—Coleridge

BLOOD
AND
GUILE

ONE

I tasted salted blood of my cut lower lip as I scrambled up from ankle-deep snow, retrieved my father's sixteen-gauge Parker side-by-side, and staggered after Drake Wingo as we climbed toward the ridge of Blind Sheep Mountain. I licked the blood and hunched my chin into my parka's fur collar.

Why am I, Walter B. Frampton II, here, I asked myself, when I could be warm and secure at my law office or apartment in Jessup's Wharf? Unlike Drake or Charles LeBlanc, I felt the urge to kill birds, deer, and bear existed only feebly in my genes. I respected the hunting tradition and the fine men who pursued it, but I would much rather have been sipping George Dickel's Tennessee Sour Mash Whisky, reading *Vanity Fair,* and listening to a Mozart quartet.

Drake had already bagged a ruffed grouse—a clean shot of the bird as it canted into hemlock shadows, which draped a dark cloak across snow. I moved obliquely through slush, the Parker heavy in my gloved fingers. Drawing hard for breath, a stitch in my side, I hurried to keep pace with long-striding Drake. Kraut, his German short-haired pointer, coursed ahead.

A shot faintly heard stopped Drake and me. He peered westward along the wooded slope. When he resumed climbing, two more shots and a laggard third—three, the agreed-upon distress signal.

"What?" Drake asked, not to me, but stared toward a gauzy stratum of meandering mist. He legged downward, and I again stumbled as I dodged fluted trunks of the great hemlocks whose drooping black-green branches released shards of snow. Drake paused and raised a hand for silence. The liver pointer stood watching and waiting for command. A slow thawing caused rivulets to run unseen beneath us. I dabbed at my lip.

Drake moved into a lope traversing the mountainside. I, following, attempted to see beyond a sea of wet, glistening laurel.

"There," he said and pointed.

The figure on the steep grade waved and bounded downward, his arms flapping, his cap gone, his camera tossed about by its neck strap—Cliff Dickens frenzied, his legs looping so high his booted feet appeared hardly to touch the ground. When he reached us, he bent over, winded and retching, and I saw the blood on his hands and hunting jacket. Where was his Beretta?

"Wendell, quick," he said.

He straightened and turned to climb back along his own tracks, his steps uneven, his body reeling, his arms swinging as if deboned. He slipped to a knee, yet rose without breaking stride. Garbled words choked his breathing, and an arm curved forward weakly to gesture us upward.

"What?" Drake asked.

For an instant Cliff slowed and looked back wildly before again flinging himself at the mountain, a drunken gait, swerving and lurching back on course. Kraut, running ahead, turned to watch.

Cliff halted, tottered, and sank to his knees at the huddled figure lying on his side in the thrashed drift. Snow melting from Wendell's body heat had diluted blood that seeped through the cashmere scarf used to stanch the wound's oozing. Wendell gazed upward from his deadpan face, his set eyes now seeing far beyond any earthly vision.

Drake knelt, laid his ear close to Wendell's mouth, and lifted away the scarf. Torn, powder-burned pieces of Wendell's Woolrich jacket and bits of a plaid shirt lodged in the imploded scarlet breach of his chest.

Drake lifted his gaze to Cliff.

"I tried carrying him," Cliff said, weaving, slumped, racked. He stared at his bloody palms and pushed his hands away as if to disown them.

"But what the hell?" Drake asked while Kraut circled wanting to sniff Wendell's body. Drake ordered the pointer to stay.

"A bird flushed," Cliff said. He sank to his knees and pushed his hands under the snow to rub off blood. "I thought Wendell was on my other side. I tried to stop the bleeding and carried him down the mountain far as I could."

"You swung into him?" Drake asked as he pushed up. He helped Cliff to his feet.

"I believed he was to my right," Cliff said. "Brought up my gun, led the bird, and fired just as Wendell stepped in front of the load."

He swayed, flung snow from his fingers, and shook his head as if to cast off memory.

Drake handed me his twelve-gauge Savage and crossed to an immature hemlock, drew his sheath knife, and hacked the blade at the slender trunk. He yanked the tree loose and arranged it alongside Wendell before rolling the body onto the boughs, causing Wendell's arms to flop and his face to find rest against a mud-smeared cheek.

"The authorities won't want him moved," I said.

"I don't want authorities screwing around on my mountain," Drake answered.

It was like him to think of possession, of Blind Sheep's being his even when confronted by the hideousness of death. He used the hemlock as a makeshift litter to begin hauling Wendell's body feet-first down toward the cabin. Kraut ran ahead, still hunting. The weight on the hemlock's branches left a streaked, orderly wake as if the snow were being harrowed in preparation for planting. I assisted as best I could, adjusting Wendell on the litter, cradling my Parker and Drake's Savage, guns I wanted to throw aside. The way down was softly treacherous. While Drake's strides continued long and sure, I took short, quick steps to slow my descent. Cliff wove his way behind us, head lolling, his body giving itself to gravity.

Melting snow dripped off the cabin's roof as well as the Bronco, the drops of water sliding from its black sides and puddling among slush. Drake released the litter to open the two-wheeled trailer's tailgate, cleared space among provisions, and nodded at me to lay down the guns and help lift Wendell.

We worked him onto the trailer. The body was still flexible, limbs dangling, the head thumping back and exposing throat. I tasted a vomit flake. Drake unfolded a shelter half and spread it over Wendell.

"We'll go to High Gap," he said and banged up the tailgate. He chained Kraut to a papaw tree as I sat in the rear of the Bronco behind Cliff in the front. Cliff worked the Nikon's strap over his head. Drake started the engine, the Bronco pitched forward and skidded sideways, and the vehicle fishtailed along the abandoned logging road, never slowing.

I thought of Wendell, a polite, quiet little man who had willingly carried more than his share of our gear up to the cabin when we first arrived and was now himself the cargo.

TWO

The Bronco's bouncing jolted me. The air seemed to have thinned, the world to have distanced itself, and I pictured Wendell's body being tossed about beneath the shelter half. Drake drove as if to punish the vehicle. His was the gift of certainty. Rawboned and wiry, he still wore his dark hair cropped and stiff in the military mode. His direct blue eyes were flecked with gold.

The Bronco drifted sideways, its tires slinging chunks of mud-soiled snow that splattered laurel and left an ugly trail. "I can't stop seeing it," Cliff said and reached to the dash to keep from tipping as the Bronco swerved.

"Just hold tight," Drake said and twisted the steering wheel. In Slash Lick Hollow he cut the wheel to miss broken remains of a split-rail fence erected many years earlier by shepherds. Wendell had said they led their sheep down from the high sod during the first snow to allow the flocks to reach low-ground pastures.

"I can't believe this happened," Ciff said.

Even during his youth Cliff had been restrained, cool, disdainful. He had become master of the arched eyebrow, and early on I had tried to model myself on him. His was a made presence during the years I had struggled to establish my own.

"It'll be okay," Drake said. A sergeant who had served three hitches in the army before mustering out, the sight of the dead had to be less stunning to him.

5

I couldn't stop myself from envisioning what the moment of Wendell's death must have been like—the hot blast of a high-brass 7½ load, the rupturing of flesh, the blood a red fountain finally draining away life like a faucet slowly closed.

The Bronco pounded along the hollow. Drake clicked on the windshield washers, and an arched brown film momentarily obscured the glass. He slowed for the turn onto the paved valley road. A plow had cleared lanes, leaving cindered snow piled high. We passed a marker: HIGH GAP 17M.

High Gap was the county seat of Seneca County, West Virginia, a town bound by ranges of steep, timbered mountains that clipped short the day's sunlight.

"I'm so sorry," Cliff said. He raised a hand, which dropped like a fallen bird.

"What you learn is that when it's done, it's done," Drake said. Curved forward over the wheel, he kept glancing at Cliff. "Just get your story straight."

"Story?" Cliff asked and lifted his face.

"What you tell the law. He'll need to make a statement, won't he, Raff?"

"He will," I said.

"A grouse flushed, you fired swinging into Wendell, nothing more, right?" Drake asked Cliff.

For a second their eyes met and held. Then Cliff turned away and nodded. He touched his temple with long, artistic fingers that trembled.

We passed the first dwellings, a few sided with tar paper patterned like brick. Firewood had been stacked on porches, smoke rose from chimneys, and dogs barked, their voices nearly silent in the Bronco's rattling interior. The mountains' outcropping of gray boulders broke the pall of snow.

"Just an accident, nothing more," Drake said. He drove well, pushing the edge of recklessness.

"I'm due in classes Monday," Cliff said.

"The college will surely allow you time off," I said.

"So damn sorry."

Drake stopped at a Marathon gas station to ask where to find the sheriff. The attendant pointed us on along the street to the concrete courthouse that appeared squatly massive relative to the size of all structures around it, bullying its neighbors with the majesty of the law. A rectangle of lawn held a rusted cannon and a flagpole.

Drake turned in at a street beyond the courthouse where at the rear the "Sheriff's Department" sign hung over the doorway of a one-story, flat-roofed brick addition.

"Wait till I see what's what," he said and sidled from the Bronco. His boots crushed slush.

"Is this going to be bad?" Cliff asked without facing me.

"Just a procedure," I answered and hoped that would be all.

Drake returned with the sheriff, not a grizzled, potbellied lifer, but young, no more than his middle thirties, his tan uniform sharply pressed, his trooper's hat set slightly cocked. As Drake walked him to the trailer to unlatch the tailgate, I stepped from the Bronco. The fair and lightly freckled sheriff flipped the shelter half from the body and leaned forward to lay fingers against Wendell's jugular. He uncovered the clotted wound.

"You shouldn't have moved him," he said.

"His hunting partner tried to get him down," Drake said. "Panic time."

"You the one?" the sheriff asked me.

"No, Mr. Dickens is in the Bronco," I said.

The sheriff walked to the passenger side and opened the door.

"You did the shooting?" he asked, his accent just a touch hillbilly, the words partially filtered through his nose.

Cliff nodded, his head bowed.

"We'll carry the body to the coroner," the sheriff said. "You men follow my car."

The sheriff walked back to the building. A uniformed deputy had pushed open the storm door and stood watching. The sheriff spoke, zipped his leather jacket, and reset his hat.

Drake banged up the tailgate. He pulled out after the black Dodge cruiser that had a rack of blue-and-yellow lights bolted to its roof. Drake stayed well back to keep his windshield clean. Three crows pecking at a flattened vestige of roadkill flapped aside and settled back after we passed to continue feeding.

THREE

The Seneca County Free Clinic was a white vinyl-sided building leveled partway up the mountainside. Drake parked on a graveled lot at the front. An artificial holly wreath that hung from a hook screwed into the door looked as if it had been in place many seasons.

The bald, elderly doctor lay snoozing on the stainless-steel examination table. A stout and dark-skinned nurse whispered questions to the sheriff before gently shaking the doctor.

He rose patting himself as if to make certain he was all of a piece. When he couldn't locate his glasses, the nurse searched for and discovered them on a shelf among stacked rolls of tape, gauze, and bandages. The elbows of his brown sweater had been reinforced with chamois patches. He worked his feet into arctics as the nurse pulled on galoshes, and the two of them walked out to the trailer. The doctor's gray pants drooped around his skinny loins. He had not bothered to buckle his arctics, which flapped.

The nurse held a clipboard and pencil tied to it by twine. Cliff stayed in the Bronco while Drake opened the trailer's tailgate. The sheriff uncovered Wendell and helped the doctor knee up inside to lay his stethoscope over Wendell's heart. The doctor's hands were palsied, and he grunted. Just holding on he was—to anything within his feeble grasp.

"All cessation of bodily functions," he dictated to the nurse, his voice rickety. "Tentative evaluation death caused by gunshot wound to the lower anterior chest cavity and upper abdomen."

The nurse checked it off on an official form and walked back inside to bring out a collapsible canvas stretcher, which she unfolded. The sheriff and Drake helped her with the body. I held the door as they carried Wendell into the building and positioned the stretcher on the examination table.

The nurse fingered Wendell's wallet from the hip pocket of his rigid new hunting britches. She drew out his driver's license, studied it, and copied information before she and the doctor began removing Wendell's clothes. When a telephone rang, the nurse answered it.

"Roof fall at the Black Eagle," she told the doctor.

"Don't it ever stop?" he asked and hastily washed his hands above the sink and again stepped into his arctics while the nurse reached him his overcoat and near shapeless fedora. Bag in hand, he listed out the door to a Chevy 4x4. At the wheel, he started the engine and, exhaust steaming, drove the pickup in winding fashion down the mountainside to the main street.

"I'll get back to you, Linda Belle," the sheriff told the nurse after he emptied Wendell's pockets of change, keys, coins, and a small wooden cross that had what looked like a tiny eye carved into the top of the upright timber. He also took Wendell's wallet.

"Won't that be a blessing," she answered.

He gave her a tight smile and we left.

"Once Old Doc Bailey was a young fellow fresh out of med school who could've practiced in Charleston or Huntington and made big money," the sheriff said. "He had this idea about serving humanity. Well, humanity's about damn near run him to death."

We drove back into the shadowed valley and to the Sheriff's Department. The white walls and green linoleum floor were brightly illuminated by overhead fluorescent tubes. He led us along a corridor and into an office equipped with a metal desk, folding chairs, and a rack of rifles and shotguns chained in place through their trigger guards. His nameplate read: *Bruce B. Sawyers.*

Coils of an electric heater glowed. Walls held tacked-up men-wanted posters, a calendar from the Appalachian Bank, and a yellow handbill listing the game schedule of the West Virginia Mountaineers football team.

"Sit," he said, indicating chairs at the front and one side of his desk. He slipped off his leather jacket and hung it along with his hat on deer antlers attached to the wall. From a drawer he lifted a mimeographed form, and from his shirt pocket he drew a white plastic ballpoint pen. "Light'em if you got'em."

Set on a black iron safe behind him I glimpsed the picture of a soldier dressed in battle fatigues and holding an M-16. He appeared more boy than man. Drake also eyed the photograph.

"Yep, that's me way back," the sheriff said. "Lied about my age. Only job I could find those days. You all in?"

"Three hitches and an education," Drake said.

"One not taught in books," the sheriff said and hunched his chair closer to the desk, studied the form, and held his pen ready. "First thing is who should be notified. You done any of that?"

"Not yet," Drake said.

"Wife, next of kin, family, somebody's got to be told," the sheriff said. He shuffled the driver's license and other cards from Wendell's wallet, the leather slightly curved from its fit to Wendell's hip.

"I'd like to help you, Sheriff," I said, "but all I know about the deceased was that he managed a food store in Richmond as well as owned the land we hunted on."

"He had a wife, but she died off," Drake said. He pushed back his blaze orange cap and scratched his cropped hair. A sliver of scalp shone through.

"Any children?" the sheriff asked.

"Not I heard of," Drake said.

"Brothers, sisters, anybody?"

Drake and I shook our heads. Cliff looked at his drooping hands, his wrists supported by his knees.

"Which of you knew him best?" the sheriff asked. His slate-colored eyes had penetration. He would need to be smart, I thought, to survive in this rough and tough country.

"Guess that's me since I brought him along but I never knew him close," Drake said. "More like a business relationship."

"I need a name and number, though I already overspent the phone budget. Cut me to four deputies and a jailer. I'm filing to run for the legislature next term. None of you can come up with further identification?"

"You could call somebody at his store," Drake said. "They'd pass the word."

"Okay," the sheriff said. "I'll turn it over to the Virginia State Police and let them handle it. What's the name of the store?"

"Food," Drake said.

"Full name?"

"That's it. FOOD."

"Some name. You got a number?"

"No, just Richmond town."

The sheriff lifted the phone, dialed, and leaned back. He knew the trooper at the other end and traded small talk before listing details. "Shoot me any feedback," he said. "And my good hello to Captain Harvey."

He collected Wendell's wallet and pocket contents, dropped them into a manila envelope, and set the envelope in the desk drawer along with the mimeographed sheet. He locked the drawer before standing and reaching for his jacket.

"What say we do a look-see at your camp?" he asked, zipping the jacket and setting on his hat. "I'll trail you in my vehicle."

We drove away in the Bronco. Cliff appeared aged and bled. I glanced back to see the sheriff following in the Dodge. Each jolt of the road whipped its three antennas.

We reached the turnoff from the county road, bounced along Slash Lick Hollow, and Drake geared to four-wheel to begin the climb up the logging road. The sheriff honked, leaned from his window, and shouted. He wanted to leave the Dodge for a ride with us.

At the cabin Drake let Kraut loose, and the pointer dashed around till brought to heel. Cliff proceeded us up the mountain, his stride jarring him as if his legs had become brittle. The fragile warming continued the slow melt, the rivulets finding channels of Blind Sheep's descent. Hemlock boughs freed of snow's weight sprang upward.

We reached the drift where Cliff had let down Wendell's body. Sheriff Sawyers circled it, and voice lowered, he fed details into a hand-sized recorder held left of his mouth.

"Stay wide around this place," he directed us. From a breast pocket of his uniform shirt he slipped a small, flat camera, a Canon. He snapped pictures and worked a broken branch of a spruce pine into the ground to mark the drift's location.

We climbed on until we reached the bloodied snow. The sheriff stepped forward alone, spoke into his recorder, hunkered, rose, and backed off. He located the over-and-under Beretta Cliff had borrowed from Drake, the shotgun apparently hurled aside, and then Wendell's Remington automatic. He didn't touch them. The guns had sunk into snow.

"Leave them lie," he ordered Drake, who had started toward the Remington. Death hadn't blunted Drake's concern for guns.

"They'll rust," he said as he drew back, startled by the sheriff's tone of command.

"The department will tag and care for them," the sheriff said and faced Cliff. "Where'd your bird flush?"

Cliff had been waiting submissively, his face partially turned away. He pointed to a laurel thicket, the dark green tubular leaves cautiously unfolding to warmth. The sheriff crossed to the laurel to scan the ground.

"No bird tracks," he said into the recorder. He was definitely no hick lawman but a professional performing a meticulous investigation.

"They could've melted," Drake said.

"You swung around left to shoot?" the sheriff asked, ignoring Drake.

"It happened so fast," Cliff said.

"Wendell Ripley could've lunged past in a rush to get in a shot," Drake said.

"A could've," the sheriff said. He definitely did not care for Drake offering explanations and dictated further hushed observations, made a penciled diagram on the page of a pocket-size notebook, and again reached for the Canon. The shutter gave off precisely engineered clicks. Lastly he grouped us and snapped our picture.

"I want full names, addresses, and phone numbers," he said and wrote them in the notebook. He also asked us to show our drivers' licenses and checked our hunting permits.

"For now that'll do but you fellows stay away from this place. I'll be back with deputies and know if the scene's been compromised."

He pulled out a Buck knife, thumbed the blade open, and cut laurel sprigs he stuck in the soil to identify the area.

We hiked down to the cabin Drake had built a year ago on land leased from Wendell. Drake had chosen a bench of the mountain below the ridge, a southern exposure that used Blind Sheep itself to block the northern shriekers, which, he claimed, blew so hard they would rip the hair off a bobcat's back.

The cabin was a rectangular plank dwelling that appeared raw instead of fully weathered to the blending that nature demanded. Drake had considered restoring the shepherd's cottage on the high sod, but the roof and supporting beams had rotted and the stones fallen in upon themselves.

To the west of the cabin ran Wolf Creek, its origin mossy seepages high on Blind Sheep that fed upon themselves till they grew and gorged downward. By the time they reached the valley they had joined to become the Wilderness River, a torrent that had carved a chasm and smashed itself against boulders, the violent water grinding them over centuries to sand and sending waves to shore that created a beach and ocean clamor hundreds of miles and thousands of feet above the sea.

Sheriff Sawyers snapped pictures of the cabin and fitted the camera into his shirt pocket before looking hard at each of us as if to set our faces in his mind.

"I know all of you are from out of state but like you to stick around a few days," he said.

"Are you telling us we can't leave?" I asked.

"You're a lawyer," he said.

"I am," I answered. He had apparently sighted my Virginia Bar Association membership card when I took out my driver's license.

"Not can't," he said. "Just a request. How about a ride to my car?"

"I'll do that thing," Drake said. "You a hunter?"

"I've been known to bring meat to the table," the sheriff said.

"Knew you were a hunter," Drake said.

FOUR

I watched Drake lay out the grouse he had killed earlier, placing it on a red-oak stump he used as a chopping block beside ice-bordered Wolf Creek. Spray from the stream had laid droplets that gleamed over ferns along the bank.

"We're about ready," I told him.

"As soon as I finish," he said and with a single short chop of his ax decapitated the plucked bird. He tossed the head to Kraut and knelt by the creek to shuck out the heart and snaky red entrails. He held the grouse positioned so that the fast flow washed and emptied its body cavity.

I crossed back to the cabin to help Cliff carry his gear. He moved like a man disoriented. When I started to lift my bag into the trailer, I drew away from Wendell's dried blood that spotted the floorboard planks. I wiped them with a sheet of snow-wetted newspaper and dropped it on fireplace embers, where it drew into itself, flared, and quivered like a black winged creature expiring.

Cliff waited at the Bronco. Drake wrapped aluminum foil around the grouse before packing it with scooped-up snow in his Coleman cooler. He set the fire screen, pulled shut the cabin door, and snapped the heavy padlock through the hasp. Kraut he allowed onto the seat beside me. The dog gave me a friendly sniff and curled himself until he found comfort. No visions of the dead on his canine mind.

Drake drove off Blind Sheep and along Slash Lick to the junction where he turned south for our descent from the high country, crossed the Virginia line to Monterey, and rolled us over Whiskey Creek to Staunton, where we picked up Interstate 64 that would carry us to Richmond.

We had left our cars at Drake's house in Midlothian, west of the city. His two-story Georgian sat above a lawn shaded in seasonal weather by towering yellow poplars, their leaves now torn away by the winter's winds.

Drake had married a lovely, cultured woman named Deborah, whose first husband died of a brain hemorrhage that sent him reeling into and spilling golf trophies off the shelves of his den. A corporate attorney, he had left her a large estate as well as their twin children. She was now three months pregnant, and Drake had thrown an Indian summer cocktail party that spread over the garden and lawn to celebrate what he called his potency.

He and I helped transfer Cliff's gear to his Thunderbird. The car had a numbered decal on the rear window that entitled him to faculty parking rights at Virginia Commonwealth University.

"Stay tonight with Deb and me," Drake offered him.

"I'll be okay," Cliff said, straightening and brushing back his lank off-blond hair as well as struggling to regain poise.

While I loaded my suitcase into my Buick, they stood talking. Drake laid a hand on Cliff's shoulder, and Cliff gave slightly beneath it.

"I'll check on you later," Drake said.

"And I'll follow you in," I said to Cliff.

"I'm able to handle it," he answered.

Drake held the Thunderbird's door for Cliff, and we watched him back out, turn, and drive along the suburban street overarched by the massive bare branches of ancient elms and white oaks.

"What can we do?" I asked.

"I'll keep watch on him. Come in for a sandwich or drink?"

"I think I better move on."

"One hell of a hunt," he said.

"Poor little man, Wendell."

"When you're dead, you're not poor, just gone."

That was Drake, the attitude he had come back with from his army service. I drove away, a seventy-minute trip east to King County's Jessup's Wharf. Laughing gulls, their plumage in gray-and-white winter phase, perched on the rusting iron bridge over the tidal Axapomimi River. They had splattered the railings and faced into the wind like feathered vanes.

I stopped by my office to check messages. Oh, the sweet flow of dollars after the lean years at Jessup's Wharf, a place I had set out my shingle as a last resort. The money was partly the result of the explosion at Bellerive Plantation some four years earlier that had caused the death of John Maupin LeBlanc III and his family as well as an aged servant named Gaius.

Charles LeBlanc, John's younger brother, had been suspected of their murder, become a fugitive, and I had defended him—at first with great reluctance. After his exoneration I had sued on his behalf a life-insurance company that had been withholding payment, collected two hundred and eighty-nine thousand dollars, and administered that money for Charles, who now lived in Montana.

Moreover, he would be receiving half a million a year for seven years from the sale of Bellerive to an Arab prince named Jamir. Edward, the third LeBlanc brother, had very generously agreed to split the proceeds, the first payment of which I expected to receive in Charles's behalf any day. Three and a half million for my client, who shortly before had been a derelict. My hands on my lap beyond Edward's sight had clenched and released when he, in his precise, solemn voice, had explained the transaction.

Though I would not leave my archaic Victorian apartment at Miss Mabel Tascott's, I had moved my office over from the narrow nineteenth-century brick building once owned by a doctor who made braces for children's crippled legs. The space I leased was on the ground floor of Jessup's Wharf's River Street, the two rooms repainted, carpets installed, the electricity rewired. I now had a lavatory as well as a reception area for clients. Would I lay my copies of *Vanity Fair* on a table for them to scan along with the *Reader's Digest* and perhaps *The Farmer's Almanac*?

Behind my desk I planned to rehang my three-by-five-foot portrait of uniformed Marse Robert that I had owned since graduating from Washington and Lee. I belonged to the Society of the Lees, an organization that required proof of blood kinship as a condition for membership, and felt his unswerving gaze warded off any temptation to compromise the standards I aspired to. The revisionists were attempting to bring the general down, but in my mind he continued to stand for honor, devotion, and valor. The latter, the real test of a man, had become particularly important to me because in truth I was still uncertain of my own.

I strove to appear sober and dignified in the practice of law and felt guilt and remorse that while my life was changing so much for the better, Cliff's had been devastated by what had happened to him on our Blind Sheep grouse shoot.

FIVE

Wendell Ripley's name appeared in the obituary column of Tuesday's *Times-Dispatch*, the cause of death given as a hunting accident. The stark, two-sentence announcement listed no next of kin, funeral service, or advice as to where to send condolences.

I had worked hauling law books and files from my old office to the new one, which had been a bakery before I contracted to have it remodeled. A faint odor of bread still hung around, embedded in walls and floors. On a shelf at the rear I discovered half a dozen loaf trays gathering dust, one holding a moldy, desiccated mouse. I had arranged to have my name painted in gilt letters over the broad window that gave out onto the King County Bank's Colonial headquarters and the white steeple of St. Luke's Church beyond.

Friday morning as I left Miss Mabel's house to walk to the office, my phone's ringing drew me back. I recognized Cliff Dickens's voice.

"I'd like to drive over at a time convenient to you," he said.

"You bearing up?" I asked.

"I've managed to hold it together. May I come?"

"You know you can. I'm on River Street now, across from the bank."

"I ought to reach your lair by eleven."

His voice, which had shed most of his Southern accent, sounded cool and in control as of old, and I was not surprised. During our years together at John Marshall High, he had twice won the Best Actor award. Because of his talent the Dramatic Club had dared attempt *Hamlet*, a production that turned out to be a near calamity except when Cliff spoke the soliloquies. Then a rowdy young audience quieted, and some of the girls' expressions became touched by something like sexual rapture.

He remained the best student among the Marauders, a gang the membership of which consisted of Drake Wingo, Cliff, and me. We had a secret handshake and in a shack built from scrap lumber behind Drake's parents' house took a blood oath by candlelight, using the single-edge Gillette blade to cut our left thumbs and touching them so that our bloods united. Cliff supplied a motto: *nunquam trado*, which meant never betray. He excelled in Latin.

Cliff grew up the best looking among us, five eleven, that lank off-blond hair frequently tossed both for control and effect, about him an easy physicality that never seemed hurried or baffled. He made the varsity basketball squad while Drake was second team and often benched. I too tried out for the team but quit when I realized as I loped back and forth along the court I appeared comically ridiculous.

After graduating from John Marshall, we three began to drift. For his college, Drake chose Virginia Tech, Cliff the University, I Washington and Lee. Drake dropped out after a single semester, not because he faced failure but believed all he was receiving was what he called a trainload of bull crap. He joined the army.

Cliff's grades and all-around talent had won him a scholarship. He acted in plays and became almost as theatrical offstage as on, often striding about wearing a full-flowing coat draped around his shoulders, a long scarf, and a black beret aslant his left brow. Deep thinking seemed to rack his face. He made everyday actions like the purchase of cigarettes or the dropping off of his laundry appear to be a venture of importance that demanded profound attention.

After he graduated from the University he entered Yale, where he studied drama and intended to become a playwright as well as a novelist. The few times I saw him during those years, he was so occupied we little more than shook hands and drank a beer or two together. He did most of the talking.

Lately he had taught at VCU, gotten into photography, and had some of his work featured in a daring exhibition of male nudes that shocked Richmond's gentry. Letters received by the *Times-Dispatch* demanded that the show be closed. Cliff had enjoyed the notoriety, assuming that nothing the general public approved of could have lasting value.

"And good for sales," he said. "Let the mossbacks writhe in their piety."

At five minutes after eleven I glanced from the office window and saw his Thunderbird pull to the curb. The car's sides had become crusted with chemicals road crews had spread to melt snow. He lifted out a 35mm camera before locking the door and drawing on his Austrian toggle coat. He adjusted his plaid touring cap.

I met him at my door. Other than lines of weariness, he appeared almost his usual self—detached and suffering boredom.

"Well, you must be rising in the world, Walter," he said. He never called me Raff any longer, a thoughtfulness I appreciated. His eyes stopped at the picture of General Robert E. Lee, and his mocking smile reasserted itself.

"It's good to know some things in this old world never change," he said.

When I positioned a chair for him in front of my desk, he sat with a tragic sort of grace—the scene played of a man badly used. As he unfastened his coat, I crossed around the desk.

"I'm not certain whether you're insulting me or not, but I'm glad to see you, Cliff, and hope all things in your life are looking up."

"Things are becoming tolerable, as we say out on the farm. I believe I slept as much as three hours last night without waking and having to blot out certain hideous displays which attempted to invade my consciousness."

"I know you've suffered."

"I doubt you know fully, but thanks, Walter. I'm happy to see some people doing well, I mean in particular my comrades of old, you and Drake."

He was referring with the latter to "The Truth of the Grouse," a pamphlet Drake Wingo had originally given away free off the counter at Grizzly's, his sporting goods outlet. A reporter for the *Times-Dispatch* wrote an article about the pamphlet, and local bookstores started peddling the tract, each copy autographed by Drake in his bold hand. Then the paper published an interview, causing sales to increase enough to justify a second printing. Drake was invited to speak before the Rotarians.

"I've been trying for years to write only to have one story published in a magazine now defunct," Cliff said. "An ironical development, don't you think?"

I had read that story in the quarterly named *Now.* A man living in a one-room tenement stares through smudged windowpanes over roofs which have steam rising from cast-iron pipes. He sees nightmarish shapes form among the steam. Why he is looking or his identity is never explained. Frenzied fish attack and swallow each other, white snakes coil, hiss, and strike. The man's vision ends when he turns away and pours coffee grains swirling down the kitchen sink.

"Did you bring that camera to snap my picture?" I asked, evading the subject because I had detected envy.

"Not long ago I saw a man do a swan dive from the seventh story of a hotel, and I had no camera with me. Now I try never to be without. Nights I keep at least one loaded alongside the Seconal on my bedside table."

He opened his coat over a red sweater. I offered him a Winston, though I knew he had stopped smoking as had most of my friends. I limited myself to ten cigarettes a day.

"I attended Wendell Ripley's funeral," he said. "I'd been trying to get in touch with his family to express *mea culpa* and my contrition. First I drove to FOOD, where he worked. What originality for a store name. I found a handwritten sign taped to the door announcing the place was closed for the burial. Also displayed was a drawn map and directions to the cemetery. When I arrived, pallbearers were lowering his wooden casket into the ground."

I leaned back, smoked, waited. If he needed to talk, pour it out, I would give him all my time he wanted.

"A commune cemetery," he said.

"You mean commune in the present meaning of that word?"

"Out in the wilds of Chesterfield County—three long barracks, sheds, farm buildings, barns for hay and dairy cows, a simple frame church, and fields where they grow vegetables. There must have been a hundred or more people in attendance. I tried to locate family members among the crowd but found no central group of mourners, so I questioned a man standing beside me, who turned out to be an employee at the store. He said they were all Wendell's family. Apparently he meant all members of the commune, at least that's my take on it. Obviously Wendell was respected and loved. I'd not been able to make much of a judgment about him at the camp, he was so nearly mute and unobtrusive."

"I was surprised Drake invited him along."

"Wendell owned the land we hunted, and because of the grouse plenty, Drake hungered to buy it."

He laid his cap across his lap and tossed his hair, the familiar gesture I had seen many times as far back as our boyhood.

"I never thought I'd ever kill anybody," he said.

"Just a terrible break, Cliff. It could have happened to any of us."

"I've never cared to hunt. A damn fool thing for me to agree to. These Virginians and their guns."

"Let's cross over to the Dew Drop Inn for a beer and sandwich."

"Actually, Walter, I'm here to ask your advice. Sheriff Sawyers of High Gap has knocked on my door."

I visualized the neat, efficient sheriff with the slate-gray eyes.

"Early this morning," Cliff said. "While I was still in my 'jamas and brewing coffee. Invited me to come back to the highlands for a visit."

"He traveled all the way to Richmond to do that?"

"The man claimed he just happened to be in the vicinity—he and his wife passing through on a vacation to Williamsburg. He told me it would be a help in completing his report, that there were details that needed to be precisely delineated. It's the expression he used, 'precisely delineated.' Fancy talk from the Appalachians, don't you think?"

"Are you going back?"

"I asked whether it was necessary. He said he was merely requesting cooperation and that the county would pay mileage and put me up a night. I told him I'd think it over. The question is, should I make the trip?"

"He likely wants to depose you for the record, though I understand your not wanting to face that scene a second time."

"I don't know anybody in West Virginia. I've really never cared that much for mountains but all my life have been drawn to the sea. I sense he's up to more than he's revealed. Any chance I might become entangled in some interstate legal complication?"

"My first inclination is to think not."

"Still, with your permission, I'll notify him he's to deal with you, assuming you'll agree to represent me. I mean on a paying basis."

"I will, though I don't foresee more than some inconvenience since hunting accidents rarely involve a charge."

"I'd feel better if I can tell him to refer any questions he has to you and then you instruct me how to respond."

"Will do," I said. "You'd never met Wendell till we went on the hunt, had you?"

"I'd never seen him, though I had heard of FOOD. He was the store manager. You require a retainer now? I brought my check-book."

"No. You want lunch?"

"I have no appetite for food. For days I've been living off cottage cheese, Ritz crackers, and deep fulfilling drafts of Dewar's Scotch uncut by water or soda."

SIX

Tuesday morning was too windy and cold for a walk downtown. Before entering the office, I heard the whistle and chimes of saw blades starting up at Axapomimi Lumber. A flight of pigeons, their wings swishing the air, swept over on their way to feed under the loading docks at the Southern States Co-op.

Jessup's Wharf was a Tidewater town centered around the brick courthouse, the drug and general stores, the doctor's and another lawyer's offices, the moldering warehouses, two churches for whites, one for blacks, the sawmill, the Dew Drop Inn, and the King County Bank.

I unlocked my office door, hung up my coat, and switched on the coffeemaker. As I sat at my desk and checked my calender, the phone jangled.

"Sawyers, Mr. Frampton," the caller said. "Bruce B. Sawyers, Sheriff, Seneca County, West Virginia. If you're going to be at your office, I'd like to schedule a visit. Can reach your place by mid-morning."

"Where are you, Sheriff?"

"My wife and I been seeing the sights in Jamestown. According to my map, that's not far from where you hang your hat."

"Come on, Sheriff."

So Sawyers was still around. I sat wondering as I looked out the window and across to St. Luke's steeple poking into a winter sky bled of color.

At five minutes before ten, Sheriff Bruce B. Sawyers arrived not in the black Dodge police cruiser with its whipping antennas but driving a white Camry. He had left his uniform behind and unbuttoned a gray overcoat over a blue pinstripe suit that fitted nicely. His red hair appeared freshly barbered.

"Pleasure to have you in King County, Sheriff," I said, standing to shake his hand. Mary Ellen Cartwright, my secretary, had greeted and shown him in. We sat.

"It's always nice to visit Virginia. There's so much history I need to read up on it again back home to sort it all out. You people been good to me this trip. Left Annie, my wife, at an antique show. She's crazy for an old wardrobe. Hard on a man's wallet."

"Yours a working vacation?"

"Might as well get two for one, don't you think?"

"How can I help you, Sheriff?"

"Mr. Clifford Dickens tells me you represent him and has advised me I'm to speak with you about him returning to Seneca County." He drew his notebook from an inside pocket of his jacket. "Be a big help to us in High Gap if he'd assist us in binding up the loose ends in regard to events that happened during your Blind Sheep hunt."

"It seems you could depose him here in Virginia just as well."

"Could but be better to have him back. Depositions hardly ever get to all the facts. The county will pay his mileage and meals. Also bed and board him if necessary."

"Sheriff, it's natural Mr. Dickens doesn't want to go back. He was greatly affected by Mr. Wendell Ripley's death. Just take his sworn statement, and Mr. Dickens will fully and truthfully answer all your questions."

"Maybe so, and you too might be able give me a few answers. Not as his attorney but as a party on the hunt. Mr. Wingo told me you all met at his house and drove up together in his Bronco."

"I wasn't aware you had questioned Mr. Wingo."

"I talked to him like I am to you right now." The sheriff brought out his micro-recorder and set it on my desk. "You object if I copy what's spoken here?"

"I might, and if so, I'll ask you to switch it off."

"Fair enough. Just trying to fit the pieces. So let's start with the four of you leaving Richmond to go on a shoot."

"We left Thursday at noon. It is approximately a four-and-a-half-hour drive to the Blind Sheep camp. Our plan was to hunt all day Friday and Saturday and return Sunday."

"What'd you do when you reached the camp?"

"Lit a fire, laid out sleeping bags on bunks, cut cards to see who would cook and do dishes that night. The second night low guns were to catch KP."

"Low guns?"

"The two who came in with the least grouse kill. We also cut cards to pair up for the hunt."

"Okay, go ahead."

"We ate steaks, fried potatoes, and collards plus a French apple pie sent by Mr. Wingo's wife. We then made our plans for the next morning, banked the fire, and sacked in."

The sheriff turned a page of his notebook.

"This Wendell Ripley, you knew him well?"

"I had never met him till I shook his hand at Mr. Wingo's house on Thursday."

"That's what Mr. Clifford Dickens stated. And Mr. Wingo has also said he knew Mr. Ripley only as a customer. Why was Mr. Ripley along with you?"

"Mr. Wingo wanted to purchase from Mr. Ripley the land he leased for the camp and hoped to make a deal during the hunt."

Sheriff Sawyers checked his notebook. Something had disturbed the pigeons, causing them to flap out from under the eaves at St. Luke's.

"What did you think of Mr. Ripley?" the sheriff asked.

"He was quiet, helpful, rarely spoke until spoken to, did camp chores willingly."

"Nothing out of line? Fit in with you other three just fine?"

"We were hardly there time enough to establish much of a relationship. Mr. Dickens, Mr. Wingo, and I are longtime friends. For us it was a reunion of sorts. The three of us hadn't gotten together for several years."

"None of you seems to have much information about Mr. Ripley. Think he knew anything about hunting?"

"As far as I could tell he handled his shotgun well. I saw him checking it the morning of the hunt."

"You all owned guns?"

"No, Mr. Dickens borrowed the Beretta from Mr. Wingo."

"Everybody checked his shotgun and ammo before setting out?"

"As Mr. Wingo reminded us to do."

"What other instructions did Mr. Wingo give?"

"He showed us on topographical maps the territory to be covered. Mr. Wingo and I were to hunt east of Wolf Creek, a stream that runs through the camp area."

"I know Wolf Creek."

"Mr. Dickens and Mr. Ripley were assigned the area west of Wolf. Mr. Wingo supplied maps and compasses to keep us from becoming lost. We loaded up and separated in pairs."

"You remmber that Mr. Dickens stated in my office that Mr. Ripley was on his right side as Mr. Dickens brought up his gun, swung on the bird, and fired just when Mr. Ripley lunged left in front of the load?"

The phone rang. Mary Ellen in the outer office answered it. She tapped on the door.

"Taking calls?" she asked.

"Not at the moment," I said, and she withdrew.

"You're questioning his statement?" I asked the sheriff.

"I'm trying to get it exactly right in my mind."

"How about turning off the recorder?"

"Glad to oblige." He thumbed the switch. "Now, I been out to the scene a couple of times, and the way I recreate events by examining the tracks, Mr. Ripley wasn't to Mr. Dickens's right but following a step or so behind and below him on the slope. He was shot primarily in the lower chest and upper abdomen. Mr. Dickens was standing higher than Mr. Ripley on the slope. He would've needed to discharge his weapon with its muzzle at an angle of decline."

"A low-flying bird."

"The laurel thicket where he reported the bird flushed was to Mr. Dickens's left as he climbed. If he'd swung in that direction, it would've been high away from Mr. Ripley. And it would've taken some lunge to get up in front of the load."

"Mr. Dickens said he believed Mr. Ripley was to his right. Mr. Ripley could have shifted without Mr. Dickens being aware of it."

"No sign a bird got up."

His eyes fixed me as he waited.

"Sheriff, memory at such moments can easily be disordered. Moreover the snow was already soft and might have melted any grouse tracks by the time you reached them."

"Mr. Dickens stated that the bird was at the edge of that laurel thicket. The likely flight would've been up and over toward the hemlocks, not down along the slope."

"My understanding is that grouse are completely unpredictable in flight, a factor that makes them such excellent sport."

"That's true, but at that slope's angle any grouse on the ground to the side where Mr. Dickens stated the bird flushed would've likely been more elevated than Mr. Ripley's chest and abdomen."

"Likely is a slippery word, Sheriff. I don't think you could know without being there."

"I don't think I could either. Still it's a question to be answered, and we in Seneca County would appreciate you recommending to

Mr. Dickens he return to help us clear up any possible contradictions and close the book on the killing."

"Killing. It sounds as if you might be preparing a case."

"I repeat I'm just trying to put it all together."

"And I believe a deposition would meet that requirement."

"Meaning you won't advise Mr. Dickens to come back?"

"If he finds doing so objectionable, not as things stand now."

Those penetrating eyes took me in before he stood and slid the notebook and micro-recorder into his pocket.

"Nice of you to see me," he said.

I walked him to the door as he buttoned his overcoat. Definitely no hillbilly sheriff he, but a police officer who might speak with a nasal twang, yet who used the language well. My sense of our conversation was that he knew more than he had revealed. He was truly, as Drake had observed, a hunter.

SEVEN

My first thought was to talk with Drake. When I phoned him at Grizzly's, his chief clerk, nicknamed Boomer, told me that Drake had left town and would not be back in the store till Monday.

Saturday morning to my delight I received a call from Josey Lynn. She wanted to see Bellerive.

"I'm on my way," she said.

"I'll be at Miss Mabel's," I said.

"Just your style," she said, another cutting remark in reference to her belief that I lived far behind the times. Miss Mabel was an aged spinster, her father a county judge who had left her the three-story house with pointed gables and the wraparound porch.

I phoned Bellerive to ask permission.

"Please as to wait," a man's voice I didn't recognize said. It sounded foreign with an emphasis on his *S*s. He returned. "The prince wishes to inform you that you are welcome and apologizes that the house is not yet open for inspection. You are to enjoy freedom of the grounds."

I buttoned on the chamois shirt and laced up the Bean boots I had bought for the Blind Sheep hunt. The day had dawned warmer, and goldfinches pitched down to Miss Mabel's sundial and pecked around her dormant peonies. The warmth felt as if the earth had been released and again breathed.

Josey arrived in her Lexus and veered fast around the circular drive before the house, braked hard, causing her radials to skid across the moist ground. Miss Mabel would disapprove of tire tracks.

I gathered myself, intending not to show too great a happiness in Josey's presence. Because she still continued to swim three times a week, she wore her coppery hair cut short and needed no padded shoulders as her freestyle crawl had muscled and broadened hers. Mounted on her office wall was her Sweet Briar field hockey stick, a statement she led a sporting life. Josey to me was like the freshness of morning.

"Raff, do me the dance," she said when I opened the car's door.

For Assembly in the tenth grade at John Marshall High, I had been coaxed by Josey to paint up and dress like a clown to perform a soft-shoe routine on stage—the performance my life's worst mistake. I was double-jointed, had a high waistline and unusually long legs, and had flung them and my arms about like a scarecrow and wildly rolled my eyes. I had pretended to share a lollipop with another student, who wore a gorilla costume.

Oh, the audience had applauded for my making a fool of myself. A reporter for the school paper had compared me to an inebriated giraffe. Raff had thus become my nickname and students called out to me to do the dance. I hated the memory and the name, which still followed me.

Drake, Cliff, and I had all loved Josephine, who became Josey to us. She had lived down the block from me and been a tomboy who played baseball for our team, able to slide into bases and spit long with the best of us.

During high school she had changed, still an athlete, but with her body forming new lines—startling legs and under her sweaters breasts that drew our eyes. We competed for her, and she had allowed us at one time or another to kiss her, do a little tonguing and ear blowing, but she always made me keep both my feet on the floor when we necked and never allowed me to touch anything below her waist. She had favored Cliff, and I suspected but didn't know for sure that she had allowed him a more wide-ranging freedom of her anatomy.

"Are you expecting rain?" she asked of the tightly furled umbrella I had carried from the house. The question bore a smirk.

"Let's take my wheels," I said.

"I do have my image, and your Le Sabre, well."

I slid in beside Josey. The interior of the car smelled of perfume and burgundy leather. As I instructed her how to reach Bellerive three miles upstream, we drove through Jessup's Wharf, the Lexus scattering pigeons feeding around the loading docks of the co-op.

White posts topped by stone pineapples marked the plantation's entrance, and sunlight shimmered off the brass nameplate mortared into bricks. A Kentucky gate had been replaced by iron pickets of closed double portals. She pulled up to a speaker system installed alongside the road, and without awaiting a word from me reached out and pressed a button. We heard a click and a voice I recognized as the man's from whom I had asked permission. When Josey gave my name, the portals swung open.

The drive wound between rows of black walnut trees, and in fields on either side were barns, silos, and brick slave quarters that had been renovated as guest houses, all painted white with midnight-green trim. Snow had melted off the fields, its weight leaving the pasture grass flattened and subdued.

Josey stopped at a white plank fence beyond which horses romped. She explained their dish faces and short-coupled bodies identified them as Arabians. They didn't appear to gallop as much as to flow like swift streams over submerged rocks.

"Lovely," she said. Of course she knew about riding horses and jumping coops and oxers. She had also taken flying lessons.

We reached the serpentine wall at the rear of the house, where another gate, this one with gilded spearlike palings, opened before us as she slowed the Lexus.

"Magic," she said and drove into the courtyard surfaced with rounded cobblestones. A copper dolphin topped a scalloped fountain. The mansion had an English basement and rose three stories in courses of Flemish bond. Construction equipment surrounded the house from which came the sounds of hammers and the piercing shrill of a table saw.

Prince Jamir walked from beneath the shaded porte-cochere. Forty or so, trimly fit, his dark hair wavy and finely scissored, he appeared a sport in an orange knit sweater, tailored Levi's, and black boots.

"Enchanted," he said, and black eyes alight smiled over teeth that contrasted brightly with his tawny complexion and dark mustache as he kissed Josey's hand. That she liked what she saw was evident in a compliant softening of her body.

"I apologize for the disorder of the house," he said. "Would you like one of my people to drive you around?"

I thought he probably did own people, though I was always skeptical when those who were not British spoke the English language so well. Still his assurance was convincing, and my instinct when I had first met him was to like him.

"Thanks but we'd rather walk on a day like this," I said, careful not to be slavishly thankful. I felt he was a man who appreciated dignity, and dignity was an aspect of my life I constantly sought to achieve. I turned my head at the sound of clanking machinery north of the mansion.

"My airstrip-to-be," the prince said. He bowed to Josey. "Please make me happy by enjoying yourself."

"We'll close all gates," she said.

He walked back to the house. Josey and I strolled the boxwood-flanked path to the front terrace, where she paused to look at the portico that Edward LeBlanc had ordered rebuilt after the explosion. Limbs of mossy water oaks were so heavy they had been chained to the trunks to support their weight. At the foot of the lawn were the dock, the prince's motor launch, and a newly constructed gazebo.

"Does he have a wife?" Josey asked. "And wonder whether he'd let me shoot some landings at his airstrip?"

"The way he looked at you, I expect he'd insist on it."

"Enough, Raff," she said.

Raff, the way she always saw me. We stopped at the gazebo. The Axapomimi ran high from snows melting upstream, the water dragging at and jerking at willow branches along the bank, causing them to appear alive and frantic.

"I finally roused Cliff out of his shell," she said. "A terrible thing that shooting, but we had drinks, and he seems to be coping. His photo exhibition was naughty, naughty, naughty. He's possessed by so many inner demons. Greatly ambitious, yet nothing seems to pan out. A case of the cat-in-the-corn-house syndrome."

"Josey, you've lost me."

"A story my father related. At the farm he had opened the corn-house door, and dozens of mice scurried for cover. Our Siamese cat, named Slink, sprang among them and darted about catching the squealing little rodents, but soon as he captured one, he dropped it to chase another. Before he could make his final choice, all the mice escaped, and Slink stood baffled that he hadn't sunk his teeth into the first juicy morsel."

"That's how you characterize Cliff?"

"Actor, playwright, writer, teacher, painter, photographer—all of which he does well but no one activity that he excels in to the point of becoming a star. He carries himself as if he's intact, but he's wounded and hurting. He feels despite his many gifts he's fallen behind lesser men."

She cocked her head. "Listen. Drums?"

"The Indian reservation," I said. "Perhaps they're doing a ceremonial dance to petition the Great Spirit for a good crop or an abundance of shad when the fish return to the river. If the breeze is right, you can hear their tribal celebrations."

We left the gazebo and let ourselves through a gateway beyond the paddock and belfried stable. Josey controlled our pace across brittle, crackly grass. Ahead a flight of crows rose cawing from a dip of ground and flew toward a bordering fringe of loblolly pines.

We climbed a plank fence and walked under limbs of a leafless pin oak toward a pond on which Canada geese cruised in stately file. Josey stopped, turned her head to listen, and then we heard another kind of drumming and looked back toward the stable.

The horse, a dappled gray Arabian, rose effortlessly over the fence and raced, mane flying, across the pasture. It snorted and struck out with its hind hooves, alarming the geese, who honked and began flapping off the water. They left disturbed wakes across the pond.

"God, the beauty of it," Josey said.

The horse neighed and pranced around the pond. It flung its head, caught our scent, and gazed across the water. Snorting, it thrust itself into a gallop and pounded in our direction.

"Whoa now," Josey said.

The animal charged us, hooves slamming the ground, head lowered, neck stretched forward, teeth bared like an attacking dog. The sound it uttered was not a neigh but more a hysterical scream. Josey and I jumped aside as it swept past, eyes wild, the heat of its body a hot wind.

"Stallion," Josey said. "Let's get the hell out of here."

When we started toward the fence, the horse shifted to a high-stepping canter, his neck arched, and intercepted us. Again the god-awful scream as he flung his head. That he was a stallion was obvious by what Josey must have also noticed—his extended, stiffly flopping penis. Each time we tried to move toward the fence, he cut us off.

"The tree," I said, and we sidled back toward the pin oak. The stallion again shrieked and bolted toward us. We ran to the tree. I grabbed a lower limb, got a leg up and over, and as I reached for Josey my dangling glasses fell. She stumbled but recovered and stepped around the trunk. The horse wheeled, tried to reach and bite her. His teeth ripped the sleeve of her windbreaker. She shouted at him and scrambled to keep the trunk between herself and the stallion. He couldn't turn sharply enough to get his teeth into her.

I hollered to Josey and stuck my hand down to haul her up, but each time she reached for it the stallion struck. Warily she kept sidestepping and circling, her hands grasping the tree's trunk. I saw something beyond fear in her expression. Escape and survival were turning into a challenge and game for her, deadly but exciting. She was both frightened and elated.

A horn sounded. At the far end of the fence a man jumped from a Jeep to open a gate. As the driver sped through toward us, the stallion swerved to face it. The prince behind the wheel kept blowing the horn and gunned the Jeep past us. The stallion pawed the ground and gave chase. It galloped after the Jeep and back through the gate, which the man who'd been left behind closed and latched.

Breathless, I let down from the tree. Josey pushed away from its trunk, exhaled slowly, and reached to remove her red brow band. With it she wiped her forehead, face, and neck. A cheek was smudged. Shaken, she stared after the horse.

"Talk about one big horny bastard," she said.

"I had my hand down for you," I said as I picked up my broken glasses. She had stepped on them.

We walked toward the fence. The prince drove back, let himself through the gate, and stopped to help Josey into the Jeep. Without my glasses, the day for me had become fuzzed.

"The groom failed to bar the door at the breeding shed," he told her. "The mares upset Grand Illustrious Sultan, our premier sire. Do you need doctoring?"

"A drink," Josey said and tucked her red wool shirt back into her tan corduroy pants.

I sat in the rear as he returned us to the mansion, where he showed Josey the way to a lavatory just inside the porte-cochere. A hefty, dark-skinned man brought out brandy and glasses on a tray.

"You know a woman in heat can arouse a stallion," the prince confided in me as we waited for Josey. He smiled.

"Lots of fun 'round this place," she said, striding from the house. She quickly drank two brandies. The prince again kissed her hand as well and held the Lexus's door open for her.

Josey carried me back to Miss Mabel's but didn't switch off the engine.

"Thanks for one swell time," she said. Her color up, she appeared exuberant.

"I did have my hand down for you," I said.

"Of course you did, Raff. You did the best you could."

A hell of a thing to tell a man. She sped off, leaving me standing in front of the house holding my umbrella and looking after her. I believed in valor, but the truth was I felt at Bellerive Josey had acted more the man than I.

EIGHT

I drove from Jessup's Wharf to Powhatan County, where Drake Wingo now had his shop. At least a shop had been the way it had started out—a small rented space in a strip mall on Route 60 west of Richmond that announced itself by a hand-painted "Guns & Gunsmith" sign over the doorway.

Drake opened the shop after his discharge from the army and became so successful he moved farther west into Powhatan County, where he bought seven acres of undeveloped land and supervised the construction of a one-story, flat-roofed cinder-block building that appeared too small for the lot it occupied.

Over time he expanded it, adding a wing here, a showroom there, until the place became barn size and sold not only guns but also upscale lines of sport clothing and camping equipment. He never advertised and rarely offered specials, but the word spread about the high quality of his merchandise and the dependability of the repair service. He named the store Grizzly's after killing an *Ursus horribilis* on a hunting trip to Wyoming.

Grizzly's sat on a grass field surrounded by a hardwood forest. At the doorway he had bolted down an outsized plastic bear reared to attack, its fangs exposed. Another attraction was a ruffed grouse in flight Drake himself had carved from balsa. It had a six-foot wingspan and was supported by an all but invisible nylon line attached to a ceiling structural beam at the center of the store.

Each night after closing a spotlight played on the white bird, which seen through the display windows appeared to be luminously soaring through darkness. As people drove past, they slowed their cars to look, and parents brought children to see what had become known as the ghost grouse.

Drake often sat on a camp chair just inside the doorway to greet customers. He remembered names, shook hands, led buyers to clerks, yet there was never anything subservient about him. Rather he made people feel esteemed by the attention he gave them.

I found him at the front counter restocking his pamphlet, "The Truth of the Grouse." He had set his safari hat at its usual jaunty angle.

"And they used to be free," I said. He now charged a dollar a copy for the pamphlets.

"Raff, people never put value on anything free," he answered. "And I know why you're here. Let's go to the office."

I followed along an aisle between basketball, golf, and tennis equipment. All Drake's clerks wore blaze-orange vests and black bow ties. He stopped to straighten a pyramidal arrangement of moccasins in the shoe department.

Walls held mounted heads of deer, lynxes, coons, foxes, and bears, their glassy eyes lustrous. Shelves displayed taxidermic partridges, doves, turkeys, ducks, geese. We walked under the outsized ghost grouse that when nudged by air currents shifted slightly and drew customers' gazes.

Firearms occupied the entire hindmost section of Grizzly's. Pistols, shotguns, and rifles were racked behind locked sliding glass panels, and indirect lighting at the base of the guns caused burled walnut stocks, nickel-plated handguns, and blue steel rifle barrels to gleam with the opulence of jewelry. Young boys often stood before them and dreamt of glory in combat.

We passed through the accounting department, where two ladies worked at computers. Drake's office had a camp cot in it and grouse tails tacked to the walls, each a tagged trophy carrying a date, place of kill, and memory for him. On the desk he'd set a color photograph of his wife, Deborah, and laid across the blotter a lever-action rifle and a flat metal box, the lid open, which held compartmentalized gunsmith tools.

"This is a Winchester .44-caliber rimfire," he said and drew the rifle to his shoulder. He pressed the worn, gouged stock against his cheek. "Earliest model, 1866. The Henry 1858 preceded it but had no forearm and grew too hot to hold after repeated firing. The 1866 is a work of beauty I'm repairing and refinishing. Comes up to you like a loving woman. It's a rifle made for joining."

He laid the Winchester on the desk gently, as if it had feelings.

"People go to art galleries and museums for their cultural highs, but I'll take a classic Winchester or Henry any day," he said. "Guns are the real American art. They should be displayed and admired like Rembrandts or Van Goghs. You feel their beauty where it should be felt—in your gonads."

"Drake, that's a unique aesthetic theory," I said.

"The balls never lie," he said.

"I understand Sheriff Sawyers has been to see you."

"Oh yeah. He looked over my merchandise."

"Did it ever occur to you to inform me?"

"I didn't consider it important. Just a lawman routinely nosing around."

"He's supposed to be on vacation, not nosing."

"Some people can't stop working, and maybe he just wanted to slip away from the mountains a couple of days and used investigating as a means of getting a trip at taxpayers' expense."

The telephone on the desk rang. Drake lifted it.

"Hold the calls," he said and sat.

"Sheriff Sawyers seems to believe he needs more detail about what happened on our hunt," I said and also let down to a chair.

"I told him it's not complicated. Wendell was a hunting

greenhorn. First time gunning game. His eagerness to cap the bird caused him to make a dumb move."

"How did you get to know Wendell Ripley?"

"His son Jerry used to work in my shoe department, and Wendell hung around."

"Wait a second," I said. "You never mentioned a son when the sheriff asked about next of kin in High Gap."

"No need to. Jerry Ripley no longer walks this earth. He quit the job years ago. I tried but couldn't reach him. Some weeks later, Wendell, all broken up, stopped by and told me Jerry was dead. I asked how he died. Wendell said poisoned. In High Gap Cliff was suffering, and I wanted to get him and us out of Sheriff Sawyers's office and away as fast as possible."

"Do you have information regarding any other of Wendell's kin?"

"Not blood family," he said and pushed back his safari hat. "Wendell lived in a commune out Chesterfield County way. Call themselves The Watchers, a religious sect. When I enlarged the store and put in a shoe department, I didn't know Wendell. The boy applied for work, and I hired him. He did his job, not much more. Wendell with a father's interest stopped by. He doted on his son and was hard hit after he died. Never really got over it."

I heard firing and turned my head. Drake had an indoor shooting range where he and his clerks trained people how to handle guns.

"Then Wendell stayed around the store even after his son's death?"

"He came in one day carrying an old shotgun, a LeFever, and wanted to know if I could fix it. The gun was rusted, pitted, and had Damascus barrels. I explained that if he used today's powder, particularly high brass shells, the barrel would untwist or explode. So I fitted him with a twelve-gauge Remington three-shot automatic that had a twenty-eight-inch barrel and adjustable choke, a gun inexpensive but reliable, the same one he carried to camp."

"Did he know how to handle it?"

"Not at first. He told me he had never fired a gun. The old LeFever had belonged to his grandfather back in the mountains. I taught him to use the Remington. It turned out Wendell was a natural shot, instinctive. First just chipped the clay pigeons. I explained that if they were real birds, he'd only have winged them and the grouse would hit the ground running, bury under cover, and die, a waste."

Drake and his passion for grouse. He had been working to extend his pamphlet to book length and hoping to find a publisher.

"I showed Wendell how to bring the stock to his cheek, not take his cheek to the stock, keep both eyes open, and continue his swing past the targets. In no time at all he was shattering them. A born gunner in talent if not temperament."

"And you found out about the land he owned on Blind Sheep?"

"He happened to mention the acreage bordered the Monongahela National Forest. His family used to herd sheep in those mountains. He said he remembered plenty of what he called brown birds. I asked him whether he'd let me drive up to West Virginia and check it out. He drew me a map, I took my sleeping bag, located the place, and stayed a night on Blind Sheep. He was right. Kraut retrieved me a broken hickory limb. The dog's way of telling me there were more birds than you could shake a stick over. I knew I had to have shooting rights on that place. I leased the land and built the cabin. I wanted to buy the land. He wouldn't sell."

"That's the reason you invited him along on the hunt."

"Get two for one—a reunion with old friends and let Wendell see we're decent people. I figured quality folks like you and Cliff would help me win him over and I could buy it."

"Can you tell me anything more about Wendell's son?"

"No explanation of the poison and how Jerry swallowed it. Wendell was grieving so bad I didn't push it."

"I can't figure Sawyers."

"Maybe politics. The sheriff told us he was thinking of running for the legislature. He might be looking for an arrest he can exploit, get publicity, win votes. A fishing expedition."

"It seems he ought to be able to find something more newsworthy than a hunting accident."

"Maybe there's not much happening up in High Gap, and he's got to use what's at hand."

Drake lifted the Henry and repeatedly snapped it to his shoulder to aim at his electric wall clock.

"What I want is more information on Wendell Ripley," I said. "You know anything about the store he managed?"

"I heard it's chiefly an outlet for what's produced at the commune."

"I'll stop by and ask around," I said.

NINE

I found FOOD located two blocks south of the alley where Cliff, Drake, and I had fought members of the River Rats gang—still a grimy neighborhood of garages, machine shops, and warehouses, most tainted and scarred by decline. The old King James Hotel with its twin turrets and arched entrance had long ago been razed, and spiky, winter-ravaged weeds sought to survive among the lot's scattered debris.

The store occupied a building close to the CSX railroad tracks that led past the abandoned Main Street Station. Outwardly the entrance to FOOD appeared neglected and off-putting. I made out the MORPHEUS MATTRESS CO. in flanking white paint on bricks under front eaves crusted with pigeon droppings.

So many cars filled the asphalt parking lot I circled twice to find a space. Inside, I faced a different world—a brightly lit, cavernous room lined with row upon row of long wooden bins. The place was clean, orderly, the shoppers brisk. Women in white smocks, their hair bound by white kerchiefs, worked the checkouts.

"Direct you, sir?" one pushing an empty shopping cart asked.

I told her I wanted the business office.

"Up the stairs at the rear, sir. Enjoy your visit with us."

I walked past heaped fragrant bins holding cabbages, lettuce, tomatoes, peppers, cucumbers, oranges, cantaloupes, and beans as well as a battery of refrigerated cabinets offering gleaming rounds of cheeses and dairy products. Prices were cheap compared to what I paid at the Jessup's Mercantile. I found no meat displayed. Despite its roof and walls, FOOD had the feel of an outdoor country market.

The stairway rose to a loft where secondhand clothing for sale hung from pipe racks. Shelves offered shoes that had been neatly arranged and polished, the laces tied. A girl trying on a summer straw hat stood before a mirror hung from a nail pounded into a wooden column.

The office at the rear had no dividing partition between it and the merchandise. The plainly clothed women working at desks appeared out of place in the company of electric typewriters, calculators, computers, and monitors.

The nearest glanced up from a printout and smiled. Young, hardly twenty, and brightly energetic, she crooked her finger at me, and I crossed to her wooden desk—a sturdy oak model of the kind that used to be seen in federal offices and were now sold at government surplus auctions.

"Hep you?" she asked, a country girl.

I told her I'd like to speak to the manager.

"Sister Maude's right over there in the corner," she said and pointed.

I tried to remember the last time I had come across a woman named Maude, this one elderly, her creased face washed to a shine. She studied an inventory list spread over her desk. When she became aware of me, her fingers released the list and let it settle.

"Did you notice the sunrise this morning?" she asked.

"I confess I didn't," I said, slid my card from my wallet, and offered it.

"The clouds were a golden pink," she said as she took the card and reset her glasses. "When the sun touched my face, I felt the hand of God."

"Yes," I said and wondered what I had walked into.

"Nice to meet you, Mr. Frampton," she said. "I hope you not out to sue us."

"No, ma'am, I've come to make inquiries about the late Mr. Wendell Ripley."

"Brother Wendell," she said with no note of surprise or regret. "Our Lord has chosen him to share eternal companionship. Won't you sit a moment and rest your bones while you tell me what in particular you're asking?"

"His background," I said and drew the wooden chair to her desk. "And does he have any family I can contact?"

"Oh, he has family. Some eighty-seven of them at last count and growing. The Watchers are all family."

"But not blood kin?"

"Kin of the spirit is stronger than blood."

"Perhaps you can tell me something about The Watchers."

"Can and will. Our doors are open to anyone who'll make God's work the primary aim and purpose of their lives and profess belief that Jesus Christ is with us this very day. We accept aspirants on a six-month instructional basis. After that if they want to stay, we vote them into our family on the condition they turn over their worldly goods to be shared by all."

"An agricultural commune."

"We don't call ourselves that. We are children of God who live to serve others by feeding them. We are brothers and sisters in the Spirit. Wendell was a good, loving man who knew no strangers, a shepherd who came to us from the mountains."

"Did he have a wife? I know there was a son."

"About those questions you'd do better talking to Brother Abram. You'll find him at the farm. He speaks for us. I'll draw you directions."

She used the back of a discarded envelope to pencil the directions. Nothing was wasted at FOOD.

"You should watch the sunrise each day," she said and gave me the envelope. "It's the Lord opening His eyes upon mankind after the darkness of night as well as His promise of eternal renewal."

I drove west on Route 360 into Chesterfield County. Richmond had expanded in that direction, the malls, marts, and housing developments giving way finally to countryside and woodland. I turned on 707 and wound along a narrow paved road among shaggy cedars that bent before the wind, their branches dipping and recovering.

As Sister Maude had indicated on the envelope, the entrance to The Watchers was a mile and seven-tenths along 707. The aluminum farm gate had been latched open, and at the end of the lane the land opened before me—fields laid out in rectangles and beyond them barns and parallel one-story buildings, all painted brown. Despite the wind and cold, bundled men and women worked using posthole diggers, shovels, and tamping bars to install fencing around a plot of fallow soil.

I stopped between a pickup and dump truck in the parking area. The sun caused me to squint as I looked for somebody to ask where to find Brother Abram. I walked to the end door of a building and knocked. I heard no sound of life inside. I opened the door onto a long corridor flanked by cots and footlockers that ran its entire length.

"Anybody here?" I called.

As I backed out and shut the door, I heard a chain saw crank up. I followed the sputtering, growling racket and came upon a man standing outside a galvanized turtle-back shed. He gunned the saw, and thin blue smoke gathered around him. His body was immense, the shoulders and hips heavy, his stomach bulging, his thighs vast as hams. He had rolled the sleeves of his brown coveralls over his hairy forearms.

The sixteen-inch Poulan appeared a toy in his huge hands. He wasn't cutting wood but carving a design on a cedar post and operated the saw with a casual expertise as chips sprayed over and gathered around his outsized clodhoppers. The rounded tip of the blade created what—an eye socket?

I stood observing until he glanced my way and used a plump thumb to switch off the saw. His beard was a luxuriant brown, and hair grew thick and curly from his head, nose, and ears as well as overflowed the neck of his coveralls.

"A blessed day," he said, his voice surprisingly soft. A smile opened over horselike teeth.

"I'm looking for Brother Abram."

"Rest your eyes, my friend." He laughed, the sound booming from the fullness of his great belly. "You may rejoice at the good fortune of having found him."

I told him my name and that I was an attorney gathering information about Wendell Ripley. I gave him my card.

"Sister Maude told me he was a member of your order and suggested I drive out to see you," I said.

"What you will find about Brother Wendell is he lies in our cemetery. Furthermore, we are not an order. That terminology is much too militant and intimidating. We are a fellowship. Anyone who comes here willing to work and live by our simple rules is welcome."

"You do own and operate the food store?"

"Yes and no. There are no owners in the usual sense of that word. This property, what it produces, all profits belong to a common fund that pays for seed, equipment, and operating expenses. We grow our edibles, make much of our clothing, wait, and watch."

"May I ask what you watch for?"

"You may. We await the end time. We believe our Savior is already among us, that He's on this earth this very instant, perhaps walking along a street, standing alone in a crowd, stopping to lay His hand on the halt and the blind. You, I, anyone may have already passed Him or He us. We won't know until we look into his eyes. One glance from Him will transform us."

"In what manner?" I asked and glanced at an old Oliver tractor hauling a wagon loaded with fence posts and rolls of barbed wire toward the fields.

"Brother, when you see into the eyes of God, all sin will be kindled to cinders and you taken up cleansed to join Him in eternity."

"Armageddon?" I asked, remembering my Sunday-school days when I had been reared as a Presbyterian and learned that at that final fiery conflict the saints would rise to meet Christ in the Rapture after which He would rule on earth a thousand years.

"Signs exist," Brother Abram said. "Wars, famine, flood, blood in the streets. Read any newspaper, listen to the radio, switch on TV."

To be amiable I nodded but believed there had never been a time without such signs. He noticed me shiver in the wind and suggested we go in by his stove.

The wood burner at the center of the shed had been made from a metal oil drum and flued through the roof. Workbenches held drills, grinders, a heavy-duty vise. Tools hung in systematic fashion from hooks screwed into wood strips above the benches. Brother Abram set his Poulan on the concrete floor.

"I expect you, like many others, think we Watchers are a peculiar, even a backward people," he said. "It might be of interest to you to know that I am an educated man, attended Columbia University, spent some three years at an Episcopal seminary, and inherited a shameful amount of money from my father, who manufactured boilers and turbines—many more dollars than I could wantonly spend. I was also a drunk who drank rivers of liquor. It filled my gut and would have flooded the sea. I swam in the filth of many gutters."

We held our hands to heat from the stove. His were meaty, roughened, and callused while mine by comparison appeared slender and fair.

"They threw me out of the seminary," he said. "In my search for God and to mortify my flesh I beat my bare body with wire coat hangers. I howled on my knees in the refectory garden until they carried me to the infirmary. It was there our Lord descended to me like a flame out of swirling darkness. He lifted me away from this world and set me back. The words I heard were not spoken among thunder and lightning but in a still, small voice which said, 'Feed my people.'"

Waiting, what could I do but appear receptive and keep nodding?

"I've done so since," he said. "I bought this land and alone began tilling it. I preached God's message, sometimes on street corners, in storefront churches, or shanties where wind blew between the cracks. And people began to come, at first just one or two at a time. We worked the fields, planted potatoes, English peas, radishes, and chard as soon as the weather broke and we could work the soil."

As he talked he seemed on the verge of more laughter, a restrained whoop that was gathering in his drooping belly.

"Mr. Wendell Ripley was one who came?" I asked.

"Wendell and his frail wife joined us, her name Sarah. They had journeyed down from mountain country where he tended sheep before he found a job providing creosoted ties for the railroad. His work brought him to Richmond town, a man whose kindly nature made us love him, his wife, and the child."

He turned away from the stove to lift the Poulan and clamp its bar in the vise. Next he selected a file that had a bulb-shaped wooden handle and drew an index finger across the bite of the rasp before beginning to sharpen the saw's blade.

"Sister Sarah fell ill. Her medical bills took all their money and more. She wasted away but held on to life long enough to bear the child, the son, his name Jeremiah. Brother Wendell mourned her, but he had joy in his son. When the boy was old enough, they worked crops together and caused happiness among us."

Brother Abram's weighty hands had a delicacy upon the saw as if the blade's teeth could feel the file and understand its beneficial touch.

"When Brother Wendell came to us, we were only a dozen folks. We built living quarters, a kitchen, and our house of worship. We first sold our produce door-to-door and alongside the highway. As we grew we dickered for more land, constructed the barn, bought milk cows. We don't eat meat."

I remembered the absence of meat at FOOD and Wendell's turning down a steak at Drake's cabin.

"It was Brother Wendell's idea when we began to garner more than we could sell to utilize the old mattress factory in Richmond. He had a good mind for figures. The decaying building stood empty and was for sale. We were able to work out terms with a bank desperate to be rid of it. We gave the store its honest name and chose Brother Wendell to run it, which he did well. In fact he made it succeed. Now that entire property belongs to us free and clear, and with our low prices, fresh produce, and dairy products we do feed the people."

He continued to file in a slow, rhythmic fashion.

"Brother Wendell delighted in his boy. He gave thanks and waited for our Savior to appear among us. He sang, had a fine baritone voice, and walked with his son singing prayers through our woods."

"I knew Mr. Ripley less than twenty-four hours," I said. "To me he appeared quiet and withdrawn."

"Yes, good as he was, Brother Wendell suffered from the weakness of not surrendering himself completely during a time of pain and travail to God's judgment. Jeremiah grew to be a rebellious son. At school he fell among bad company. He fled us and Brother Wendell, who searched him out in the city, but Jeremiah never returned."

"What happened to him?"

"Gone."

"You mean dead?"

"Dead, yes."

"I heard he was poisoned."

"That is true."

"In what way and by whom?"

"One among the company he kept."

"Was anyone prosecuted?"

"The police showed little interest."

"Are you able to tell me anything else?"

"Yes, brother, keep watch."

He removed the saw from the vise and gripping it made to leave the shed.

"And Mr. Ripley's buried in your cemetery?" I asked.

"With his wife, Sarah, the plots just past our church on the hill-side."

I hadn't recognized the plain boxlike building he pointed to as a church, though unlike other structures it was painted white.

"Rejoice, brother, Our Savior moves among us and will bring us understanding, peace, and love," Brother Abram said as he adjusted the Poulan's choke and repeatedly jerked the cord to start the saw.

"What's that to be?" I asked of the cedar post he'd been carving.

"One of two to be planted on each side of our entrance," he said. "By the way we had another visitor inquiring about Brother Wendell, a sheriff from West Virginia. So much earthly distress over a man who found the most glorious good fortune of all—he resides with his Lord."

So Sheriff Sawyers had also been to The Watchers. I drove toward the cemetery—not much of a hill, merely a low rise of mowed field that grew a single locust tree from its center. I parked beside a black Pontiac.

Orderly mounds lined the field, but no gravestones or markers provided names or dates. I assumed their absence involved church doctrine, possibly the belief that those who died left nothing of their old selves behind but had put on new bodies as the apostle Paul had written.

I stopped at the church, climbed its three wooden steps to the door, and slipped inside not a narthex but a white room furnished with plain benches on either side of a center aisle. No pulpit rose above them, no curtains hung at the windows, no carpeting covered the floor. If the worshipers sang, they did so without a piano or an organ.

As I turned away, I almost missed the young woman. She sat in shadows to my left just beyond a fan of faint sunlight. Her floppy hat matched her tan raincoat. Head bowed, eyes closed, her gloved fingers steepled to her chin, she silently wept.

She abruptly realized I was watching and quickly stood and left past me. From the doorway I looked after her as she hurried toward the Pontiac in the pigeon-toed manner that women have of running. Her knee-length black rubber boots skirted frozen puddles.

Leaving the farm, I slowed to pass workers unloading posts and wire from the wagon. Again I thought of Sheriff Bruce Sawyers, who was turning out to be a watcher of a different sort.

TEN

The day before Christmas I flew to Tampa, where my mother waited at the sunny airport. In her mid-sixties, she played tennis twice a week and remained a slender, active woman. She had also been studying Italian in order to read the *Divine Comedy*.

While I was a law student at Washington and Lee, she and my father sold our Richmond house and retired to Venice and a white stucco condo that had a balcony which overlooked the intercostal waterway. My father learned to identify boats as they passed. "A Bertram," he would say, "a Hunter," or "Choey Lee." He kept score on a pad but did not count the number of drinks constantly refreshed.

"Need to put out the fire," he would say, a tic lately developed causing his right eyelid to flutter. In his attempt to protect friends prosecuted for an under-the-table land transaction with the Virginia Department of Transportation, my father got caught up in a scandal, considered his reputation forever besmirched, sold his real-estate ventures, and resigned from the Society of the Lees.

The sun-blasted Christmas seemed as unreal as the artificial wreaths tied with shiny red plastic bows. My mother roasted a turkey we ate after we opened our presents. They had bought me a wristwatch, a wallet, and two button-down Oxford-cloth white shirts. I gave perfume and books to my mother, and for my father I purchased Bushnell 7x35 binoculars he could use to watch the boats.

"The cards we're dealt," he said the morning I left. "I apologize for the heritage I've left you."

"Dad, I won't hear any more of that."

He believed himself the cause of my not being able to find a job with a prestigious Richmond law firm and ending up in Jessup's Wharf—a partial truth I had put behind me. I loved him and what he stood for.

"God the dealer," he said.

There was no breaking through to him. My mother carried me back to Tampa and my flight to Richmond.

"He's promised to take walks," she said and kissed me in sunshine so bright our shadows on the white concrete lay black as paving tar.

At Jessup's Wharf, newly hired, ginger-haired secretary Mary Ellen Cartwright sat at her desk in my office. She was aged thirty or so, formerly married to an army pilot killed in Germany, where his helicopter crashed. She had picked up quickly on legal procedures that were routine but tricky and almost indecipherable to people not trained in their use. She had laid out the mail chronologically on my desk and set a potted Christmas cactus on the windowsill.

She hummed and smiled to herself as she worked, perhaps thinking of her young son or remembering the days years earlier when she had reigned as Miss York County. Her back was to me, and her dark skirt had pulled up over her knees as she turned aside to finger paper clips in a glass dish. She had legs softly rounded in ladylike contrast to Josey's spare shanks slimmed to muscle.

"Mr. Frampton, my mama won't be home today, and is it all right for my Jason to stay here after school? I don't like him returning to an empty house. I promise he'll be no trouble."

"Fine," I said and hoped the boy's stopping by wouldn't become a habit. I liked the way she'd used "mama" instead of mother.

I fanned through the mail and list of calls. Nothing from Josey, though I'd had Talbots send her a pair of black leather riding gloves. Charley LeBlanc had phoned to wish me a Merry Christmas. Cliff had also called, but when I dialed his number I got only his answering machine. His recorded voice was the old Cliff's—curt and edging on haughty.

He rang me up just after lunch, and he sounded urgent.

"That sheriff's notified me that if I don't return to Seneca County for questioning they might seek a writ," he said. "Can they force me to go back when I live in another state?"

"Not without probable cause and a warrant."

"What do I do?"

"You might consider returning."

"I don't like it. I've told them all I know. If the sheriff has more questions, let him come to Richmond instead of inconveniencing me. Walter, the man's spoiling my days."

"I'll talk to him. Possibly the situation's resolvable."

"He didn't sound like it."

"He could be playing poker. I'll call you back."

I phoned Information for the number of Seneca County's Sheriff's Department and told the woman who answered I wanted to speak to Sawyers. She said he wasn't in his office but would give him my message.

I looked out the window. Snow had again begun falling, rare for Tidewater Virginia. These were random lazy flakes. I walked to the courthouse and the clerk's office to check out a title for Prince Jamir. Benson Falkoner was just leaving.

Benson was King County's commonwealth's attorney, a ruddy, fleshy man who talked as if he had a mouth full of molasses and made two out of one-syllable words. His eyelids hung heavy. He and Felix Bonnet were Jessup's Wharf's other attorneys.

Benson had lately become particularly cordial, hoping to share any spillover from Prince Jamir's business coming my way.

"How's life treating you, Walt?"

"Can't complain, Benson."

"A person who can't complain's not alive. Man's first utterance in this world is a cry and protest against life."

"Didn't realize you were a philosopher, Benson," I said as I drew out a heavy gray property book and opened it on the counter. Hands had been turning its pages for two hundred and fifty years. I never wanted to be standing between Benson and a dollar bill.

When I walked back along River Street, snow had collected on parked cars. I ate a bowl of spiced-up chili at the Dew Drop Inn before returning to my office. Sheriff Sawyers had called collect at two-thirty.

"I been expecting to hear from you," he said.

"I hadn't thought you'd still be investigating an accidental death so doggedly," I said.

"In the code there's no such thing as accidental death. It's manslaughter and punishable."

"There's excusable homicide."

"You contending that Mr. Wendell Ripley in some manner threatened Mr. Dickens and that provides justification for shooting him?"

"No, I'm saying what we have here is an unfortunate happenstance that is not routinely brought to trial or at most is treated as a misdemeanor both in Virginia and other states."

"Here in the mountains we don't consider any death routine, and there are details about this one that beg further investigation. Mr. Dickens alone can explain more fully what happened on that Blind Sheep grouse hunt. By not cooperating he's making problems for us and himself."

"He can and is willing to answer all your questions down here in Richmond."

"Not the same. Our district attorney, Mr. Sam Tuggle, wants him back. If your client's being up front with us, what's spooking him?"

"He's not spooked, as you put it, but has his life and work in Virginia. I believe I know all the facts and that he's told them to you."

"Let's be real, Mr. Frampton. We both know clients don't always square up with their attorneys."

"Sheriff, how about being more specific?"

"I have a gut feeling about this one."

"Gut feelings don't count in a court of law."

"But they do before the court convenes."

I looked out the window at the snow layering the sidewalk. Women walking along the street carried umbrellas, their boots and shoes leaving imprints.

"I understand you been out to The Watchers," I said.

"Mr. Frampton, you might be surprised where all I been."

"My guess is you don't intend to tell me."

"Not at this point. Convince Mr. Dickens to return, and the district attorney will lay it all out on the table."

"Lay it out, as you put it, here in the Commonwealth."

"Okay, Mr. Frampton, I don't guess there's any need for us to continue sparring. Seneca County means to get Mr. Dickens back one way or another."

"And I might have to make the process difficult for Seneca County."

"We'll see about that. The law has a long arm. Thanks for your call."

When I hung up, I watched the snow fall more heavily. In my mind I again went step-by-step over the Blind Sheep hunt. So Cliff in his state of shock may have described events there in a confused fashion. Surely that wasn't enough to build a case against him.

At three-fifteen a yellow school bus stopped in front of the office, and a small, pale boy stepped down to the street. Mary Ellen hurried to meet him. I guessed his age as about seven. Mary Ellen made him clean his feet on the mat and helped him off with his jacket and knit cap. His short hair was whitish blond but had no luster. She used her handkerchief to dab away snow melting on his face.

"Mr. Frampton, this is my son, Jason."

"How you, Jason?" I asked and extended my hand.

The boy didn't shake it or answer me. He kept his eyes averted. He was scrawny and maybe sickly.

"He's shy," Mary Ellen said and placed a chair by her desk, sat Jason, and fondly touched the top of his head. The boy's feet didn't reach the floor. He drew a book from his backpack and opened it across his lap.

When I offered him a peppermint from the Dew Drop Inn, he lifted his eyes. They were not honey-colored like his mother's but a much deeper brown, a bottomless hue and much too large for his small, narrow face. Quickly he looked away but not before I'd seen a shape rise beneath the pupils like a creature from the depths. The shape's name was fear.

ELEVEN

I couldn't locate Cliff. I left messages on his answering machine and drove by his carriage house, where the gate through the stone wall remained locked. I felt he damn well should have notified me before leaving town.

I had received an embossed invitation to Bellerive for a New Year's Day hunt meet and breakfast, and though I'd never owned a horse or been a rider, I did consider foxhunting an aristocratic sport and envied those who followed the hounds.

The snow had partly melted, but the ground firmed up from an overnight freeze. I dressed warmly and wished I owned a shooting stick. I also carried my umbrella and reminded myself to stay composed and not talk or laugh too readily.

When I reached Bellerive at eight, the entrance portals stood ajar, and along the walnut-flanked drive a farmhand directed me into a line of parked cars. Tables covered by linen cloths had been set up in the crusty, sole-deep snow. On them thermoses held hot tea and coffee. The ranks of liquor and wine bottles dimly reflected the sun's rising above the cold fog of the pine woods. Servants wearing overcoats tended bar.

Vans and trailers pulled into the pasture. As I walked among them I noted license plates from Richmond, Williamsburg, and Virginia Beach. Prince Jamir did not have to make connections. They were attracted to him like iron filings to a magnet.

I asked for a pewter mug of hot buttered rum, and its good

warmth spread ease through me. Appear sophisticated, bored, and wealthy, I counseled myself.

Riders wearing hunt attire saddled their mounts—sleek animals whose manes and tails had been intricately braided. The horses' nostrils steamed, and their eyes flared at the excitement of the chase. They stomped hooves and pulled at lead lines.

The hounds arrived in a closed truck that had FOX HAVEN painted on its sides in block white letters. Their rich coats bespoke a good worming program at the kennels. The truck belonged to the Gaffneys, a couple who had moved to Virginia and King County from the north and become close friends of the LeBlancs.

The huntsman opened the tailgate to allow the hounds to boil out. They didn't run about wildly but clotted, obedient to his commands, and when two snarled at each other, he cracked his whip over them, and they cowered like reproved children.

Prince Jamir made his appearance. His hunting Pinks displayed a pale blue collar, and he moved like royalty, a hand grasping his bone-handled whip as a king might a scepter. He wound among the mounted guests offering sherry from a silver goblet. A servant followed holding a bottle in each hand to keep the goblet filled. When the prince passed, he turned back and extended the hunt cup to me.

"My local legal representative," he said and smiled. I was pleased and craved his bearing and sense of certainty.

He strode on greeting guests, nodding and receiving tips of hats until a groom brought his horse, a glossy chestnut whose leather tack gave off a deep, opulent glow. The groom joined his palms, the prince set a knee in them, and allowed himself to be hoisted to the saddle.

He conferred with his huntsman, a hook-nosed, weathered man hired from Charlottesville. The prince had ordered his carpenters to panel much of the property so that the fox could be pursued without the necessity of slowing to open gates.

As if he also controlled the climate, the sun broke fully through thin, tearing clouds and gleamed off brass buttons, spurs, and the silver bands around whip handles. The procession did have a beauty and grandeur. I regretted I wasn't mounted on a blooded horse and part of this American nobility.

The huntsman raised his copper horn to sound a long, wavering note and moved off, the hounds trailing his heavy bay and ever mindful of his whip. The prince and members of the field dropped in behind. While I counted the riders, thirty-four in all, I spotted Josey.

She appeared elegant in her Melton, derby, and knotted stock, her gloved hands light on the reins, her shoulders curved forward slightly, her body secure in the saddle and, as always, positive of its competence. She hadn't noticed me among the crowd, and I didn't call out but stared at her black gloves. They could've been those I sent.

The hunt field moved away down toward the river and along the edge of the woods. I wished for the binoculars given to my father.

"We supposed to wait 'round here till breakfast. I'm ready to chow down."

It was Felix Bonnet, the other lawyer in Jessup's Wharf—middle-aged, his face marked with liver spots, dark glasses masking his rheumy eyes. He suffered from stomach ulcers and chewed Tums, his teeth methodically crunching them, the sound audible during court proceedings.

"We can't eat till they serve," I said. "You should have brought a horse."

"I've never ridden and don't plan to start now. Two asses on one animal."

As I was about to return to my Buick, I heard the huntsman's horn and his whooping in what sounded like a falsetto voice. I caught sight of the white-and-tan hounds racing up from the bottom after a red fox that moved in a seemingly unhurried hippity-hop fashion toward the rail fence.

The prince and the field galloped after the huntsman—all headed straight for the spectators. We scattered to the side. The fox slipped between rails, and the huntsman, the prince, and Josey jumped the fence, their horses heaving themselves upward, arching, their hooves striking and slamming the turf and throwing clods. I felt the animals' pounding weights through the ground and smelled their sweat.

Other riders took the fence, though two horses refused, and a man went over his gray to the ground. The gray leaped the fence without him while the man was left cursing and brushing dirt from his white britches. It was Harry Gaffney, and he slogged away, pulling a flask from an inner pocket of his Pinks.

The bar remained open, and I carried a double bourbon in a paper cup to my car, started the engine, and switched on the heater and radio. I wondered how Josey had worked it to be among the guests chosen to hunt. Actually she didn't have to work anything. Her presence was an automatic invitation anyplace she wished to go.

I would have driven off except for her. I became comfortable sipping, dozing in the sun, and listening to *Don Giovanni* broadcast from Tidewater Public Radio.

I roused when I heard the huntsman's horn and stepped from the car to glimpse the field straggling up from the bottom, the horses quiet now, heads drooping, their flanks foaming. I looked at my new watch to find it nearly noon.

The riders were relaxed, calling to one another, passing flasks. I meant to speak to Josey but rather than stopping among the vans she rode off at the prince's side toward his stable. I stood looking after them.

As servants closed the bar and folded tables, the guests began filing toward the mansion. I joined them and climbed the brick steps of the portico, where at the house's entrance a black domestic wearing a white jacket and bow tie opened the door for us. The prince's bodyguard, a swarthy Arab, eyed all who entered. People called him Al, I assumed short for Abdul or Aladdin, and the rumor around Jessup's Wharf was that he carried a pistol in a shoulder holster. He awarded me a cheerless nod.

Three chandeliers lighted by teardrop bulbs hung over a series of trestle tables being loaded with food by the kitchen help. China serving platters displayed hams, roast beef, partridges, shrimp, and oysters as well as an array of salads, vegetables, corn bread, and urns of coffee and tea.

A bar occupied the end of a wainscoted living room, which held a Steinway grand, Persian carpets, hunt tapestries, and a fireplace whose andirons were topped by polished brass fox heads. Above the mantel hung an oil portrait of the prince dressed as a sheik in a flowing white cloak, his legs astride a reared Arabian steed.

I looked for Josey. Those who had been on the chase had begun to join the party. They still wore hunt attire except for the caps, toppers, and whips left behind. They had also wiped their boots.

Most headed for liquor, as I had. I positioned myself beside a towering antique secretary and watched the parade of class and wealth. Hilarity opened moistened mouths wide, voices gave thrilling reports of viewing two reds and a gray as well as praise for the working of the pack, who had torn the gray to pieces as it tried to climb a tree.

"You've got to give them blood occasionally or they won't hunt," a stout, jowly gentleman remarked to an aging woman with netted yellow hair. I wondered whether she had ridden with her fingers so jeweled beneath her riding gloves.

On the second-floor landing a jazz band assembled and began to play—trumpet, tenor sax, double bass, drums, and vibraharp. I knew I should be eating but instead decided to down one last bourbon.

"Banquo got in under that fence," Harry Gaffney said, explaining his fall to people gathered around. "It was his last chance. I'm letting that plug go."

As a small-town lawyer I would likely always be an attendant to most of these people. I knew my manners and might be invited if useful and pleasing to the outer fringes of their inner circle, yet nothing more. I felt the sting of it.

Prince Jamir made his way among guests, stopped to smile and chat. He kissed the hands of the ladies. Josey entered not through the front door but from somewhere at the rear of the house, perhaps the porte-cochere. Her stock was held in place by a gold safety pin fastened through the knot. I watched her remove her net and shake out her hair.

As I moved toward her, she stepped up to stand beside the prince. She was taller than he. He kissed her not on the hand but the cheek, and for an instant his mouth lingered as he whispered at her ear.

I backed off and merged into the crowd. I meant to ease unnoticed out the door, but before I reached it a voice called my name—not Walter but Raff.

It belonged to Jefferson Burford, a student I'd known at John Marshall and Washington and Lee. A Kappa Sig, he had passed out drinking Salty Dogs and been left propped under the shower by fraternity brothers, where he almost drowned.

"Hey, Raff," he said, drink in hand, "do the clown dance for us."

Guests turned to him and me. The combo on the landing had just started playing "Take Five."

"He can do this crazy clown dance with a gorilla," Jefferson announced. "It'll break you up. Come on, Raff, show the folks."

I hated him, and I had drunk too much.

"Screw you, Burford, and I hope you've gotten the worming the vet advised you needed," I said and made for the door. I escaped down the portico steps, staggered toward the parking area, listed off course, and pushed among box bushes until I bumped the scalloped rim of the courtyard fountain, which had been emptied for the winter. I puked into it.

TWELVE

I caught up with Cliff on a rainy Thursday evening. I had been to Richmond both to carry Lee's portrait for framing to artist Phoebe Laratta and to visit my dentist for a routine checkup. When I first parked alongside the curb at Cliff's Gothic-style carriage house and rang the bell, the rain beat my umbrella, and I received no answer.

As I started to leave, he drove his Thunderbird into the service alley, his tires splashing puddles. The double doors opened on command from his remote and closed after he drove through. I walked back to the stone wall, again rang, and Cliff buzzed me in.

"I've been on a trip to the sea," he said. Rain dripped from his Irish hat onto his toggle coat's shoulders. "The humpbacks are running."

He hurried to the Thunderbird's trunk to lift out camera gear and a duffel bag. I helped carry them into the carriage house, which was cold and clammy. The first floor held his living and dark rooms plus a small kitchen, the second his bed and bathroom. I shook out my umbrella.

He switched on lights before kneeling at the fireplace to strike a match to rolled-up newspaper shoved beneath kindling and logs laid over bricks used for andirons. Smoke drifted uncertainly until the draft began to draw. The paper uncurled in flames, kindling crackled, and sparks swirled into the flue.

"I feel the need of a tod," he said. "And I've got a bottle of good rye bought in Baltimore."

From the kitchen hidden beyond a black lacquered screen decorated with a golden Chinese dragon he carried a bowl of ice cubes to mix the drinks on a battered upright piano, the top of which doubled as his bar.

He set mine before me on a black coffee table painted to resemble a white octopus, its tentacles spread over the edges and down the legs. Literary quarterlies lay fanned across it. The room's walls displayed his work, the near one studies of males, a number stripped of clothes, that must have come from his recent show.

"Some great shots of the whales," Cliff said as he checked his thermostat and removed his coat and hat before sitting on the sofa opposite me. "We boated so close their flukes wet us and I tasted the salt."

He lowered his drink to study me.

"Why don't you just go on and take an honest look at the pictures? Obviously they interest you."

"I remember you told me notoriety is its own justification in our day and time."

"Sorry you didn't attend the exhibition but not surprised. You're from another age, Walter, a living flesh-and-blood relic."

I shrugged and sipped at the rye.

"And gays bother you."

"Not they but what they do."

"What do they do, Walter? What are the mechanics?"

"You know."

"Of course I know, but they do it in privacy and it's all just too abhorrent for you to speak the words. The truth is, Walter, fucking of any variety lacks decorum or artistry. Do something for me. Say 'shit.' I've never heard you speak the word."

"No."

"Walter, it's the shit generation. Babies come from the womb using it. Everybody does."

"I don't."

"All right, I give up. Why so solemn?"

"Sheriff Sawyers is set on bringing you back to High Gap. I'm trying to turn him, but the next move's his. We will see."

"Wonderful news," he said and drank.

"Can you think of any reason why he's so determined?" I asked.

"I have no answer."

"I've known you most my life, Cliff. Despite your dramatic talents, you were never the best poker player in the gang. Drake was, and this isn't a situation you can dance around."

"I was a good dancer and still am," he said, yet his reply sounded disheartened. I waited for more. He tossed back his hair. I unbuttoned my overcoat in the expanding heat. Flames of the fire lit one side of his face, the other remained shadowed.

"I want you once again to go into details of the hunt," I said.

"You were there, you know."

"I wasn't with Wendell. Maybe you overlooked something."

"I arrive home elated by whales and have to face this," he said and sighed. "All right, Walter, if it has to be. This is strictly privileged between you and me, right?"

"Correct."

"Okay, on Blind Sheep after we separated into pairs the morning of the hunt, Wendell, silent as usual, followed me up the mountain. We climbed till we reached the beech flat below the ridge. Then he surprised me by breaking the silence and beginning to talk."

"About what?"

"'I wanted my son Jeremiah to learn about these mountains,' he said and told me five generations of his kin had herded sheep on the sod. He thought it a thing his boy should know but never got around to it he was so busy at The Watchers, a plan put off and never taken up. He regretted it. He lagged behind me, and I slowed so he could draw alongside.

"'My son was in your class at the college,' he said. I tried to remember. So many students. They came in hairy droves. A vague handsome face associated with the name Jeremiah took shape in my mind.

"'He bought a magazine with a story you wrote in it,' Wendell said. 'You'd signed your name across the top of the page for him. Kind of you.'

"I told Wendell it had been a pleasure, though most of the students were in fact sucking up for higher grades.

"'They must look to you for more than being a teacher,' Wendell said. 'To them you'd likely seem to know the answers to 'bout everything.'

"I answered it was a sobering responsibility. He dropped back again as we hiked upward.

"'I know you impressed Jeremiah,' Wendell said. 'For a time he talked about becoming a teacher and writer.'

"Before I could answer I spotted a grouse feeding near the laurel—head raised, its neck stretched high. The bird flushed, I swung and shot, and simultaneously Wendell lunged in front of my gun. That's it."

He stood to freshen his drink. I had only sipped at mine and set the glass on the coffee table. He used the poker to stir the fire, causing logs to sink into the licking aroused flames, and again sat across from me.

"Why didn't you tell me before this that Wendell had spoken to you about a connection with his son?"

"Hardly a connection. The boy might well have brought me a copy of *Now* when the magazine appeared, certainly nothing more."

"I find it difficult to believe the son being in your class and Wendell on the hunt are a coincidence. Sheriff Sawyers must feel the same way."

"Jesus, how did everything go so wrong?" Cliff asked and rubbed his face. "Why can't it be somebody just got shot in a hunting accident and leave it at that?"

"The same question I'm asking you."

"You can't defend me with what you've got?"

"No, Cliff, I need it all."

"God, to be a whale gliding majestically through blue seas. I'm so damn tired, Walter. I feel I've been punctured, the air let out."

He drank, let his head fall back, and talked toward the ceiling, his eyes half-shut.

"When I spotted the grouse, I told Wendell not to fire unless it flushed.

"'You'd never shoot a bird on the ground, I reckon,'" he said. "'I sure admire your high standards.'

"There was a harder edge to Wendell's voice, and I would've faced him except for the grouse. It didn't flush but footed away making trilling sounds as it peered back at us.

"'We'll step up the pace,' I told Wendell and lengthened my stride to close the gap and force a flush.

"'Maybe that bird's so young it don't know it should be scared,' Wendell said.

"'I'll give it further motivation,' I said and scooped up a handful of wet snow, patted it into a ball, and threw it. The grouse flushed and angled up and over the laurel. We watched it curve around and glide downward, its shadow skimming the snow.

"'Gone away,' Wendell said.

"'We didn't exactly respond with the killer instinct,' I said.

"'Killing's new to me,' he said.

"I looked at him, but he continued to gaze off in the direction the bird had flown. As we began to work around the laurel, I turned to Wendell and found him watching me.

"'Something?' I asked.

"'Hate dirtying clean snow,' he said and used his gun barrel to indicate the tracks left by our boots. They had stirred up mud from the thawing ground.

"'I feel the same way,' I said.

"'Like something good made bad,' he said, and those pale eyes leveled at me. 'You consider yourself a writer or teacher first of all?'

"'I don't think it's an either-or proposition,' I said over my shoulder.

"'The minds of the young,' Wendell said. 'Like bread dough. Pat them into all kinds of shapes.'

"'A great responsibility,' I said.

"'Drop the wrong word, and it might lodge in the brain of a boy, take seed, set him off bad the rest of his life.'

"'I try to be guarded in the sensitive areas about what I tell my classes.'

"'Jeremiah told me you always went the extra mile for your students.'

"'I attempt to,' I said.

"'A man and his wife grow a beautiful child,' he said. 'They give him the fullness of their days, their toil, and their love. They clothe and protect him from hunger and cold. Then he's thieved away and corrupted, lured into sin by an older man he admires, his teacher.'

"'You're accusing me of that?' I asked, again turned. Fury had transformed that deadpan face. He raised his gun barrel.

"'I seen your exhibition,' he said. 'Walked through that place. Naked men on walls. Sodomites.'

"'Those photographs were no moral statement but an exercise and study in black-and-white,' I answered him. 'And I'm in the dark why you're talking to me like this.'

"'You in the dark all right,' he said. 'You belong to the dark.'

"'Wendell, we've gotten off wrong here somehow, so let's forget the hunt and straighten this out,' I said.

"He drew back the Remington's bolt, released it, and aimed the gun at my genitals.

"'I been trying to do right,' he said. 'I asked God for release, but the Lord's not granted it. You got to provide me that.'

"'You're actually meaning to use that gun on me?' I asked.

"'I am,' he said and clicked off the safety.

"'Mr. Ripley, for God's sake let's be rational here.'

"'God and rational don't come into this,' he said. 'I studied it out.'

"'How will killing me help you or anybody? Consider the consequences.'

"'I been living with consequences long enough. Time to wipe the slate.'

"The Remington was still aimed at me. I watched his index finger snug to the trigger.

"'You'll end up in prison or worse,' I said.

"'Maybe not. During hunting season you can hardly pick up the paper without seeing somebody's been shot. The authorities expect it.'

"I was trembling," Cliff said. "Everything was quiet except for the sound of water trickling under the snow and calls from ravens up toward the ridge. I swore to him I'd never had any relationship with his son.

"'No jury'd convict me,' he said.

"I turned away and glanced down over rounded contours of the white land before I again looked behind me. He'd lifted his shotgun to his shoulder and was squinting along the barrel. He meant to do it. I saw the hate. I had no doubt, took a step away, pivoted, and fired. Oh, Jesus, the blood, all that red blood spurting out over the white snow."

His head hung forward, and his eyes clenched against seeing it.

"Why haven't you told the truth about what happened?"

"I thought I could keep it simple. Wendell was right about hunters often being killed. I would avoid being charged and possibly taken to court."

"Tell it now."

"Who'd believe it? And he called me a sodomite. The furor

caused by my exhibition would resurface and stamp me forever in the public's eye as a deviant. Walter, I've been seeing a girl in Baltimore. We're serious about each other. She was with me and the whales. Her father's a prominent doctor who doesn't approve of me as it is."

"There's no way you could have been mistaken about Wendell's intent?"

"I saw the contorted loathing on his face. He meant to kill me all right."

I tried to make sense of it and waited for Cliff to give me more. He sat holding his glass in both hands, his eyes open now but still directed to the past.

"You know nothing more about Wendell's son, Jeremiah?" I asked.

"Nothing."

"You haven't heard he was poisoned?"

"It's news to me, and I've told you all I can. See Drake."

"See him about what?"

"The son worked for him."

"I know."

"Well, Drake can help, and will, and that's all I have to say."

THIRTEEN

I drove to Grizzly's and walked past the plastic bear, which had a loudspeaker inserted inside its belly that produced a low cyclic growl, the result both frightening and delighting children. They drew toy pistols to aim and shoot at it.

The chief clerk, a muscled Virginia Tech ex–football player named Boomer, told me Drake had driven to his Blind Sheep cabin for two days hunting. Boomer had been selected second-team All-American but was slipping into a softening, settling body, though you could still see muscled remnants from his days of gridiron eminence.

"He go alone?" I asked.

"Un-huh, Drake likes solo hunts. He told me he gets his best ideas by himself up on Blind Sheep."

"Boomer, were you here when Wendell Ripley's boy Jeremiah ran the shoe department?"

"Sure was, though we never called him Jeremiah. Just Jerry."

"Why did he quit his job?"

"Can't help you there, Mr. Frampton. He upped and left without telling anybody. I worked the stockroom back then. Jerry never said good-bye or collected his last week's pay."

"You hear anything about his being poisoned?"

"I did but got no details. Lots of talk, nothing nobody could pin down."

A customer entered, bringing along wind with him, and the

ghost grouse stirred on its nylon line. Boomer signaled a clerk to wait on the man, who carried a pair of ice skates.

"You knew Jeremiah's father?" I asked Boomer.

"I sure did. Mr. Ripley liked being around here near his son. Came in and hung out even after Jerry left. He never talked much, though he eyed everybody who walked through the door."

"Why would he do that?"

"Lonely, I guess. Maybe hoping for somebody. He was bad tore up."

"You able to tell me anything else about Mr. Ripley?"

"Well, he was kind of country, you know, the sort that'll sit around for hours without needing to talk. I guess he had nothing much else to do. He did ask me and others if we knew a sailor named—hold it a second, I got it—Leonard Dawson. I told him I didn't. I think he hoped to see that fellow."

"He never explained why?"

"No, sir, he never explained hardly anything."

"What did you think of Jerry?"

From the back of the store came the sound of grinding. The clerk was sharpening the man's ice skates.

"Nice, clean-cut boy, had a way with women customers who came in to buy for their men. More citified than his father. I liked and missed him around here."

Again I drew on what Cliff had told me. Wendell had used the word "sodomite" and talked of a youth lured and defiled by a man trusted and admired. Possibly the sailor Leonard Dawson was in some way connected to Jeremiah's poisoning?

I thanked Boomer, drove off, and in Richmond stopped by stockbrokers Bunker, Rose & Diggs, where I left my umbrella beside the entrance and glanced after the fleeting market tape. At her desk Josey studied the monitor as she scribbled on a pad. Her white seashell earrings set off her tan. I pushed my new glasses higher on my nose before I made my entrance. A pearly conch shell served as a doorstop.

"I've been missing you," I said as I watched her slim, proficient fingers move rapidly over the keyboard, the nails clear and shiny from a natural polish. The sun had bleached downy hair along her wrists.

"Just returned from Grenada and blue waters," she said and had only a glance for me.

"I've always wanted to go to Spain."

"Not Spain. Long *a*. The Grenadines and scuba diving. I looked a sand shark right in the eye and stared him down. The guy turned tail."

Her phone sounded a musical tone, and she lifted it. I listened to arcane talk about expiring options. She had dated lots of men, a couple from the first flight of Richmond's blue-blood society.

I started to light a Winston. I was careful not to hold it in the thumb-and-finger reversed palm style I preferred. She and others had made fun of that as they did my umbrella. She waved a hand side to side in front of her face and shook her head. I returned the pack to my pocket.

"You live an active sporting life," I said when she finished talking.

"You should too, Raff. Take care or one of these days you'll become portly and look like a lawyer. You're already just a tad short of being a stuffed shirt."

A man stepped through the doorway, one of many who worked for the firm, a nearly total enterprise of eligible males, most if not all more physically attractive than my thin, reedy height.

"The Flannigan account again," he said.

"Tighten the screws on those turkeys and no compromise," Josey said, and he left nodding. Command came naturally to her.

"How you abuse me," I said.

"Loving abuse."

"I saw you chasing the fox at the prince's hunt breakfast."

"You didn't speak to me," she said and turned away from the monitor.

"You appeared fully occupied."

A second time her phone sounded. Again I adjusted my glasses. I continued to wear them because contacts irritated my eyes and during the fall term I had lost the left lens during a traffic case before the General District Court, the resulting disruption causing the bailiff and everybody else except the judge himself to help find it. The clerk on his knees had located the lens beneath the defense table and come up with it atop a fingertip.

"Actually I witnessed a bit of your exit," she said as she set the phone down.

"I had to leave but noticed you and the prince hit it off well."

"He's now doing business with Bunker, Rose and Diggs. The fact is he asked me to execute a significant order."

"You go to Grenada with him?" I asked, though I had not meant to. The question formed and was spoken before I considered any loss of aplomb.

"We flew in his plane."

"And looked sharks in the eye."

"Raff, I believe it's time for you to leave. I'm very busy. Visit me when the market's not rollicking."

She again turned to her monitor. I had wanted to talk about the stallion, the pin oak, and the hand I held to her. Well, not this day, if ever.

"I'll do that," I said and started off.

"And stop thinking those bad thoughts about me," she called.

As I walked past the ironfronts to the parking garage I passed a specialty store that sold toys. Through the display window I looked at a simulated American Indian village—scattered red-and-yellow autumn leaves, a tepee, birchbark canoe, bow and arrow, calumet, feathered headdress, and stones of a circular fireplace.

Children's books had been upended among them, one titled *Blood Brothers*. On the cover a buckskin-clad frontiersman shook hands with a bare-chested, war-painted brave. They solemnly eyed each other. In the background stood an Indian maiden, who held a clay cooking vessel. I bought a copy for Mary Ellen's young son, Jason.

My thoughts of Josey pictured her and the prince together, two beautiful people, their sun-toasted bodies entwined. I created pictures that aroused, angered, and shamed me.

FOURTEEN

Before heading for Jessup's Wharf, I again thought of Wendell's son, Jeremiah. If he were poisoned, there should have been an investigation. I drove to the Department of Public Safety building located behind Richmond's white, tombstone-style City Hall—the police like poor cousins housed in the older, shabbier structure.

I told the uniformed deputy at the desk I wanted to speak to a detective.

"The purpose of your visit?" he asked through a circular two-way speaker set into bulletproof glass.

I explained who I was, gave him my card, and told him I needed information concerning a missing person.

"See what I can do," the deputy said and lifted a phone. "Citizen herc on a look, anybody open?" he inquired. He listened and set the phone back. "Through the door and ask for Detective Bush."

He pointed me to a locked double door and buzzed me through. I walked along the beige corridor until I saw the "Detective Section" sign. The windowless room was filled with cubicles and resembled more what one might see in the office of an insurance agency than the jumbled disorder of a squad room as represented on TV. The detectives wore shirts and ties and might have been salesmen or executives except for handcuffs and snub-nosed pistols holstered at belts. There was, however, a certain weighing and sharpness of eye.

A female officer directed me to Detective Bush at the rear of the room. Thin, with graying hair, he appeared resigned and weary. I introduced myself as I gave him my card. He studied it before looking me over and indicating a chair. On the desk he'd set a color photograph of a border collie jumping to catch a Frisbee.

"And the person you're looking for?" he asked, his voice unhurried, yet not so much relaxed as fatigued, his body posture defensive and suggesting he expected nothing that could bring happiness into his life.

"His name is Jeremiah Ripley. I have no middle initial."

"Is this a criminal matter?"

"At this point I have little information about him."

"Spell his name for me."

I did, and he methodically two-fingered the name into a computer and scrolled the monitor. The lobe of his left ear was gone. Shot or bitten off? He exhaled and shook his head slowly.

"No wants on him," he said. He continued to scroll, pulled up a page, and scanned it. He was not a man to speak without laboriously ordering his thoughts, and his weariness seemed to gray the atmosphere that surrounded him.

"A Jeremiah Daniel Ripley reported missing by his father some three years ago. He was never located."

"Were there any leads?"

"None." He waited passively. I had the feeling he would never speak again.

"Do you have anything else?"

"The monitor has a description."

"Is he presumed dead?"

"We don't presume in this department."

I considered a moment.

"What about a sailor named Leonard Dawson?"

"His name's here, an inquiry about him. Again no record or other information and no description."

"If something turns up on either man, would you please get in touch with me?"

"I'll make a note," he said and did with a resigned effort. He looked at me out of faint blue eyes that surely belonged to a much older man. They were hooded as if peering from a burrow. He carried his burrow with him. "Your father Walter Frampton?" he asked.

"I'm his son, yes."

"Thought you resembled him."

I waited for more but no words came. Was he recalling my father's troubles? He opened a drawer and lifted out an amber Smith Brothers cough drop he placed on his grainy tongue. A good man, I thought of Detective Bush, who had likely encountered so much of humanity's mayhem and vileness that they had seared and withered all emotional responses and left him bound and deadened by scar tissue.

I headed to Jessup's Wharf and parked in front of my office, where I looked out the window. The snow had become slush along River Street, and water ran along the gutters into storm drains. I watched the red-tail hawk circle in and make a pass at the St. Luke's church steeple. The pigeons flung themselves into flight and escape. The red-tail didn't give chase but sat at the base of the steeple knowing he could take one for a meal anytime he wanted.

FIFTEEN

I needed to talk again to Brother Abram, but it was too late for me to drive back through Richmond to Chesterfield. The next morning, a cold misty day, I drove out to The Watchers. No workers sowed or reaped in the gray fallow fields. The ground had frozen again overnight, and a pond grew a dull, gray skim of ice.

I found Brother Abram not at his workshop but in one of the barracks-like buildings, from which I heard clattering. When I opened the door at one end, I faced two rows of Singer sewing machines with both men and women sitting before them. They were making brown coveralls of the type they wore themselves and I had seen for sale on the second floor of FOOD.

Brother Abram ambled among the workers until he noticed me, then approached in his heavy, rocking gait. Sewers' eyes had lifted to take me in. The place was so noisy Brother Abram led me into a small office whose desk was a section of half-inch plywood laid over sawhorses. I avoided looking at the hair growing so thickly from his nose and ears.

"I can make you a good price on a pair," he said as he closed the door. Again he seemed on the point of laughter. "Or is it you're thinking of joining us? You're surely welcome."

"Not yet, but thanks for the gracious invitation. What I'd like is to ask a few more questions about Wendell Ripley."

"Dead to this world but alive in the Lord."

"His son Jeremiah also?"

"I seem to remember I told you he was poisoned."

"And died from it?"

Brother Abram hesitated, and the corners of his merry mouth leveled slightly.

"In the spirit, yes."

"You're insinuating not the body?"

"The body is a flimsy garment."

"Brother Abram, it's important I know for certain."

"He's gone from us. We prayed for him and still do."

"Why pray for him when he's dead?"

"We pray for all the damned. Surely you've heard of Hell."

"Rarely lately. How was he poisoned?"

"Evil is a poison in the bloodstream," he said and lifted a large pair of tailor's shears from the desk to snip at an irregular scrap of discarded cloth.

"It seems what you're telling me is the poison was spiritual, not actual."

"Spirit is actuality, the most enduring gift God grants us."

"I won't dispute that, Brother Abram, but who did the poisoning?"

"Jeremiah became enticed and perverted," he said, and I saw he was fashioning a small star out of the scrap of cloth.

"Please help me by being more specific."

"Why should I?" The shears stopped snipping.

"Because I think you're a good man who believes in justice."

He laid down the star, and his cinnamon eyes lifted to mine.

"Jeremiah became enticed by and consumed with the desire for the bodies of other men."

"Who did the enticing?"

"An evil one."

"Are we talking about Satan?"

"Who else but the father of all evil?"

"Yet not a flesh-and-blood person in the here and now?"

"In the guise of one such. The devil can assume any shape he wishes except that of Our Savior."

"Does that shape have a name?"

"Most people do." The shears clicked away at emptiness.

"Is the name Leonard Dawson?"

"I have heard that name mentioned by Brother Wendell. I know Mr. Dawson not."

"But Jeremiah, his body, might not be physically dead?"

"To those of us here he is whatever the nature of his present state."

"Brother Abram, I very much need to know his whereabouts if he's alive."

"I can't be of help to you, sir. He left us and never returned. We would have taken him back and washed him in the blood, but sin conquered and defiled him. We have not closed the book on Jeremiah Daniel Ripley. He closed it on himself."

As I then turned to leave the office, I thanked him. He saw me to the door, which he shut behind me over the din from the rhythmic clacking of sewing machines. I walked to my car and driving out had to stop for plodding cows being herded across the road by a scowling, albinic man whose long colorless hair swung around his neck. He turned furious and swept an arm about in a gesture meant for me to leave.

"Sir?" I called to him after I lowered my window.

In a long-legged country stride, he moved away after the cows and gave me a fierce look while he again swept his arm as if to wipe me off the land.

I drove to Jessup's Wharf, where steam from Axapomimi Lumber's black stack flattened out over the river, the sign of a falling barometer. I fretted how to find Wendell's son, Jeremiah, whether he were dead or alive. On the slimmest chance I had overlooked the obvious and he might still live in Richmond, I checked his name in the phone directory. No such luck.

I dialed Grizzly's to see whether Drake had come back, and he answered the phone.

"I'm on my way," I told him.

I drove through the city on the Expressway to Powhite and cut over to Route 60. A tractor at Grizzly's pushed aside the last of the snow, the blade leaving black swaths across the wet asphalt. I spoke to Boomer, who stood among basketball equipment where he had fixed a hoop to a roof-support column. With a balled-up sheet of paper he made what appeared to be a delicate shot for such a large man into the center of the hoop.

"Two," another clerk called out.

I found Drake in the stockroom using a knife with a curved blade to cut open large cardboard boxes that contained fishing rods and brightly colored artificial baits.

"Preparing for spring," he said and laid the knife on the box. "I expect you'd like to talk in private."

He walked to his office. On his desk this time lay not a 1866 Winchester but an unframed oil painting of a grouse drumming atop a mossy log shaded by a hemlock forest. He lifted the canvas and examined it.

"In the larger edition of 'The Truth of the Grouse' I'm hoping to get published, I want illustrations included," he said. "The chances are I can push sales beyond the local area, maybe even interstate."

"I've been talking to Cliff," I said as I sat. "He told me what really happened between Wendell and him during the hunt. At least I'm working on that assumption as regards the truth."

"Yeah, he told me too," Drake said and laid the painting back on the desk.

"And you just went along with the story of a hunting accident without telling me?"

"Raff, it seemed the simplest way out for him and everybody concerned. I didn't want scandal any more than he did. Dangerous for him and bad for Grizzly's and my proposed book. The story would've worked except for that sheriff and still will if Cliff hangs tough."

"But you should have told me."

"Agreed and I'm sorry."

"I can't defend Cliff if he's lying."

"Sure you can, Raff. Lawyers do it all the time. Make those shit-kickers in West Virginia bring a charge and prove it. They can't now with what they got."

"Maybe they know something we, or at least I, don't."

"No," he said and sat. "And without Jerry Ripley they lack the evidence for conviction."

"What could they do if they had Jerry?"

"Who knows?" he said. He again lifted the oil to gaze at it.

"Drake, how about saying what you mean?"

"All right, what I keep thinking of is Cliff's faggy downtown exhibition. Why the hell did he have to get into that?"

"I think I don't like where you're heading."

Without comment, Drake again laid the painting on the desk.

"Cliff's one of us," I said. "And has a girl he's serious about who lives in Baltimore."

"You seen her, Raff? No? Me neither. Look, nobody's been charged yet, have they? I believe the sheriff's bluffing and this thing will blow over if everybody stays cool."

"I think you're wrong about Cliff."

"That would make me happy."

"And I need to find something definite on what happened to Jeremiah Ripley."

"Wasted effort, Raff. Jerry's gone for good one way or another, and my bet he's six feet under and wearing a grass skirt."

"You ever know any of his friends or acquaintances?"

"Jerry drove here to work from the city, did his job, and left. He never spoke about himself."

"And quit with no explanation or asking for his last week's pay."

"As I told you before, I tried to find him. I had his phone number, but he never answered, and the phone was disconnected a couple of days later. I sent his check in the mail, and it was returned by the post office, no forwarding address."

"It never occurred to you there might be trouble bringing Wendell along on the hunt?"

"It was his land. How could I know he had anything against Cliff? And Wendell wanted to come."

"He manipulated you into the invitation?"

"Looking back on it, that could be. When he heard I was going, he said he'd like to see his home place once again. The land now belongs to The Watchers. I'll never get it unless they put it up for sale. Maybe kick my tail off Blind Sheep when my lease runs out."

"I'm not certain what to do next?" I said and reached for a Winston.

"Play it cool, Raff. It's the only way. The sheriff's got nothing substantial on Cliff."

"He was at The Watchers snooping around."

"Doesn't mean he found anything. As I said before, maybe he enjoys traveling at taxpayer expense." He lifted and turned the painting to me. "So you like this picture?"

"That picture I like," I said.

SIXTEEN

D riving away, I thought about Drake and his book. People around Richmond and increasingly elsewhere had begun to call him "the Prophet of the Grouse." That appellation had its origin in Letters to the Editor columns of the *Times-Dispatch* when the shooting and resulting death of a jogger along a suburban road aroused the antigun, antihunter factions. Their protests filled mailbags, and voters petitioned the General Assembly for more severe firearm and game regulations. One letter read, "It is time mankind sheds his barbaric atavisms and joins the twentieth century."

Drake composed his own reply and posted it. He wrote: "What's so wonderful about the twentieth century? Many of its years we've been at war and buried tens of thousands of young men.

"Face it, to eat is to ingest something that has been alive. We live on life. Which is better, to award wild game a sporting chance or to herd cattle into a slaughterhouse and hit them with an eight-pound sledge between their eyes? Can you respect a slab of cow or hog meat on your plate? It's just food. I believe God provided man fish in the sea and game in the forests not only for his use but also his guidance. True hunters in the pursuit of game learn respect for this created world."

Drake's bringing God into the argument caused more letters. One correspondent wrote, "Sure, the Lord's trekking through the woods with a .45 strapped to His hip." Another stated that "God holds out His hand to offer life, not death."

When the General Assembly at its fall session debated a law that would further restrict gun ownership and use, Drake closed himself in his office and wrote the pamphlet explaining what hunting grouse meant to him. The hundred copies he ordered printed he laid out on Grizzly's front counter for customers to carry home and read. By the end of the week all the copies were gone, and he ordered two hundred additional ones printed. Moreover he began to receive requests over the phone and by mail for the pamphlet as well as invitations to speak before private and civic organizations.

I attended a debate at the Public Forum held in the St. Jude's Episcopal Church's auditorium. A sincere, collared young priest took the affirmative on the proposition that "Hunting Is a Dangerous Historical Vestige, a Nostalgia for a Time That Will Never Return." He spoke well and convincingly and ended with the words, "Let us share the goodness of this earth with our fellow creatures and rejoice in living together at peace."

Drake rose from his chair on the stage and crossed to the podium. He appeared professional and distinguished in his charcoal business suit, vest, and maroon tie. He showed neither nervousness nor discomfort.

He had brought no notes. After a pause that allowed the talking and shifting about of the audience to die, he rested his hands lightly on the podium and spoke. He kept his eyes raised and moving over the assemblage to make contact. His voice was conversational, yet authoritative. He did not seem to debate as much as to share indisputable truths of life.

"Some years ago after I returned from the service, I was unemployed, near broke, and felt I walked alone on this planet," he said. "Oh, I heard people talking, but they were distant voices across gaps from another land. I spoke just enough to get through the day and also slept a lot. The fact is the bed became the biggest part of my world.

"When I was on my feet, I drank with the same intent as a man looking down off a bridge into the invitation of dark water. I thought of slipping away from this life, just letting go and drifting off like flowing out with the tide.

"What changed me was a hike I took, this one on a mountainside in northwest Virginia, up in the high country around Monterey and across the state line into West Virginia and the uprearing of Big Allegheny. I'd been invited to a hunt by a friend. We had served in the Second Armored Division together. He'd built a shack on the mountain—one room, two bunks, a potbellied stove. We dressed in darkness by lantern light and stepped into a cold January morning. That sharp forest air cleaned out the lungs, and our boots crunched ground rime as we climbed into a hollow named Sawmill Run on the chart.

"As we hiked, a stream narrowed and divided around an island of birches. My friend instructed me to take the left fork and he took the right. We'd meet again higher up where the water junctioned. Ferns, moss, and running cedar grew along banks of the stream. Laurel glinted as frost thawed on the leaves. I walked under a hemlock gloom that had never known a full thirst.

"I had bird-hunted but never yet met a ruffed grouse and seen only pictures in sporting magazines. I knew that compared to partridges they were larger, rarer, and more difficult to bring down. My friend Mike told me hunters were lucky to gun all day and carry home a single bird.

"As I passed under a hemlock that dripped moisture, a grouse flapped from the tree. Because of the loud batting of its wings, I believed it a turkey till I saw it had a shorter neck extension and smaller body. I lifted my shotgun, but the grouse banked low and put big laurel between itself and me. Too late to shoot.

"I climbed on. I was accustomed to lowland hunting, and my calves ached. As I stopped to rest, a second grouse flushed behind me. I'd walked right by him. He flew not away but at me. I ducked, saw his dark glinty eyes as he passed, felt the fanning of his wings.

By the time I righted myself and lifted my shotgun, he'd become a shadow within shadows and gone.

"Such energy and rocketing into life. These birds gave their all at full throttle. I now hiked up the hollow with no thought for aching calves. A third bird flushed. I glimpsed him and fired. The load blasted into an ironwood bough and caused it to swing broken.

"The stream narrowed as it angled to the junction. A fourth grouse busted up beyond a stand of alders. I got off a snapshot, and the bird dipped but kept going before setting down from an awkward crippled flight ahead of me.

"I marked the spot and hurried to it, my Savage at the ready. The bird was running, dragging a wing. He left drops of blood on the leafy ground cover. I tracked him twenty or thirty yards until he toppled and lay watching me from his fully opened, shiny eyes.

"Calmly he waited for death, no whining, bitching, no panic or begging, the grouse way, all or nothing, live high and die without flinching. Fly hell bent and measure life not by extent but intensity.

"The bird gave up the ghost in my hands, a last faint flutter and gone. I felt saddened and loving. The intricate beauty of its bronze feathers and its will to survive in such rugged country inspired me. I drove back to Richmond thinking I could at least give life all I had left. I borrowed money to start a gun shop, a business where I not only repaired and sold firearms but also tried to teach the truth of the grouse, which is bravery and endurance, no compromise with surrender.

"I hope the theologians don't become upset when I say on Big Allegheny I refound the God I'd lost. The grouse became my communion. I mouthed its white flesh with reverence and tasted the forest and goodness of creation. From that day to this my God runs the ridges with me, lives and breathes in high clean air and beside the pure water and mighty hemlocks.

"Some men are barbarians during hunt season. They are pigs, meat hunters, hogs for the kill. They are lawless and in no way will be changed by acts of the legislature. But there are others who are ennobled by what they hunt and honorably kill. They are first to come to the aid of an endangered species, to spread feed during the heavy snows, to save the ducks by building breeding grounds, to care for the wounded fawn or the eagle that has taken shot. They are law-abiding men who shouldn't be penalized for the sins of others. They preserve more than they kill.

"I give thanks for the grouse and honor the gallant bird. I feel I'm a brother to him. There are nights when I wake in the dark and think of them perched on thrashing limbs of wind-whipped hemlocks in the high country. I lie hearing in the pumping of my blood the birds' drumming and beat of their wings. I give thanks for the grouse to the only place it can be awarded, to God, the Master Architect of all things."

Drake paused a moment before walking back to his chair on the stage. A single clap of hands started applause that built to a standing ovation.

"To say the least a very out-of-left field theological position," the young priest spoke in rebuttal. But he had lost the debate and knew it.

SEVENTEEN

As I walked back along River Street, Prince Jamir sped through town on his sun-dazzled Harley, its engine speaking rumbling, bridled horsepower. He appeared dashing in a visored black helmet and awarded me a wave.

At the office Jason sat in his chair beside Mary Ellen's desk. He held *Blood Brothers* open across his knees.

"It's his favorite book," Mary Ellen said. "And kindly of you to give it to him."

"Would you rather be the Indian brave or the frontiersman?" I asked Jason.

He didn't look up or speak, but his small index finger moved slowly and touched the war-painted Indian.

"Me too," I said and glanced at Mary Ellen. At least his response was to me directly, meaning I had made progress in our relationship. Mary Ellen was pleased.

That afternoon as I worked at my desk with the door closed I raised my head, then stood and moved quietly to the door and listened. She was singing softly to Jason. I peeped through to see him sitting on her lap, her arms around him, her lips close to his ear:

> There is a land not far away
> Where children love to run and play,
> Where trees are hung with lemon drops
> And all the clouds have ice cream tops.

When she glanced up and caught me watching, she placed Jason on his chair and handed him the book. His delicate hands took hold of it. She came into my office.

"Mr. Frampton, I didn't know you could hear us. And we won't disturb you again."

"I never heard the child's verse you were singing."

"It's one I made up. They reassure him."

"Mary Ellen, I've noticed he doesn't arrive with the other children but is let off by another bus earlier."

"He's enrolled in special education and has a shorter day," she said.

"I seem to scare him," I said.

"Not you, Mr. Frampton, but all men. He won't talk to them. The women, yes, a little, but not the men."

She turned away quickly with no further explanation and hurried into the outer office, where she kept her back to me. I sat uncertain what to do next. Apparently I'd disturbed her. Then she again walked into my office and closed the door.

"The night my husband Ben died in Stuttgart, the German TV showed his crash on camera—the helicopter hitting the power line, exploding, falling in flames. They had a close-up of his body black and steaming, his face bloody and agonized."

She stopped and drew breath. She was trying not to cry.

"The hospital called me while I was playing cards with other servicemen's wives. When I left the hospital and reached our living quarters, I heard Jason screaming and the baby-sitter trying to quiet him. She had been in the kitchen and hadn't realized what he was watching on the TV. He had seen his father on fire and screaming. Jason too screamed, for hours, until he dropped asleep exhausted, and when he woke he wouldn't talk or look at anyone. Not a word or glance. He kept his eyes shut and felt his way around his room as if blind."

Fighting to maintain control, Mary Ellen swallowed and lifted her chin.

"It's taken two years for doctors, psychologists, and special teachers to bring him to where he'll speak, and that for a time just to me. Not until last spring has he spoken to others, but only women. He can read and count, do his written exercises, but he won't talk to men. The psychologists believe this will pass, but he should be protected from further traumatic experiences. There are times during the night he still screams."

She again turned, opened the door to walk to her desk, and sat by Jason. I stood, stopped behind her, and touched her shoulder. Again about to break, she bowed her head and gripped her hands, squeezing the blood in her fingers to their tips.

"I have business in the clerk's office," I said and left her.

Valor, I thought. During the heat of battle it displayed itself chiefly in men, but long term and over the wear of years the women owned it.

"A Mr. Sam Tuggle called," Mary Ellen said when I reentered the office.

Jason was still reading and didn't look up.

"Mr. Tuggle identified himself as the Seneca County, West Virginia, district attorney and requested you contact him. I have his number."

If he wanted me, I thought, let him pay the bill, and I considered calling collect. No, better to stay on the best terms possible with all legal authorities. Oil over the waters.

"Mr. Tuggle," I said after I was passed through to him by his secretary.

"Call me Sam," he said, his voice husky, deep, energetic. "Get that out of the road."

"Fine. I'm Walter."

"What's the weather down your way?" He sounded expansively genial.

"Sunny, cold, wind from the northeast," I said, thinking he was talking on my nickel. "Twenty-nine degrees."

"Don't tell me about wind. Blowing hard enough 'round here to scalp you. People carrying weights to keep their feet on the ground."

I wasn't about to trade small talk about the wind or weather and waited.

"It's my understanding you represent Mr. Clifford A. Dickens," he said.

"That's correct."

"We'd appreciate it here in High Gap if you could persuade Mr. Dickens to pay us a visit."

"Sam, traveling back out to those mountains would cause Mr. Dickens both anxiety and great discomfort. He is more than willing to offer himself here in Virginia for deposing at your convenience."

"Afraid that just won't buy it, Walt. We want him here with us one way or another."

"You're thinking of charging him?"

"We may feel compelled to do that very thing."

"On what count?"

"Involuntary manslaughter. Now, I know you're going to tell me the shooting was just an accident, but I'd like to remind you that under the code in your state and mine that there's no such thing as accidental homicide."

"I'm aware of that, yet believe it's pushing the code to bring a charge in this instance."

I had raised my voice a bit, and Mary Ellen looked through the doorway at me. She held the green can with a long spout she used to water her African violets.

"Your client killed another man in the negligent and reckless use of his firearm. Prima facie case."

"At worst a misdemeanor."

"A misdemeanor under the code of West Virginia that's punishable at the discretion of the court by fine or imprisonment or both."

"Why inflict either in this case?"

"Because we're clamping down out here and trying to put a stop to the taking of human life. Too many good people dying needlessly. We investigate all homicides. We want the word to get around that Seneca County won't put up with the careless use of firearms."

"My opinion is that such a procedure can be carried too far," I said and glanced out the window to see the pigeons flying around St. Luke's steeple.

"Saving a single life justifies lots of prosecution. Of course the court can also just reprimand and fine a man, put him on probation, turn him loose. But that's up to a judge or jury. They good people around here and not out to stick it to anybody from out of state. I'd like you to believe that, and we'd appreciate you advising your client to come on up and see us. We'll treat him in a manner that could benefit him in any further legal action. You're also invited."

"You would appreciate it?" I said, thinking that the correct plea if necessary should be self-defense but that I could not use it without subjecting Cliff to an investigation leading to Jeremiah and the possible allegation and airing of a homosexual association. I also thought of Cliff's relationship to his girl and her father, the doctor who already disapproved.

"Save everybody time, sweat, and money," Sam said.

"It would save more if you just took his sworn statement here in Virginia."

"We don't seem to be getting very far down this road, do we?"

"I believe any charge is excessive under the circumstances."

"Well, if Mr. Dickens doesn't comply, I got no alternative than to request a Seneca County magistrate to issue a warrant for his arrest, such warrant to be forwarded to the commonwealth attorney's office, city of Richmond, Virginia. But I'll hold off awhile. Action won't be necessary if Mr. Dickens presents himself to my office within three days."

"I will get back to you."

"That'd be real nice," he said and laughed. "Let's do all we can to keep everybody happy and full in the belly."

When I hung up, I immediately phoned Cliff's carriage house. No answer except the reply from his damn answering machine. I called every hour as I sat working and fidgeting at my desk.

Just after three that afternoon he lifted his phone during the recorded message. I explained my conversation with District Attorney Sam Tuggle.

"If I go to High Gap voluntarily and they try me, I'll receive just a slap on the wrist?" Cliff asked.

"Likely, but no guarantee. It's your decision."

"No way, I'm not doing it. What if I take a vacation for a while?"

"Cliff, I can't be a part of your evading arrest if it comes to that."

"It hasn't come to that yet, has it? Give you time to work things out for me and get them off my back. Walter, my thanks and talk to you later."

He hung up, and I tried raising him again, but he wouldn't answer. I laid my legal tablet before me on the desk and in For and Against columns listed all the facts I knew about what had happened on Blind Sheep. I definitely wanted to cut this thing off before it reached the indictment process. The fact was that even if we were forced to use a plea of self-defense in court, it would not hold up without collaborating evidence.

The missing link was Wendell's son, Jeremiah, probably dead but no verifiable facts about his death, and if alive, where would he now hang his hat? I reviewed what I knew about him: brought up among The Watchers, a Virginia Commonwealth University student, apparently an admirer of Cliff, a shoe clerk at Grizzly's, from what Brother Abram told me involved in homosexual liaisons. Wendell, according to Cliff, had used the word "sodomite."

I considered hiring a private detective. Costs would be substantial, and though I was doing all right financially, I didn't want to spend the money if I could find another way. I thought about Richmond's gay community. At least the possibility existed that someone in that community had associated with Jeremiah and could answer the question whether or not he lay in his grave. Might I ask around in the right quarters and find answers? I didn't know how or where to start? If I frequented the homosexual bars and their other haunts, who would talk openly to a prying attorney?

A thought emerged. Philip Garrow. I'd known him at John Marshall and liked him, though he'd never been as close as Drake and Cliff, my blood brothers.

EIGHTEEN

I knew what had become of Philip Garrow. He had attended Dartmouth, lived for a time in New York, and returned to Richmond where he opened the Left Bank Café in Shockoe Bottom, a once seamy section of Richmond where Confederate deserters hung out during the Civil War. The Left Bank had done so well he had bought an old saddlery in Shockoe Slip and turned it into a classy restaurant named Le Gallic. I had never eaten there. He had also been seen in the front rank of those marching during Gay Pride Day, an act which had disconcerted me, yet I conceded his leaving the closet so openly demonstrated valor of a different sort.

I couldn't get away from the office till noon and at Richmond found space in an underground municipal garage eerily lighted by mercury vapor lamps that cast spectral shadows on dingy yellow walls. I walked along Cary Street to the Slip, a deteriorating commercial area during my youth that in more recent years had transformed itself into a region of style and fashion. An elegant hotel rose among smart shops, bistros, and art galleries. Youth, money, and as yet undaunted hope created excitement and vibrancy.

The entrance to Le Gallic appeared modest, a single door with a large brass knob, and unlike other eateries along the street, no menu had been posted. A carelessly penned note announced that Le Gallic would not open until six o'clock.

Using my car key, I tapped on the door's frosted glass. No one answered, though I heard voices inside. I rapped more loudly. Still no response. I walked up the street to the Windsor Arms Hotel, located Le Gallic's number in the directory of a public booth, and called.

"We're taking no reservations until Tuesday," a voice told me before I asked.

"I'm phoning to speak to Philip Garrow," I said, thinking business had to be good. I remembered Philip always accented the second syllable of his last name.

"The nature of your business, sir?"

"That's confidential."

"Your name, *s'il vous plaît*?"

I told him.

"I'll see whether Monsieur Garrow is available."

I had heard the waiters spoke with French accents but that only a few could converse in the language. Reportedly the service was flawless, yet if you failed to leave an adequate tip, you might receive dark looks and insolent remarks on your way out.

"That you, Walter?" Philip asked, no French accent, just softly Southern and cultured. "It's been such a very long time."

"I knocked but nobody answered."

"Le Gallic's found it sound business to be difficult to reach and that impertinence pays." He laughed. "What can I do for you? Anything, just ask."

"I'd like for us to talk."

"I'll be waiting."

At Le Gallic he opened the door and shook my hand. His white bow tie contrasted brightly against a dark blue shirt. He had taken on weight since college days, a glow to his skin, a bemused expression about his eyes and mouth.

"So good to see you, Walter," he said. "I've often thought of you and heard you've become a barrister. Life's treating you well I hope."

"Well enough. I read in *Richmond After Dark* about Le Gallic's success."

"The public loves a bit of fakery along with food, and our fare is honestly good," he said and raised a hand as if to present his restaurant on his palm to me. Milky globed lights illuminated the high room and dark paneling relieved by alternating gilt-framed mirrors and prints by Matisse, Picasso, and Rouault. The bar had a speckled marble top. White linens covered round tables set at the center with crystal carafes.

"Impressive," I said.

"Come eat as my guest," he said. "We serve a rack of lamb so delicious it would melt hearts at the IRS."

"I'll do that," I said, though I knew I wouldn't. "Spare me a moment in private?"

He smiled, raised a finger, and led me to his office off the kitchen, where a white-clad chef and assistants darted about among steam from simmering pots. Philip closed the door against rattling and clashing.

His desk held a French telephone set beside a silver inkwell on a green blotter. As we sat, I faced a shelf behind the desk on which was displayed a piece of sculpture that had been made from painted tin and twisted copper wire—the representation of a naked tightrope walker who held not a pole to balance himself but a fire extinguisher in one hand and flames of his burning palm in the other. The implication was that if he tried to put out the fire he would fall into a chasm beneath.

"Fetching, don't you think?" Philip asked.

"Who or what's the figure?"

"You could say mankind perhaps, or possibly Job, or take your choice. The artist gave it no name. The point is it resonates in the mind. You know him by the way, your friend Clifford Dickens."

Cliff. Of course he would have an acquaintance with Philip and others here in the Slip. There had been the exhibition, and his work necessarily meant he moved among artistic people. Was there a closer association with Philip?

"He is still your friend?" Philip asked.

"I spoke with him only yesterday."

"Clifford's an authentic genius but needs focus. Always hopping around from one project to another, different genres, a little of this, a little of that. I read about the hunting accident and trust it hasn't shaken him too greatly."

"He's surviving, though stressed."

"And your father? I felt terrible about all that publicity created by the ravenous wolves of the press and media. You haven't married, have you?"

"I have designs on a lady," I answered, wondering whether his question had subtle implications.

"Designs, a good word. Like blueprints for a structure that needs to be built brick by brick and not on shifting sands. Well, I wish you luck. Look, Walter, you're not uncomfortable with me, are you? You seem, well, a bit fidgety."

"No," I lied.

"I have no designs on you if that's what you're worried about, but I am fond of you and wish we could have a drink and converse now and again about the old days."

"That's generous of you, Philip."

"All right, now what's on your mind? You're not after money, I hope. I'm very close with it."

"Do you see Cliff from time to time?" I asked, again looking at the gaunt tightrope walker.

"He's been in to dine occasionally, but not for months. When he does come, I send a good bottle of wine to his table. I paid him twenty-five hundred for that piece. Really an artist of the first degree."

"My interpretation of the figure on the wire is that he's desperate but doesn't have a chance," I said.

"Very good, Walter. Man, or mankind, is desperate—also brave, at times pitiful, heroic, a coward, a survivor, weakling, giant, himself a work of art."

"It's one man I'm looking for. I thought perhaps you could help."

"Connected to one of your law squabbles? I won't be drawn into any sort of litigation."

"I'm not asking that but attempting to find what's become of a youth named Jeremiah Ripley. You've heard of him?"

"Why should I have done so?"

"I was told he used to live around the area."

"You're suggesting he's of a certain persuasion?"

"I think he is or was."

"And of course that means I would know."

"Please, Philip, not you personally. Just a chance shot you could put me in touch with someone who might remember him."

"You're very sure you're not dragging me into a legal thicket?"

"You have my word."

"Good enough for me. Fact is I do know a little something about Jeremiah. He was quite a handsome, sought-after young man. Heads turned when he passed. He had beautiful blond hair and an aristocratic nose like the Prince of Wales."

"What's happened to him?"

"I have no idea. He hasn't been seen around the Slip for several years. He applied for a job at Le Gallic, was hired, yet never arrived for his training."

"Would you ask about for me?"

"I'm not to be involved?"

"I'm just after information. And what about a man, a sailor, named Leonard Dawson?"

"There I draw a blank."

"I would greatly appreciate your help."

"I'll do what I can. Humanity, Walt, members come and go."

I didn't know whether that was another innuendo or not and drew a card from my wallet to give him.

"Jessup's Wharf," he said. "Quaint village. Are you happy there, Walter?"

"I'm doing all right, thanks."

"The roads we travel, eh? A curiosity. What do you think the good Lord had in mind when He started it all?"

"Philip, I haven't worked that out."

"Sometimes I believe it's entertainment. Celestial follies. He and the angels draw chairs to the brink of the firmament and watch the show. I'll do what I can for you."

He escorted me to the street. I looked back at waiters moving among tables and setting napkins they shaped like a pope's miniature white miter. Again Philip shook my hand.

I walked into the world, my mind still relaying the vision of the naked man on the tightrope, his palm burning and the destruction that waited beneath.

NINETEEN

Since I was in the city, I walked from Shockoe Slip up to East Main and past Richmond's contradictory mixture of antiquated iron storefronts and contemporary steel-and-concrete towers of the banking and financial district. At Bunker, Rose & Diggs I found Josey leaned back in her chair, her hands joined behind her head, a posture that lifted her breasts beneath her yellow knit sweater. She looked, well, victorious.

"What's happening, Raff?" she asked and cocked an unshod, nylon-encased, beautifully arched foot on an opened lower drawer of her desk. A black leather pump lay toppled on the mouse-gray carpet.

"I'd like to take you to dinner."

"Can't tonight, old buddy of mine. I'm full to busting anyhow. Digesting a good day on the market. The Dow's up—a fine seventy-points-and-change meal."

"You made a killing?" I asked and sat carefully so as not to entangle my legs. I had come close to stepping on her conch shell doorstop when I entered.

"Oh, I made some bread this day. When you bringing me your dollars? I just happen to know of a situation I believe has tremendous potential."

"Tremendous is quite an enormous word," I said.

"Well, admittedly a bit overstated. As you know it's part of the trade. At Bunker, Rose & Diggs, we live on a diet of adjectival superlatives."

"This situation have a name?"

"No mon-ee, no tick-ee," she said and flexed her arms.

"You and the Prince Jamir still doing business?" I asked.

"None of your concern, but, yes, I receive a nice order from him now and again."

"And I assume you continue to pursue the fox and engage in other sporting events."

"Raff, let's not drop into your haughty mode. Indeed we, along with the Gaffneys, chase Reynard from time to time. We ran a red fox into the outskirts of Jessup's Wharf, and the little beastie turned at the river, where he escaped through a culvert. Buckshot, our lead hound, got stuck, and the Rescue Squad had to sledge the pipe to save him. The prince intends to pay them and the Virginia Department of Highways the cost."

"You ever going out with me again, Josey?"

"Old buddy, you're my lifelong friend. Of course I'll go out with you but not to bed. It would be an unnecessary complication to both our lives."

"I'm all for complication."

"You're sweet, I love you, and wish it had worked out for us, but it's not to be."

"I may go home and shoot myself," I said as I stood.

"Wait, I can make you some money. It's pretty nearly a sure thing."

"Put me down for five thousand," I said.

"Five's the best you can do?" she asked and made a wry face.

"Well, ten."

"Afraid this investment trust has a twenty-five-thousand entry."

"Too steep for me at the moment," I said and thought if Charles LeBlanc had not been spending his insurance money so freely I could have made the investment for him.

"Alas," she said, dropped her arms before standing, and fitted her foot into the fallen pump. "Kiss my cheek."

"I would prefer other regions but can't refuse even such a meager portion," I said and brushed her cheek while at the same time inhaling the full womanly scent of her to carry along with me.

I was back in Jessup's Wharf and my office by three. Mary Ellen had left a note which read: "No calls." She had left early to take Jason to a female Richmond orthodontist. Rain pelted the window. I had neglected to bring my umbrella from the car.

I'd not eaten lunch and considered crossing to the Dew Drop for a bowl of hot vegetable soup before settling to work. As I stood and reached for my hat, Cliff called.

"They're holding me under arrest," he said.

"Who's holding you?"

"The police in the city's Detention Section. Two detectives were waiting at the carriage house."

"I'm coming," I said, thinking District Attorney Tuggle had jumped the gun. I bundled up and drove through rain to Richmond's modern John Marshall Courts Building on Ninth Street, where I explained to the receptionist that I represented Cliff and wanted to see the charge listed on his arrest warrant. She had dark eyelashes so long they resembled antennae and told me Gerald Horner, the commonwealth's attorney, had gone for the day.

"But I believe I can line you up with Mr. DeVan, his assistant," she said. She too was ready to leave.

I sat on a leather chair waiting to see Mr. DeVan. Except for a large, decorative Virginia state seal on the wall, the carpeted anteroom could have belonged to a dentist and lacked only outdated magazines and elevator music, yet from this place the process began that sent men to prison and occasionally death.

Mr. DeVan—black, intense, and harried—asked me into his small, first-floor office that had semitransparent gauzelike drapes over the lower half of the ceiling-to-floor window, its glass tinted a pale green.

"Give me a minute to find what's transpiring," he said as he sat at his computer keyboard.

I waited. People walking past on the street appeared like apparitions moving through an aqueous world. I wanted a cigarette.

"We received an extradition warrant delivered by fax, the demanding state West Virginia, specifically Seneca County," Mr. DeVan said as he turned from the monitor. "The charge is voluntary manslaughter."

I stared unbelieving. Not involuntary but voluntary, its definition a felonious taking of life without premeditation, conspiracy, or malice. The cause was typically great provocation. What could they know in Seneca County that I didn't?

"How do I arrange bail?" I asked.

"Bail's denied at this time by our magistrate since Mr. Dickens is a fugitive from another state."

"He's no fugitive. He hasn't fled this jurisdiction."

"He was arrested on a fugitive warrant, so in terms of the law he is. Moreover Seneca County requests that bail not be granted."

"That is not Seneca County's or West Virginia's province."

"Agreed, it's not binding, but the magistrate in that jurisdiction can request whatever he wishes."

"When's the hearing?"

"Nine in the morning, General District Court. The Commonwealth's practice is to bring a fugitive before a judge as quickly as possible to inform him of his rights. We do it for other states, they for us. At the hearing a detective will be present with a prepared waiver of extradition in the event your client chooses to execute it."

"Might Mr. Dickens surrender himself to Seneca County voluntarily?"

"That can't be decided by this office or at this juncture in the process."

"I want to see him."

"I'll call over to the lockup," he said, lifted his phone, and spoke into it, his chair swiveled away from me. Droplets of rain streaking the window had a greenish hue. He again faced me. "They know you're coming."

"May I use your *Michie's Jurisprudence* a moment?" I asked, eyeing the law books on his shelves.

"Be my guest."

I stood, looked up the penalty for voluntary manslaughter in West Virginia, and thanked Mr. DeVan. The city lockup was across Ninth Street in the same Department of Public Safety building where I had talked to Detective Bush. Rain splashed in puddles, and I hunched under my umbrella tilted against a wind that flapped patrolmen's yellow slickers.

I knew that Richmond's Sheriff's Department operated the Detention Section and took the escalator down to the lower level, where I showed my identification to a desk officer. He turned me over to a deputy who led me through a corridor at the end of which we passed through two electronically operated steel doors of a sally port, the second one opening onto the lockup. Prisoners wearing either tan or orange coveralls stood in line under guard waiting their turns to arrange bail before a magistrate who sat behind what reminded me of a movie theater's ticket window except if those under arrest had the money, their admission costs would provide them tickets out rather than entrance in.

Everything in this lower level was painted the same dingy beige—the brick-and-mortar walls, the floors, the bars of the holding cell that the deputy showed me to. A fluorescent light buzzed, the tube protected by a ceiling cavity. Cliff waited, his clothes disheveled, his long hair in need of a comb.

"I thought you'd never reach here," he said, wiping at his hair. "They've fingerprinted, photographed, and strip-searched me. Look at the bunk." He pointed. "It's steel and has no mattress. Am I supposed to sleep on that? They told me they don't allow prisoners to have anything they can set fire to. They've emptied my pockets. Where would I find a match to start a fire? It's inhuman, Walter. Spring me from this loathsome place."

"Easy, Cliff," I said and touched the back of his hand that gripped a bar. "We'll get it worked out."

"Don't I have rights?" he asked and looked about him, his expression agitated and frightened. "What are they accusing me of?"

"Essentially that you provoked Wendell or he you, causing tempers to flare and a resulting death."

"I wasn't provoked into hot temper. I acted to save my life."

"The charge indicates their belief they have proof of a dispute or conflict between you and Wendell."

"That's insane."

"My guess is the sheriff suspects your past relationship with Jeremiah is the basis for the warrant."

"There was no relationship. I had him in class and signed his magazine. Nothing more."

"Still it's a connection from which a relationship might be inferred."

"They must be desperate to pursue that reasoning. Christ, you smell the fear in this place? It's in the walls. There's no other stink like it. Help me, Walter."

"I intend to, but we'll have to wait for the hearing in the morning. Extradition's been requested by Seneca County. Nothing can be done until that's decided."

"Walter, this thing's gotten grossly out of hand. Make Drake do something."

"Do what?"

"He can come testify for me," he said and ran fingers through his hair.

"I'll call him soon as I leave here."

"What happens in High Gap if I go back and am convicted?"

"In West Virginia voluntary manslaughter is punishable by confinement in the penitentiary for not less than one or more than five years."

"You hear what you're telling me? They're ruining my life."

"Do you want another lawyer? I can recommend good ones but none that can get you out before the hearing."

"It's not you." He stepped away from the bars and then back. "I mean you do realize I am actually here in a jail and facing prison?"

"I realize it. You want to tell what else happened up on Blind Sheep between you and Wendell?"

"Nothing else happened."

"Sheriff Sawyers has apparently convinced Seneca County's district attorney that you're lying."

"Get Drake over here."

"What will he do for you I can't?"

"I need to talk to him."

"Why would you want to talk to him and not me?"

"Just please do it, Walter, and don't ask questions."

I started to refuse, but even if he were keeping the full truth from me, a meeting between the two of them should bring it all out, and I could assess the situation from that point forward.

"Okay, Cliff. I will seek him out."

TWENTY

I left Cliff looking miserable, frantic, and lost under the harsh, unforgiving cellblock light. Back through the sally port I used the pay phone in the corridor to phone Drake at Grizzly's. Boomer said Drake had gone to a Lions Club meeting in Petersburg to give his grouse talk.

I drove through the dark to Jessup's Wharf and Miss Mabel's. As I hung up my overcoat, she tapped on the door that separated her side of the house from the section I rented. She often did so at odd hours. Though I'd been living with her some three years, I'd never been in her quarters. She was a spinster, a protector of the old bygone ways and manners I considered better than those of my own generation. She apparently believed it would not appear proper for her to have the company of a single man in her parlor without another lady being present. Often her small mouth rounded as if awaiting a kiss, yet at the same time she had the look of a graying, erect women who for many years had faced into a stiff wind.

She remained concerned about my health, telling me I looked pale and puny. Often she brought me oatmeal, fried liver, greens, grits, beaten biscuits, and slices of rare beef. "You should eat more meat," she instructed me. "Don't listen to the voguish nonsense on TV about calories and fat. For women yes, perhaps, but all the great men of this nation were meat eaters."

As she stood at our joint doorway she would also try to peer around me. I believed she suspected I kept liquor and was attempting to sniff out where I hid my Old Crow and George Dickel. So far I'd been able to foil her. If she sneaked into my apartment to look while I was away at work, I'd never found evidence of it. Actually I believed her too honorable to commit such a deceitful act.

"You'll catch your death running around in this weather without your overshoes," she said and offered me a plate of fried pork, snap beans, applesauce, and a glass of milk. I thanked her, and again she tried to look over my shoulder before pulling the door shut and locking it.

I ate, had my bath, and as I buttoned on my pajamas found among the covers I'd left tossed that morning the library copy of *Moby Dick* that I had been reading. As usual I lifted the color photograph of Josey in her slick black bathing suit posed to dive off the three-meter board, one knee raised, her arms leveled before her, drops of water glistening on her skin. Cliff had snapped and enlarged the picture for me.

I gave myself to the bed, reviewed events, and sank into sleep trying to decide my next move in Cliff's behalf. At seven minutes before midnight my phone rang, and I flung covers aside to reach it. I recognized Charles LeBlanc's voice, but didn't complain about the hour. The time was earlier in Chinook, Montana, and he was a person I greatly admired, a former felon and outcast who had the aspect of a rawboned man that had endured long suffering and become stoically ennobled by it.

"How much in my bank account?" he asked, no opening pleasantries, his voice sure of the words, no trimmings. Music thumped in the background—a twanging guitar, fiddle, and whacking banjo.

"You're taking it down fast," I told him. As of now he had only what remained of his insurance money. "According to the last statement from the King County Bank, you've reduced your balance to some thirty-seven thousand dollars."

"What about the half million?"

"Your first payment's in escrow until the prince exercises the lease-option agreement and it becomes a seven-year amortized loan. According to your brother Edward, that should be by February fifteenth at the latest."

"I'm fixing to buy a ranch, and I'll want the money."

"I'll notify you as soon as it's available, and I strongly recommend you put aside ten percent of all income you receive in a retirement account."

"Not yet, Walt. I been needing a touch of the high life. Bought another Cadillac car, a remuda of cutting horses, and a diamond ring."

"Charles, I can't see you wearing a diamond ring."

"Not for me, Walt."

I waited for him to tell me about the woman, but he didn't.

"You're still at the Buckskin Motel?" I asked.

"Till I get the ranch."

"Charles, you were a hunter. You ever shoot grouse?"

"No grouse—partridges, duck, geese, turkey, and deer. You thinking of doing some gunning?"

"No, but I'd like to pass something by you, get your opinion, if that's okay."

"You got to be pretty hard up for advice to consult me if that's what you're doing."

I told him in detail about the Blind Sheep hunt, Wendell's death, and Cliff's story of what had happened.

"How does it all strike you?" I asked when I finished.

"Don't see how the man could've been shot in his chest if he lunged past the shooter. My thinking is one big thing's missing and somebody has to be lying—maybe two or three lies going 'round at the same time."

"My thinking too. Charles, I wish you were here."

"That it, Walt?"

I told him it was.

"Send me another couple of checkbooks," he said and hung up.

TWENTY-ONE

At six-thirty my alarm clock woke me. The rain had stopped, but wind ruffled water in Miss Mabel's birdbath lit by a streak through the window from my ceiling light. I drank a cup of hot tea, smoked, and waited until seven before phoning Drake's house. He answered, and I told him the police had Cliff locked up.

"He wants to see you," I said.

"I heard," Drake said. "I got a collect call from him not twenty minutes ago."

"Tell me what's going on between you two."

"Don't get your drift, Raff."

"When I saw Cliff yesterday, he was extremely anxious to speak to you."

"We've talked on the phone. I just hung up. No big secrets. I told him to tough it out."

"Why is it I'm not convinced that's all there is?"

"Look, we're the Marauders, *nunquam trado*, never betray, aren't we?"

"I don't like it."

"Just cool it, Raff. Make them prove the charge, isn't that an attorney's job? Maybe we can turn this whole thing around during the hearing. I'll be there."

At eight-fifteen I entered police headquarters and waited in the corridor for a deputy to bring Cliff out. As the sally port door opened, a voice from back in the lockup called, "One day the lawyers gonna be in here and us out there."

"Give me a minute with him?" I asked the pug-nosed deputy whose plastic name tag read *Leo.*

"Maybe two," he said and stood by.

"I need a shower, a shave, and clean clothes," Cliff said. He was pale and red-eyed, his face stubbled by a sandy beard. They had fastened no cuffs or restraints on him. "Will this take long?" he asked.

"I don't know but straighten up and get hold of yourself. Body language counts."

"I feel I have bugs crawling on me," he said. He tightened his belt and smoothed down his sweater.

"We fumigate the bugs," Leo said. "Time to move."

I followed while he escorted Cliff on the escalator up to the General District Court. Again I was reminded of theater because the seats were fold-up red plush, had armrests, and faced the lofty judge's bench front and center, which in its way was a stage flanked by flags of the United States and Virginia. They formed a proscenium arch topped by the state seal depicting the foot of Justice on the prostrate neck of Tyranny. Let, I thought, the show begin.

Leo seated Cliff between us on the front row. A housefly that had survived the winter in the courtroom was revived by the warmth and buzzed around a ceiling light. A brisk young brunette walked in and sat in the clerk's box beside the bench. She held a bundle of warrants bound by a thick, brown rubber band. She checked and adjusted the tape machine before flipping through the warrants as one might a deck of cards.

Next Drake appeared carrying his overcoat and hat. He reached out to shake Cliff's hand.

"Don't touch him," Leo said, causing Drake to step back.

"It'll work out," he said to Cliff, who was staring at him.

A dark-suited man carrying a document folder introduced himself as Detective Norman Hale. He had a deeply furrowed forehead and the drained, soulless eyes of men who had seen too much war, combat, and death.

"You and your client made a decision about extradition?" he asked me.

I told him no.

"I have the papers if you decide to waive," he said and moved away from us to sit and open the folder, which he centered on his lap.

"All rise," a bailiff called. "Judge Augustus P. Oliver, presiding."

The portly judge's black judicial robe swept behind him as he made his entrance. More theater, I thought.

"All right, what do we have here?" he asked, settling himself in the high-back regal chair. He adjusted his bifocals. The clerk switched on the recorder and arranged warrants before him. The judge studied them and handed the first to the bailiff. People entering the courtroom seated themselves in rows behind us.

"Clifford Arehart Dickens," the bailiff called.

Cliff and I stood and walked through the bar to stand at the defense table. Detective Hale crossed through to the prosecution's side.

"You're Mr. Dickens?" the judge asked. The fly buzzed around him, and he slapped at it.

"I am, Your Honor," Cliff answered.

"I have before me an arrest warrant issued in response to an extradition demand from the state of West Virginia asking for your return to face a charge of voluntary manslaughter." He focused on me. "Who are you?"

"Walter B. Frampton, sir, representing Mr. Dickens."

"All right, let's get through this. Mr. Dickens, the purpose of this proceeding is to explain to you your rights. First of all you have a right to counsel, which I see you have retained.

"Secondly the State of West Virginia has requested this

Commonwealth to extradite you back to that jurisdiction to undergo judicial process. Now let me tell you about extradition. Its implementation is not determined by this court's weighing of evidence but solely upon the fact that you are charged with a crime in another state. Therefore, any attack on these proceedings based on the claimed innocence of the accused, which is you, is immaterial. We are not having a trial here. Follow me?"

"Yes, sir," Cliff said.

"Now, you can waive extradition. If you do so, the waiver and consent are executed before me, after which a copy is sent to the governor and the accused is held for delivery to authorized agents of the demanding state. We in effect turn you over to the West Virginia authorities. Their people have ten days to take you into custody. It is that simple and results in a more expeditious resolution of all accusations against you whether you are innocent or guilty."

He again slapped at the fly.

"Or you can defend yourself against being extradited. You have the right to counsel, the right to the issuance and service of a governor's warrant of extradition, and the right to seek habeas corpus to test the legality of your arrest. If the above rights are exercised, the court shall rebail or recommit you.

"I must call to your attention, however, that extradition proceedings can involve an extended period of detention. The accused may be kept in jail thirty days, but in the event the governor's warrant of extradition does not arrive within that time limit, the judge may recommit the accused for an additional sixty days during which period you will be incarcerated in the city jail to guard against your fleeing either state. Got me?"

"Your Honor," I said.

"Mr. Frampton, why do I expect to hear from you a little song and dance?"

"Your Honor, Mr. Dickens was on a grouse hunting trip among

friends. He accidentally shot and killed a companion. The proper charge, if any, would be involuntary manslaughter. I believe the warrant is incorrectly drawn."

"You're telling me it was a misadventure?"

"There was no provocation, no *furor brevis,* simply an unfortunate action on the part of the deceased, who moved impulsively in front of Mr. Dickens's gun in an effort to get a shot at a grouse."

"Apparently Seneca County, West Virginia, disagrees. No bad blood between you and the deceased, Mr. Dickens? No past history of dispute or controversy on the day of the homicide?"

"None, sir."

"But you did shoot him?"

"I didn't mean to, sir."

"Still the fact is you held the gun, pulled the trigger, and he died in Seneca County, West Virginia. Probable cause in and of itself."

"Your Honor," Drake said and stood. "My name's Wingo and it was my grouse hunt. I can testify to the shooting being just an accident, no bad feelings involved."

"You the man who wrote the pamphlet getting all the attention?"

"Yes, sir."

"I've read it. Inspiring piece of work. And you are telling me what?"

"Mr. Dickens and the deceased didn't even know each other till the day of the hunt. The shooting was just ordinary human error."

"You were present the moment it happened?"

"Not the exact moment."

"It's the exact moment that counts, and death is never ordinary. Some word or misunderstanding could have ignited provocation, perhaps whose gun brought down a bird, an inflammatory remark, politics, a woman."

"Sir, there was no bad feeling between them."

"Bad feeling can spring up in an instant from a multitude of

causes, Mr. Wingo. But even if that were not the case, as I said earlier, an extradition hearing does not weigh evidence or judge innocence or guilt. The only question is whether or not you, Mr.
Dickens, will waive the proceedings."

"Your Honor," I said, "would you consider a stay of a week to
give Mr. Dickens time to put his affairs in order?"

"I would not, Mr. Frampton. A life has been lost, and we must
allow for some inconvenience."

"Will Your Honor grant a recess to allow me to talk to my client?"

"Ten minutes, Mr. Frampton. No more. Deputy, you will remain
with Mr. Dickens and his counsel during their consultation."

The judge stood and left through a door which opened behind
the bench. The clerk switched off the recorder as Detective Hale
stood to chat with the bailiff. People in their seats whispered,
yawned, stood to stretch.

"You all talk," Leo said. "I'll stand by but won't listen." To Drake,
"Remember, no touching or exchange of anything."

He backed off, folded his arms, and spread his legs to balance
himself comfortably—a man used to waiting.

"Ninety days?" Cliff asked, his voice lowered. "They can keep me
locked up for ninety days and then send me to West Virginia and
put me in a cell all over again if we don't waive?"

"It's how the law reads," I said.

"What are the odds he'll have to go back if he fights it?" Drake asked.

"A near certainty. Extradition is chiefly a time-taking formality
during which the governors treat each other politely and rarely
refuse one another's petitions."

"What do I do?" Cliff asked. He was looking at Drake, not me,
when he asked the question.

"You talking to him or me?" I asked.

"Will he be able to get bail up there?" Drake asked.

"Only a slim chance since he's not a resident and could become
a fugitive."

"I can't believe this is happening," Cliff said.

"You can be acquitted," Drake said. "Mountain people are used to hunting accidents. They'll understand."

"My chances?" Cliff asked me.

"Without a bill of particulars I can't predict."

"How can they prove provocation?" Drake asked. "They're bluffing."

"I don't know," I said. "Maybe something Sheriff Sawyers dug up. Without it they'd need to reduce the charges to involuntary manslaughter, a misdemeanor there, but still open to jail time, though rarely invoked. Either of you have anything else to tell me?"

Again Drake and Cliff faced each other.

"I'm waiting," I said.

"If my back's to the wall, can't I tell the Seneca County district attorney what really happened on Blind Sheep and plead self-defense?" Cliff asked.

"It's doubtful you could prevail without a witness," I said.

"Drake?" Cliff said.

"Your call," Drake said. "I'd go back, take my chances, get it over one way or another. We'll stick by you."

"I'm not licensed to practice in West Virginia and would need to find an associate there," I said.

"But you'll go?" Cliff asked.

"I'll go."

"Bring me a change of clothes. They emptied my pockets, and you have to get the key from the lockup's property clerk."

"And?" I asked.

"We'll waive," Cliff said.

TWENTY-TWO

L et the record show that Clifford Arehart Dickens has re-
sponded affirmatively," Judge Oliver ordered as he rapped his
gavel. Detective Hale allowed me to look over the waiver of extradition before it was signed in triplicate by Cliff and the judge.

"Just like that," Cliff said and raised his hands to look at the steel
cuffs Leo had fastened on him. "Incredible what a few words
before a judge can do to a man's life."

"I'll bring you clothes," I said.

"This will work out, old friend," Drake said. He hugged Cliff and
patted his back. "Just believe it."

"Let's go, fellow," Leo said and held Cliff's left elbow to return
him to the lockup. I followed down on the escalator to get his keys
from the property clerk. I watched the sally port's door close
behind Cliff.

The deputy clerk had me sign a release. I drove to the carriage
house and switched on lights in Cliff's bedroom, which had once
been a hayloft. The windows on both gabled ends were Gothic-
shaped—one offering a dismal view to the wet narrow street where
a trash can had been overturned, the other to an elm from whose
scaly limb a child's swing dangled and swung, prodded by the
wind.

I opened his bureau for shirts and underwear, drew slacks and a

126

jacket from his louvered closet, and stuffed socks into a pair of loafers. I glanced at the cluttered cove he used as a darkroom, then turned back to examine a photograph hanging from a drying clip of a dark-skinned girl with bare shoulders and frizzy black hair. His Baltimore girlfriend and perhaps a black herself? Just like Cliff to go against all conventions. A reporter had written that if you threw Cliff in the James River, he would float upstream.

"He won't be able to use them out Fairfield Way," the deputy at the lockup told me as he inspected the clothes. Fairfield Way was the city jail's location. "All inmates required to wear prison garb, but I'll see these get tagged through to West Virginia."

I talked to Cliff in the same holding cell of the Detention Section.

"How long before they come for me?" he asked.

"As the judge explained, they have ten days."

"Just don't leave me hanging."

"I'll check daily. Anything else you would like to tell me?"

"No, and I guess for a while I'll be catching up on my reading."

"I can bring you books."

"*War and Peace*," he said. "I never got around to finishing *War and Peace*."

I left recollecting Drake's embrace of him. Cliff had stood passively and allowed it. Like a tape my mind rewound to the day of the hunt when we returned to Richmond, and the frame stilled at the memory of Cliff's shoulder sliding out from beneath Drake's hand and the private look that had passed between them. Somehow I had to break into the confidence they shared and were withholding from me.

Using a public phone, I first tried to reach Drake at Grizzly's, then his house. Deborah told me he had left town.

"It's his book," she said. "He's talking to a publisher."

I asked her to have him call me soon as he returned.

"I'll do that, but you've been neglecting us. The portrait I had painted of Drake is back. Promise you'll come see it and have a drink—and I mean soon."

I promised, drove to Jessup's Wharf, and worked at my desk reviewing the homicide laws, a generic term that covered manslaughter and murder. Luckily the West Virginia and Virginia codes aligned because they had formerly been one and the same state.

I also used the *Attorney Directory* to look up names of lawyers in High Gap and found seven listed. Hiring one as an associate would mean more expense for Cliff, or me if I had to pick up the tab.

At five Mary Ellen readied herself to go home. She drew on her coat and hat as well as zipped up Jason's jacket.

"You like Brunswick stew?" she asked at the door. "We have a plenty if you'd like to break bread with us."

"I'd better stick around here awhile longer," I said.

"We'll hold dinner for you."

"Don't do that but thanks. I need to be alone with my thoughts."

She left, Jason beside her, his book bag strapped over his slender shoulders. I wondered whether Mary Ellen was just being gracious or trying to move us onto a more personal footing. Already darkness had settled like a veil along River Street. I stayed at my desk till seven-thirty, ate beef Wellington at the Dew Drop, and in case Cliff called, walked back to my office to check the answering machine before driving to my apartment. The red light blinked. The message was not from Cliff but Philip Garrow. I dialed him at Le Gallic.

"You might try around Grizzly's," he said.

"Try what?"

"An acquaintance informs me Jerry Ripley had what might best be termed a special friendship with somebody in the vicinity of that bizarre gun store."

"Philip, give me a name."

"I wasn't able to close on that. My source claims that he heard Jerry while in his cups allude to it."

"What does vicinity mean?"

"I really have no idea."

"Anything else?"

"Nothing substantial but still delving into the matter."

"I need to know bad."

"Bad can be used as an adverb," he said, "but I prefer badly, which has a more harmonious tonality."

TWENTY-THREE

Who in the vicinity of Grizzly's and did "vicinity" define just the store itself or a wider range? I thought of Boomer. Despite what he had told me about his casual association with Jeremiah, they could have been lovers.

First thing in the morning I headed for Powhatan County. The early sun caused frost on Grizzly's roof to steam as it thawed. The spotlighted grouse mobile at the center of the store gave off its white gleam as I walked to the entrance to find the doors locked. I peered through glass to see clerks wearing their blaze-orange vests moving about organizing wares. Boomer stood at a cash register, noticed, and allowed me to enter.

"You early, Mr. Frampton," he said. "Drake's not here yet."

His football linesman build had given way to pliant shoulders, but his bulk still suggested inherent power. I asked when Drake was expected.

"This morning sometime," Boomer answered as he closed the cash register's drawer by pressing his stomach against it.

"No matter. The fact is I came to talk to you further about Jeremiah Ripley."

"Sure, old Jerry." He leaned against the counter.

"You told me you two worked together," I said and watched for a reaction of consternation or evasion.

"Not with him. He was in shoes. I sold mostly football and baseball stuff, other gear in season."

"But you were close?"

"Just here at the store, the way everybody is."

"You didn't consider him a special friend?"

"We spoke and helped each other out during rush times, sometimes ate lunch together. That's about it."

"How did Jerry get along with the other clerks?"

"We all got along good. Anybody that doesn't fit the team is out at Grizzly's. Drake sees to that."

"Was Jerry particularly drawn to any particular one of them?"

"Nope, not that I remember. Friendly and all, but stuck to himself, though not standoffish. A nice kid."

"You know anything about his life outside the store, for example, in the immediate vicinity?"

"Not much immediate vicinity 'round here and never talked with him about himself. His running and stocking of the shoe department was a classy act. We got a good man now, Eddy Turner over there, but Jerry was hard to replace. He talked Drake into starting the department and built it into a profit maker. Designed the display shelves and lighting. Drake didn't want to go along with the idea at first, couldn't see money in shoes."

"It was Jerry who convinced Drake?"

"Sure and it was Jerry who came up with the idea of hanging the ghost grouse, making it the store's emblem," Boomer said and glanced at the mobile. "Drake paid him a bonus."

I remembered my conversation with Drake and his telling me that Jeremiah had been no more than ordinary help, certainly nothing special. Drake had also taken credit for the shoe department and the ghost grouse. That was unlike him. He was not small minded or given to envy.

"Are you able to remember anything you haven't told me about Jerry?" I asked.

"Like I said, his father used to come around looking, but nobody seen Jerry after he quit us here. Hey, there's Drake now."

Drake crossed the parking lot and entered the store. He must have come straight from the airport, for he carried an attaché case and could have passed as a downtown attorney.

"Raff, something happening?" he asked. "Come on along."

I followed him through the store to his office. He laid his attaché case on the desk, removed his hat and gloves, and began flipping through mail as he unbuttoned his overcoat.

"I'm assuming you're here to talk about Cliff and how we can best help him," Drake said. "Listen, my checkbook's open. Spend anything you need."

"I wish this were just about money," I said.

"If not, what?"

"You and Cliff leaving me out of the loop."

"Who's got a loop? Grizzly's can sell you a lasso. Sit and rest your bones."

"Something's going on between you two that you're keeping from me."

"Raff, nothing you need to know."

"I insist on knowing."

"All right," Drake said as he tossed his overcoat to the camp cot. "It is the money situation. Cliff doesn't like people learning about his financial problems, but for the last year he's been one hop ahead of the bill collectors. I been assuring him I won't let him sink no matter the cost."

"That's generous of you."

"He'd do the same for me or you if he had it," Drake said, again at the mail. "Now, I continue to believe this whole situation is overblown. At the worst Cliff will get off with probation and a fine."

"I don't like the feel of it."

"I don't either, but if we stand by him, everything will come out right. Have a little faith. When's Cliff leaving?"

"As soon as the West Virginia authorities send deputies to take him back. They work in pairs."

"Nothing more we can do at the moment?"

"No," I said, unbuttoning my own coat as I sat.

"Okay, we're on instant standby to help him. Now I'll tell you the good news. I got a publisher for 'Truth of the Grouse.' He patted the attaché case. "Been negotiating since November. It'll be a hardback edition with illustrations, an advertising budget, a book tour."

"I'm happy for you, Drake."

"Things are definitely breaking my way. I hate to be feeling so good when Cliff's having troubles. But it'll be okay if he just stands tall, which I keep advising him. Anything else on your mind?"

"I'm still trying to track Jeremiah Ripley, who his friends were, what finally happened to him."

"In his grave," Drake said and sorted through envelopes.

"Where's that grave?"

"On that I got no idea. Lots of ground to lie under in this old world."

"You worked close with him. Can you think of any way that might help me find out for sure?"

"I worked close with him?"

"Helped him start his shoe department and spotlight the grouse."

"Hold it, he was helping me, not me helping him."

"Those weren't his ideas?"

"Hell no, I planted them, made suggestions, allowed him to ride shotgun. He was proud of his work, bragged about it, but they were my concepts. He didn't know a grouse from a turkey buzzard."

"But you paid him a bonus."

"Sure, him and others earned overtime working nights. I didn't want to interrupt business while installing a new department. We had to reorganize floor space."

"You're not able to add anything that would help me discover specifically what happened to him?"

"Raff, we going in circles here. I've told you all I can. I never got into Jeremiah's personal life while he was my employee. He could sell shoes, a high markup item and very profitable to Grizzly's. I have no idea why he left and didn't collect his last week's pay. You know as much as I do about the rest. Anything else?"

"No," I said and again congratulated him on his success with the book before I walked from the store.

TWENTY-FOUR

I drove off reviewing the contradictions between what Boomer and Drake had told me about Jeremiah. Boomer was a man I hardly knew, and there was no way I could trust his word more than my friend Drake's, whose nature was direct and devoid of deception. We were Marauders and had joined our blood.

I wanted to pick up my portrait of Marse Robert reframed for me by Phoebe Laratta, a second-generation Lebanese, dark of eye, her skin olive, her straight black hair hanging long and low over a back often bared.

A reckless child of the sixties, she had carried all that wanton baggage with her until she finally crashed and the police found her wandering at night naked and sobbing on Church Hill during an Easter snowstorm. First committed for treatment and rehabilitation by the court, after her release she survived day to day. A number of years ago, prior to Phoebe's fall, and before Drake met Deborah, he had lived with Phoebe until they fell out and he was replaced by a series of other men. Her slinky body and libertine ways drew them.

She now worked for Très Chic, a downtown store, as an illustrator and window decorator, yet had always considered herself a serious artist, her studio and home a narrow ivy-covered house that provided a view to the red-brick American Tobacco factory, its lettered "Lucky Strike" smokestack, and a ravaged flow of the James.

I stopped at an Amoco station, bought gas, and phoned first the store, then her house. We had come to know each other during her days with Drake when I attended one of the bohemian parties that took place among an ambience of guitars, drink, and pot, plus clutches in a shadowed hallway. She had allowed her blouse to slip and reveal a breast, her nipple's aureole the color of Burgundy wine.

"Bring your checkbook," she said.

I drove up the hill and parked beside a honeysuckle tangled fence of broken iron pickets around a small, neglected yard. To a porch post Phoebe had tacked a black palette, her street number painted on it in blue letters. The door had an oval glass panel that rattled loosely when I knocked. She opened it and kissed me full on my mouth. It meant nothing. In her late forties, her slanted eyes often seemed to be sighting objects far distant beyond where she stood.

"Come with me before you freeze your vitals," she said and drew me into the house. The paint-splotched denim shirt over a black leotard reached almost to her knees. Her worn and mottled face was a startling contrast with her still-shapely body of a much younger woman.

"I expected you to be at the store," I said.

"I've taken leave. Weary of lingerie displays and repairing mannequins, and I've been given a promise of an exhibition down in the Bottom."

What had been the parlor she had transformed into her studio. A bay window let in a northern light, and tables and shelves held tubes of paints, brushes, tools of the craft. Several easels stood about, all empty except one that held an oil of what appeared to be two glittering red eyes peering up from a darkened pit.

"Hell?" I asked.

"Daily life," she said. "Want a drink? I have Lebanese wine and a slab of goat cheese."

Canvases placed around represented mostly conventional and commercial scenes, evidence that she needed money—a willow-draped pond, a fading sunset, kerchiefed black women selling daffodils, Laurel Street's Sacred Heart Cathedral under a misting rain. The sad fact was her true talent and curse lay in producing conventional art.

I told her no, and she sat me on a ratty green divan to wait while she brought and displayed General Lee bordered by a two-inch beveled Confederate-gray frame.

"Exactly what I wanted," I said, honestly pleased.

"One hundred fifty dollars," she said and began taping brown wrapping paper around the portrait. "Tax included."

I wrote a check knowing no tax would ever be paid. She slipped the check under an Aztec ceramic jug on her mantel before coming to sit by me, sighing, and drawing away her hair in a distracted fashion. A strand fell back aslant her cheek. She smelled of turpentine.

"You used to be afraid of me," she said. "That the reason you stopped coming around?"

"No, with you I could have become desperately overwrought and lost my bearings."

"You believed I would devour you?"

"The problem was I hoped you would."

"Liar. You were shocked and very much disapproved."

"I was also envious of Drake," I said, though not the whole truth. I had been aroused by her but knew better than to return.

"You fled me." Again she drew at her hair, her face saddening. "And Drake too. Raff, I finally figured what love's all about. It's a brew God supplies to drive us mad."

Her eyes became unfocused, seeing or not seeing what?

"Well, I'll go," I said.

"No you won't," she said, rousing. "Not without telling me about him. You can skip the part about his being married to a rich bitch who's a member of the DAR."

"Drake's doing fine."

"Of course he's fine. You've seen him recently?"

"Little more than an hour ago."

"My bold, hot-blooded lover who now flourishes not only in the realm of commerce but is also becoming a celebrity."

"His grouse book's going to be published."

"Will it have illustrations?

"I believe so."

"Raff, do me the favor of suggesting to him I'm available for the job."

"Of course, Phoebe."

"The sonofabitch," she said. "Everything was always his show. I gave him all the loving a man could ask for, anything he wanted. I lived for Drake. For once during my life I thought more of someone else than myself. I did until I found he couldn't keep his prick just for me."

"I don't think I want to hear this," I said.

"You will anyway. I became suspicious when his heat slackened suddenly, and he spent more time at the store. I became convinced when I put on some rather fancy shows for him, garter belt, fishnet stockings, a silk chemise, the works, and his response was less than rapturous. I put the question to him. He told me it was the pressure of business."

Her fingering back of her hair was like the drawing aside of a curtain from her oval face.

"I took pressure under consideration. I also thought maybe my hygiene wasn't as sweet as it should be. I devoted myself to appearing alluring. He was somewhat less inflamed than the moment called for."

A phone on her worktable rang, the old-fashioned sort that had a rotary dial. She stood and crossed to it. The floppy heels of her mules slapped the floor.

"Later," she said and dropped the phone back to its cradle. She crossed her arms and began slowly circling a worktable on which lay soiled rags and a paint-encrusted putty knife. "I shadowed him on nights when he called to tell me he had to work late. I drove out and parked not in Grizzly's lot but across the highway on the shoulder of a secondary intersecting road. I used his army binoculars to watch the store's entrance and that damned spotlighted grouse. No lie, he was working late. I'd beat him home and be waiting when he walked in the door."

Again the phone rang. She ignored it.

"I believed he was exhausted from running the store till the October night he drove away early and got ahead of me. I nearly panicked he'd reach the house before I did. I planned to tell him I'd gone out for cigarettes. But he didn't take the home route, and as I followed he crossed the river south of the city to the Shady Spring Motel, a place that had seen better times, its neon sign missing an *O*. There he met her."

"Met whom?"

"No one I knew. She had already parked. It was windy, and there'd been a quick cold shower. He registered and got the key. She was a cheap, trashy young thing, I could see that, and her spiked heels made her ass stick out as they walked from their car to the room. He stood aside for her, followed her in, and closed the door."

Phoebe came to sit beside me.

"They stayed ninety minutes in the room. When they walked out, I snuck away and drove off. Back here in the house I helped myself to a drink, not wine, but Drake's bourbon.

"'I know you're tired,' I said to him when he came in.

"'Sort of,' he answered.

"'Ain't fucking hell?' I asked.

"He just looked at me. Didn't get mad or make excuses.

"'Yeah,' he said and climbed the steps to the bed.

"I slept that night on this divan and waited for him to come down in the morning. We drank coffee, and he told me he was sorry. I said we had a chance if he gave her up. He agreed to but didn't. I kicked his ass out. 'Couldn't help it,' he said. All the loving I was giving him, and he had to have more. He claimed it was a sickness. What shit."

"I better be going, Phoebe."

"Sure, I didn't mean to dump on you. Just can't cut Drake out of my mind. The truth is I once wondered what it would be like for you and me to make love. Where would all the arms and legs go? We might find ourselves tangled up in a knot and have to call the fire department to get untied."

She managed a one-bark laugh, we stood, and I lifted the portrait. We walked to the door, she holding to my arm.

"I'll speak to Drake about the illustrations," I said.

"Don't tell him I asked you to."

"You have my word."

"I trust you, Raff, but I don't much take words any longer. The human race would be better off if words had never been invented and all we had was the sign language. Words are more dangerous than bullets and bombs."

I had expected her to ask me about Cliff. There had been a short account of his arrest in the *Times-Dispatch*. Maybe she didn't read the papers. She opened her fingers and released me.

TWENTY-FIVE

If not Boomer, the possibility still existed that someone else at Grizzly's might have been intimate with Jeremiah. I could ask Drake for a list of people who had worked at the store during the period Jeremiah was employed there, trace and question them, though a daunting procedure that would possibly require more time and expertise than I possessed.

I also continued to be nagged by the incident of the fierce-looking herdsman at The Watchers who had waved me off their farm. He had not appeared to be the sort to belong to a pacifist, vegetarian sect that lived humbly to serve God.

I was desperate enough to drive out to Chesterfield, a calm day, the sky covered by gauzy clouds that let through a pale lemony light. Again Watchers toiled in the fields, and a tractor pulled a plow whose blade curled up rolling waves of dark moist soil.

I parked and first checked the building where they made coveralls and found rows of sewing machines waiting silent, the chairs vacant before them. I next tried the corrugated work shed where I'd first seen Brother Abram. It too was empty. I continued on to the barn and located stalls of the milking parlor bedded with fresh straw, the ammoniac odor of urine strong.

"Anybody around?" I called.

Through an unlatched open door I glimpsed Holstein cows in a pasture circling and feeding on rolled hay. I left the barn and walked toward a garage where I heard tapping and found Brother

Abram sitting on a stump of wood before the wheel of a jacked-up John Deere gleaner. He dipped a dabbing stick into a can of grease and packed the bearing.

"Well, looka here," he said. "You becoming a regular visitor to our acres."

"It's a pleasure to see a well-run farm," I said. Again his sleeves were rolled above his hairy arms. His knees flanked his great belly as if they supported it.

"Making ready for spring planting," he said, and when he sneezed his breath rippled his long curly nose hairs. "Generally put in our first crops early as February if God has it on His calendar. Do something for you, Mr. Frampton?"

"I'm still attempting to find what finally happened to Jeremiah Ripley."

"Finally's a long time. Finally's forever in a place where there is no time."

Using a rubber mallet he tapped the bearing cap in place and twisted the lid on the can of grease before using a rag to wipe his hands and heave himself to his feet.

"What about the here and now?" I asked.

"Puff and it's gone," he said. He moved around to another of the gleaner's wheels, set the stump of wood before it, and sat to remove the cap. "Leaves blown on the wind."

"Is there a chance Jeremiah could be in your cemetery here?"

"Not unless somebody snuck in after dark and buried him."

"You're suggesting that's a possibility?"

"No, sir, and if he's occupying ground, it's somewhere else. Don't let me get this grease on your overcoat."

"Brother Abram, the last time I was here a man herding cows ordered me off the property. He acted angry, though to my knowledge I'd never seen him before."

Brother Abram stopped, again sneezed, and looked up at me from his ruddy, bearded face.

"That's Brother Lucas," he said and rumbled into laughter. "He's our unofficial sin sniffer."

"Your what?"

"As a young man he used to work high steel down in Norfolk town. Up eleven stories he fell off an I-beam and broke his back and most of his bones. He did a lot of talking with the Lord, and the Lord spared him and gave him a gift. Lucas can walk around a man and scent the sin on him—a smell he describes is like sulfur rising off rotted flesh."

"You don't believe that?"

"With God anything and everything's possible. Sure, why not? You think sin don't stink?"

"Did he smell it on Jeremiah?"

"Claims he did. Lucas appears scarier than he is. He's never hurt anybody and has a way with animals. You can't fool animals. They're the best judges of character."

"How well did he know Jeremiah?"

"Everybody at The Watchers knows everybody else. No secrets."

"I'd like to talk to Brother Lucas."

"All right, Mr. Frampton," Brother Abram said, set the dabbing stick on the grease can, and strained to lift himself. "We'll do that very thing."

Legs straddled, his drooping belly pushed ahead, he moved forward and began whistling "Bringing in the Sheaves" as we crossed the road back to the barn and a stone building that adjoined it at the far end. Brother Abram opened a door onto a room that had a concrete floor. A small man stood at a deep laundry sink washing a galvanized bucket with soap and a brush. Ranks of electric milking machines and a stainless-steel storage tank shone with surgical cleanliness.

"Brother Lucas, Mr. Frampton here would like a word with you," Brother Abram said.

Lucas turned to me warily. The albino's coveralls hung loosely from his leprous body, and stringy blanched hair coiled around his neck. He set the bucket and brush in the sink, stepped away, and moved slowly toward me in short, shuffling steps of a man much older than he appeared.

"Do him?" he asked, his voice surprisingly deep.

"Sure, go ahead," Brother Abram told him.

Brother Lucas's head wove side to side as he approached like a setter winding game.

"Don't you move," he commanded.

He stopped in front of me and peered out of pink aqueous eyes set so deep his colorless brows shadowed them. He leaned forward and began sniffing at me as a dog might a bush, tree, or fireplug. I resisted drawing back. He began circling slowly and continued to sniff. I looked at Brother Abram, who smiled, rocked side to side, and nodded.

Brother Lucas reversed the circle, closer now, his nose almost touching mine as he passed. I felt his breath on my cheek, ear, the back of my neck. I smelled milk, soap, sweat, and sweet feed on him. Again he stopped in front of me, his face bony, his expression hawklike. I thought of Old Testament prophets preaching in the wilderness.

He stepped back, his eyes now hooded.

"Got me a score?" Brother Abram asked.

"Four," Brother Lucas answered.

"Four's not hopeless, in fact it's about average," Brother Abram explained. "On Brother Lucas's sin scale, the grading goes from seven, which is the highest good of man, and descends to one, the lowest. Four means you have a way to go yet to be beyond the reach of redemption."

"One is Satan," Brother Lucas said.

"Lawyer Frampton wants to ask you a question or two and would appreciate you helping him out."

Brother Lucas's eyelids raised, and he glared.

"You knew Jeremiah Ripley?" I asked.

"Started out seven," Brother Lucas said. "He'd sunk to three when he left."

"Can you tell me what happened to him after he left?"

"Three is a slippery slope and nigh a sure path to destruction."

"You believe he's been destroyed?"

"It's the road he chose."

"A road to where?"

"The bowels of Hell."

"Do you know where he might be?"

"Hell is a place," Brother Lucas said and turned away to cross back to the sink. He lifted and began washing another bucket, the water from the spigot splashing inside and causing soap suds to foam over his long, glimmering hands.

"Then you don't know?" I asked.

He didn't respond, and I looked to Brother Abram. He shook his head and gestured me toward the door. Just as we reached it, Brother Lucas spoke again.

"Jeremiah 17:9," he said.

I followed Brother Abram out, and he walked me to my car. His expression continued to be one of restrained merriment.

"You take him seriously?" I asked.

"He's often been right. Frequently those like him who seem out of step with the mass of mankind are given special talents. It's the Lord's way of compensating. Look at the amazing variety of His creatures, each a miracle of invention. God does what He wishes. He is the Master Creator and Magician."

I thanked him and drove off. At the apartment I looked up Jeremiah 17:9 in a King James Bible Miss Mabel had left on my bedside table. It read, "The heart is deceitful above all things and desperately wicked: who can know it?"

TWENTY-SIX

As I drove toward Richmond, I decided to detour and keep my promise to Deborah by stopping at Drake's and her Midlothian house. Despite cold and the wind that had stripped the poplars, winter jasmine grew down over the terrace, the yellow blooms' freshness startling in dappled shadows laid by the trees' limbs and trunks.

Deborah and Drake reared the twin girls fathered by her first husband, a corporate attorney and Richmond's amateur golf champion named Louis, and she dressed them like princesses of the realm. Drake carried them in crooks of his arms, danced them around, and lifted them high and squealing above his head. I wondered whether or not the woman he had met at the Shady Spring might have been Deborah. No, Phoebe had said that girl was cheap and trashy, and I could never believe Deborah would become part of anything as sleazy as an affair in a rundown southside Richmond motel.

Behind the house Drake had built a pool used during summers to keep fit and give the twins swimming lessons. Deborah provided a pony cart to drive them over the bluegrass lawn and through the sheltering woods. Everywhere you turned in the house—the parlor, library, den—photographs of the twins had been placed to greet the eye.

I saw Drake and Deborah several times a year, always on his

birthday, usually for a cocktail party during the Christmas season, and at Easter when we all attended Grace and Holy Trinity to hear the music and afterward ate a long, leisurely dinner in the garden, weather permitting. Cliff was ritually invited but of late had made excuses, offering prior commitments, his absence vexing Deborah and causing Drake's face to tighten.

"He's not doing anything that's so damn important," Drake had said. "You'd think he was in demand all over the country."

Deborah's Volvo station wagon turned into the driveway just ahead of me, and I followed. She stopped before a bay of the three-car garage, inched the car forward, set the brake, and stepped out. She was a stylish woman who made an ordinary gray down jacket and plaid skirt appear elegant. A gust of wind that roused her dark blond hair seemed in league with her grooming. When she turned, the closeness of my Buick startled her, and I legged out to apologize.

She embraced me, presented her cheek, and because of my height, I needed to bend over to kiss it. Her complexion was fair, with a touch of color. The first time I met her I had expected to hear the languid accent of the satiated rich, but her voice was always warm, lilting, and enthusiastic.

"What's all this about Cliff?" she asked. "I can't believe they put him in jail. I want to visit him, but Drake says Cliff would hate for his friends to see him that way. Drake's terribly upset. What can I do?"

"Nothing at the moment. I check with Cliff daily and look after him."

"But he's imprisoned, and it's barbaric," she said. "How could such a thing happen?"

"An overzealous sheriff and district attorney are my best explanation."

"All right, I won't press you. I just want him to know I'm here and concerned. Please tell him that. Now, you come in the house with me this instant."

"I should have called first," I said as I lifted groceries from the rear of the Volvo.

"You never have to call. Around this place you're one of us."

A door led from the garage to a covered walkway connected to the kitchen. Ivy entwined the square white columns, and I glimpsed the covered pool, a sliding board, and a log playhouse, a window of which was cracked and needed replacing.

Lotte, their aged, shrunken black maid, opened the kitchen door to help with the groceries. I wiped my shoes on a mat just inside as Deborah toed off her boots and slipped her feet into Docksides. She clicked the counter's automatic coffeemaker before leading me into a paneled den where over the fireplace Drake's oil portrait hung.

His leather armor-corps helmet removed, his goggles hanging loose around his neck, he held binoculars as he stood in the command turret of the sand-colored Abrams tank. His skin was sunbronzed, his cropped hair sweat-soaked, his gold-flecked blue eyes fixed as if to make out the enemy in the distance. Behind the tank the shattering glare of dunes receded in parallel descending contours. I thought of Prince Jamir on his Arabian steed at Bellerive. Each man in his own way a desert warrior.

"What's your opinion?" Deborah asked. She had removed her jacket and insisted I turn my coat over to her. Her pregnancy was just noticeable—an ultrasound had revealed that Drake would father a son.

"He's an up-to-date Lawrence of Arabia."

"You're not mocking me, are you?" she asked and raised fingers to her chin to study the painting. The chin had a cleft that appeared decorative. "Drake scoffs at it. He claims it glamorizes him and that war is organized butchery."

"No, I'm envious," I said and was. I had once dreamed of becoming a fighter pilot, of flying F–16s and after battle zooming down the conqueror onto aircraft carriers. The hope had been vain because of my poor eyes and lack of coordination. Nor did I have the temperament and character of a warrior. Despite my love of valor, particularly after the incident with Josey and the stallion at Bellerive, I had come to doubt even more forcefully that such a heritage had been bequeathed to my genes.

"You're a dear friend who doesn't visit us enough. I tell Drake he ought to bring you more often. You want to keep on the good side of me, you better not stay away so long."

She sat gracefully on a love seat, a person prepared for charm through breeding and expensive schools, also provided a life of money and ease laced with the responsibilities of charities and good works that go with being a Richmond lady. She gave off sexuality, not raw and up-front like Josey, but with a refined suggestiveness seen in the brushing of graceful fingers along her lap to straighten her skirt or the way she positioned her body in demure invitation.

I told her I was sorry, promised to reform, and asked about the twins.

"Come along with me," she said and stood. I followed her up the carpeted steps to the second floor and the nursery, where the three-year-olds lay sleeping in miniature white beds, each covered by a white canopy. Dolls had been arranged on window seats and colorful Humpty-Dumpty tiles fixed along the pale pink walls. The twins were lovely children, their mouths opened slightly in sleep, their small fingers curled on top of quilted counterpanes, their golden hair spread over lacy pillows.

"There's nothing more beautiful than the innocence of children," she whispered as we left and pulled the door quietly to.

I loved being with Deborah. She made me feel like a person of consequence—the manner in which a true aristocrat treated everyone. I thought of General Lee.

"It's great news about Drake's book," I said downstairs. "I expect an inscribed copy."

"It's marvelous for him. Except from me he never received much

encouragement on the project—that's what he called it, a project—and to be frank I wasn't certain anything would come of it.
'The Truth of the Grouse,' a means for a man to pattern his own life
on the habits, bearing, and courage of a wild bird. Who would have
believed such an idea could catch on?"

"Not I."

"Drake's always been a man to choose his own path," she said
and looked at the den wall where she had mounted and encased in
a shadow-box frame his silver star and other medals. "And he
saved me, Walter. After my Louis died, I sank into a seemingly
hopeless and bottomless depression. Drake reached out and
brought me back to life, really a modern-day resurrection."

Lotte carried in coffee on a silver tray.

"I know people believe he used my money," Deborah said. "It's
not true, never a cent for Grizzly's or the book. And talk about
being proud, his becoming a father is all but popping the buttons
off his shirt."

She served my coffee not in a mug but a delicate porcelain cup
that I stirred with a small silver spoon. For me her gentility mixed
with the elusive sexuality was an exciting combination. Drake might
be rough and profane at camp or work, but when with Deborah he
acted the gentleman, knowing all the moves of the socially elite.

"Walter, I have a lady friend I'd like you to meet. She's a docent at
the Poe Museum. I think the two of you would enjoy each other's
company."

"Don't tell me you've gotten into matchmaking."

"I worry about you. This is a delightful woman, a master gar-
dener, and she loves books, art, the ballet."

"I don't think so, Deborah. Not at this time."

"You're still seeing Josey?"

"Only occasionally."

"Ah," she said, turned her head slightly, and gave me a tender
look which I interpreted to mean that any chance of my ever turning Josey to my cause was not only misguided but also futile.

I finished my coffee and told her I had to leave. She fussed, insisted on holding my coat for me, and walked me back through the connecting walkway to the garage and out to my Buick. She pressed my hand in her special way, a touch signifying *I cherish you*.

"You were kind to come," she said. "Drake will be pleased."

"I always leave here feeling good, and it's never just the liquor."

"You take good care of our Cliff, you hear? Carry him my love. How long will they hold him?"

"It shouldn't be but a few more days."

"Will they allow me to send him a cake and magazines? Surely I can write a note."

I promised to find out, and she again embraced me. As I left, she stood on the terrace, her hair and skirt blowing in the wind. I held that picture in my mind while I drove away to Jessup's Wharf and felt both jealous of Drake and downcast at the loneliness I was returning to.

Though it began to rain, I stopped by the office. Somewhere I had misplaced my umbrella. Mary Ellen had locked up and left no messages on my desk. I sat and looked out the window to the illuminated steeple of St. Luke's. If there were pigeons, they huddled in shadows of the eaves.

I nodded, almost dozed, and rallied myself to retire to Miss Mabel's. Though the iron radiators warmed my fingers, my rooms felt cold and damp. Light from the converted gas chandelier that had once been a dining room fixture seemed feeble, casting a faded yellowish tint on things, like old paper or linens brought up after lying long years in a basement trunk.

A plane flew low over Jessup's Wharf, possibly the prince returning to or leaving Bellerive. More rain tapped the roof. The temperature of my window thermometer was just above freezing. Wearily I surrendered myself to the sound of a gutter dripping and its final overflow.

TWENTY-SEVEN

At mid-afternoon the next day as I was about to phone Drake and ask him for the names, addresses, and the terms of service of his ex-employees, I received an agitated collect call from Cliff, who told me that two sheriff's deputies from Seneca County had arrived to take him into custody and transport him to West Virginia.

"They're carrying me off in ten minutes," he said. "You know what belly cuffs are?"

I did, a chain with handcuffs attached to its links locked around a prisoner's waist.

"And shackles," Cliff said. "They've fastened them on me as if I'm a slave to be deported to another continent."

"Cliff, it's just a procedure."

"'Just,' huh? You know how it feels to walk past people who gawk at and whisper about you as if you're monstrously depraved?"

"I'm on my way to Seneca County. Soon as I get myself together and can pack a bag."

"They signed me over like meat to be delivered to the market."

I tried to reach Drake at Grizzly's to give him the news, but he had left town on a buying trip. I told Mary Ellen I would stay in touch by phone and also explained to stately, gray-haired Miss Mabel I needed to be away a few days.

"Turn down the heat in your apartment," she said. Though far

152

from poor, she often repeated the adage that if you watched your pennies, the dollars would take care of themselves.

I gassed up before starting out. By five o'clock it was dark, and with my eyesight I hated driving at night. Moreover, the weather report announced a storm watch. I reached Staunton before the first flakes flattened against the windshield. My wipers labored to swipe them away in clean arcs, but they rapidly reclotted.

I sensed the mountains before I made out their looming darkness within darkness. The car's six-cylinder engine shifted down to pull harder. Still I made good time till I crossed the border beyond Monterey and headed toward High Gap. Yellow and red lights of road crews' trucks and plows flashed over mounds of snow, creating a grotesque landscape. I thought of Dante's *Inferno* and the concurrent presence of ice and fire.

Though two lanes had been partially scraped, snow again covered them. I braked behind an eighteen-wheeler logging truck, the tires of which flung up cinders that rapped my windshield. The cleaning fluid sprayed from the engine compartment's reservoir couldn't handle the job, forcing me to stop and use my handkerchief to wipe the glass. When I finished, I tossed the soiled handkerchief to the rubber floor mat.

Rolling again at only twenty miles an hour, the tires hit a patch of black ice, and when I braked, the car did a leisurely spin near the edge of the road before straightening and continuing on course. Sweat collected under my armpits.

By the time I reached High Gap I had been driving six hours. I felt tired, my eyes burned, I was nauseous. The fuel gauge's needle hovered toward empty. Under the snow nothing about the town appeared identifiable, and I lost my sense of direction until I recognized the Marathon Station where we had stopped the morning we carried Wendell's body in from Blind Sheep. The same attendant, his cap pulled low over his ears, took my money.

"Reckon winter'll ever turn us loose?" he asked.

I reached the courthouse, the lighted windows of which were steamed to opaqueness, and found the parking lot. Heat swept out to me as I opened the door of the Sheriff's Department. The green tile floor had been sullied by snow melting from shoes and boots. I found Sawyers's office locked and walked the corridor until I reached a glass window behind which a uniformed, overweight woman with full rosy cheeks sat at a console on which tiers of green and red lights blinked from a control panel.

The name tag pinned to her breast pocket read *Bess*. Behind her were file cabinets, a computer, and radio equipment. The large wall-mounted electric clock read 11:57. She had been flipping through *Cosmopolitan*.

"I'm Mr. Clifford Dickens's attorney," I said. "He is being held here?"

"Sure enough and can I see some identification?"

I slid my Virginia Bar Association card and driver's license through the slot at the bottom of the window. She held them at half an arm's length under the concentrated light of the desk.

"I want to see him," I said.

"Mr. Frampton, it's way too late for visitor hours."

"I'm no visitor but an attorney who has a right to confer with his client."

"Now don't get all hot and bothered," she said and swiveled her chair aside to pick up a phone, finger a button on the control panel, and wait to speak. "Hey, Bruce, lawyer fellow here by name of Frampton wants to see prisoner Dickens. Un-huh, tall, thin, wears glasses. Don't make a bit of difference to me."

She held the phone and touched another button. "Gilbert'll be here in a sec," she said to me.

"Gilbert?"

"Our jailer. Like a cookie?" From a small round tin she removed the top, which was painted with yellow tulips, and pushed it through the slot. "Chocolate chips I made this afternoon."

I took one so as not to offend her, nibbled it, told her it was delicious, and received a matronly smile. She glanced through a second window at her side and pressed another button on the control
panel. The lock of a black steel door released with a clank.

Gilbert limped out. His tan uniform shirt was open at the collar,
his holster emptied. He dragged a foot and surprised me by offering to shake my hand and apologizing for having to pat me down
and look through my briefcase.

"I wouldn't ordinarily do that to a lawyer," he said. "But we don't
know you 'round here yet. Okay, if you'll come on along with me,
Mr. Frampton. Bad night to be out 'less you got polar bear blood."

He led me through the doorway, which Bess relocked after us.
She watched from the second window that gave her a view of the
block. The ten cells were numbered and equipped with peephole
and waist-high portals that could be slid open. The walls had been
painted sky blue.

I couldn't tell how many cells were occupied. Two carried the
designation WOMEN, meaning not only the inmates were of that sex
but also the cells were to be entered only by female deputies. I was
not surprised that Sheriff Sawyers ran a modern, efficient jail.

Gilbert stopped before No. 5. He looked back toward Bess, and
she released the lock. He opened the door onto an antechamber
furnished with a metal table and two metal stools, all bolted to the
floor. Behind bars Cliff swung his feet from a fold-down bunk that
had a brown blanket over a thin, plastic-covered mattress. The
stainless steel sink and toilet reflected light from a caged bulb. The
cell had no window.

"We want a conference room," I said to Gilbert.

"No need, Mr. Frampton. I can just shut this outer door here,
and you got all the privacy a man needs."

"Is this cell wired for communication?" I asked and looked at the
ceiling and walls. They too were sky blue.

"It is, but neither me or Bess'll be listening. Come morning, you can speak to the sheriff about other arrangements. Holler if you need me."

I started to demand a conference room but then thought I shouldn't cause any bad feeling with a jailer when Cliff, not I, might have to pay for it.

"They took my clothes," Cliff said after Gilbert shut us in. The laces were gone from his shoes, and he sadly fingered out his over-sized orange coveralls. "Tommy Hilfiger, right?"

"They treating you okay?" I asked. He needed a shave, his hair was disarranged, the skin under his eyes puffy.

"Wonderfully. You ever taken a tour in the backseat of a patrol car enclosed with rat wire? And they've been at me with questions. I've refused to answer and told them they had to talk to you. Walter, my head's about to bust, and I'm living a nightmare."

"I can do nothing till I see the district attorney. Have you eaten?"

"I turned down food. I'm unable to swallow."

"Anything I should bring you?"

"My freedom."

"I'll be working at that first thing in the morning."

"Does Drake know I'm here?"

"I tried to reach him. He's away on business."

"It's important he finds out."

"I'll see to it, but give me a reason, and don't tell me it's so personal you can't reveal it to your attorney and friend."

"Walter, you've come with me this far, please, I implore you, stay one more step."

"All right, Cliff. I don't like it, but we'll wait until after I visit the district attorney. Try to sleep."

"Oh sure, sleep, what's that?"

I rapped the door for Gilbert to let me out. Our feet echoed along the cell block. I asked Bess where I could find a room for the night.

"The Mountain View Lodge," she said. "Want me to call for you?"

I thanked her. She rang up the lodge and gave me directions. I drove away from the jail, through the silent, ghostly town, and up a grade so steep my tires slipped. The motel's red sign emerged through snow like a fogged beacon at sea. Only a few blanketed cars were parked in the lot. I walked across the heated lobby to the desk and signed the registration card for the polite young clerk who looked no more than high-school age and had been studying a Spanish textbook. His radio played beneath pigeonholes that held keys. I recognized Willie Nelson's voice.

"I could use some food," I said.

"The kitchen's shut down but can fix you a sandwich and a glass of milk."

My room was comfortable enough, a queen-sized bed, TV, and a balconied window that overlooked High Gap. No cars moved. The snow fell with a quiet hiss and caused the town's solitary lights to appear hazed, their beams broken.

I sat on the bed and phoned Drake's home number. When Deborah answered, I apologized for calling so late.

"He's attending a gun show in Kentucky," she said. "Is this an emergency?"

"No emergency but important. Soon as you hear from him, ask him to reach me at this number."

"It involves Cliff?"

"He's jailed here in West Virginia."

"But not hurt or being mistreated?"

"He's all right, but we need Drake."

"Let me write down that number. Oh, God, look after Cliff, Walter."

When I hung up, I stood at the window and watched the snow fall into the night. The clerk brought my grilled-cheese sandwich, two sweet pickles, a glass of milk, and a paper napkin on a tray.

"*Gracias,*" he said as he left after I tipped him.

I munched the sandwich and watched the snow smother the town's lights, reducing them to erratic embers.

TWENTY-EIGHT

I was so exhausted I sank into a hard sleep that left me more drained than refreshed. Waking, I felt addled, unsure where I lay in the first unearthly white light of morning. I held my watch over my eyes, the time 7:27.

I showered, shaved, and sat in a leatherette booth of the motel restaurant, where I ordered tomato juice and coffee. I was the only customer. I bought a copy of the Seneca *Register* as well as *USA Today* that I would carry to Cliff. The headline on the *Register* read COUGAR REPORTED KILLING SHEEP.

I left word at the desk I could be reached at the courthouse if calls came for me. Wind blew curling wisps of snow over the town. I scraped the Buick's windshield, and the car slithered along the road driving down the hill to the courthouse, its stone facade snow-blasted. A trustee wearing tan coveralls used a blower to clear parking spaces. A second trustee shoveled off steps.

I studied the lobby directory to locate the district attorney's office. The elevator to the third floor felt slow but determined. Mr. Tuggle's young secretary was eating a glazed doughnut as I entered, biting at it daintily, her purple fingernails carefully positioned to protect them. She laid the doughnut aside and licked at her thumb.

"He's waiting for you," she said and with a small, pinched mouth announced me through her intercom.

Sam Tuggle met me at the door, a ruddy, vigorous man as tall as I and a good seventy or eighty pounds heavier. The grip of his hand edged on being painful. As he showed me in, he took my overcoat, patted my back, and pulled out a chair for me beside his desk.

"We glad to have you here in our fair state, Mr. Frampton. Hope everybody's been showing you a friendly face. If not, you just point 'em out and we'll nail their hides to the barn door."

On walls hung diplomas, glossy snapshots of himself with politicians, commemorative plaques, and over the window behind his desk the mounted head of a wild boar, its fangs exposed. There was also a large color photograph of him as a coal miner, his face blackened except around the eyes, his teeth gleaming in a minstrel's mouth. The helmet held an attached lamp, and an insulated wire ran from it to a battery pack at his side. Knees of his filthy, baggy jeans were protected by strapped on leather pads. His grimy hands held a lunch pail and thermos.

"Way I started out," he said. "Dug black diamonds eight years before I went to night school and passed the bar. Was near born under a lump of coal."

"It's a good picture," I said.

"The voters like it," he said, unbuttoned his gray double-breasted jacket, and sat. "Sorry about the snow. Well, part sorry 'cause we encouraging skiing around here. Got us a good slope up the road with a lift and half a dozen runs. We hoping lots of Virginians coming our way and bringing money. You ski?"

"I never got around to it."

"Be glad to give you a complimentary pass for the lift. Ten-dollar value. Had your breakfast? Gail'll bring you a doughnut and a mug of battery acid."

I declined. The fullness of his face, the florid good-ol'-boy manner, failed to mask his sharply focused hazel eyes. He struck me as being a fit, energetic man with a swift brain behind a broad brow, his folksy language a smoke screen.

"Mr. Tuggle—"

"Call me Sam. Thought we got that out of the road over the phone."

"And me Walter."

"Everybody 'round here calls me Sam. Even the felons."

"Yes, sir, well, Sam, as you know I represent Mr. Clifford Dickens, who at this moment resides in your jail."

"Not my jail. I don't own any jails. It belongs to the county, and the sheriff runs it."

"Right. I guess what I want from you first is a bill of particulars."

"Well now, I try to be accommodating to my fellow officers of the court, but as to a bill of particulars, you see, Walter, there's this question about you."

"You're going to ask whether or not I'm licensed to practice law in this state. The answer is no, but I intend to take on a local attorney as an associate if necessary."

"It will be necessary."

"I'm hoping, however, you'll extend the courtesy of talking to me at this stage of the process."

"Always try to be a good neighbor to my fellow man." He leaned back in his chair, his hands settled on its arms.

"Thank you, Sam. I confess I continue to be somewhat mystified at the trouble your office has gone to in bringing my client all the long way from Richmond to High Gap."

"Mystified? How so?"

"By what appears to be an all-out press against Mr. Dickens. You are sticking with a charge of voluntary homicide?"

"That's how it's marked up."

"And carrying it to a grand jury?"

"Already done, and they brought forth a true bill of indictment."

"You didn't waste time."

"Justice swift is justice served."

"At the heart of the matter as I see it, Mr. Wendell Ripley's death was caused by human error, and I find it a far stretch to make a case for voluntary homicide, which requires disagreement, provocation, and anger between the parties."

"The heart of the matter," Sam said, his thick fingers tapping the chair's arms. "Wonderful phrase. Get down below the skin, the fat, the muscle, the bone, and you find a heart pumping out blood and beating like a tom-tom. Got to figure what message the tom-tom's sounding."

"I don't see where you're headed."

"You wouldn't be trying to fool around with this old country boy, would you, Walt?"

"I'm here to advise my client to agree to a charge of involuntary manslaughter subject to what punishment will be imposed for that plea. I assume you would rather save your taxpayers money by not going to trial."

"Sorry to have to break the news to you but things are turning out more complicated than they first appeared."

"Sam, voluntary manslaughter is a felonious homicide committed in the heat of passion, *furor brevis*, the bloodshed growing solely from incitement to conflict."

He grinned and pointed at the wall.

"Don't you suppose I know that? There's a diploma right up there that proves I been to law school."

"What happened on the Blind Sheep hunt doesn't meet the definition."

"We don't happen to agree with you around here. Something else went on up on Blind Sheep."

"What else?"

"You don't need to know at this point since we thinking of nol-prossing voluntary manslaughter."

"You're dropping it?" I asked, surprised and relieved.

"If we do, we'll go back to a grand jury for an indictment of murder two."

I sat stunned and attempted to order my thinking. Murder in the second degree was different from murder one that required willful, deliberate, and premeditated killing. Rather, murder two involved the sudden transport of passion that the law called *furor brevis* plus malice. In Virginia it was a class three felony punishable by confinement in the penitentiary for a minimum of five to as much as eighteen or twenty years. West Virginia law would likely impose a similar penalty.

"I don't believe what my ears are telling me," I said.

"Believe, Walt. It's no joke 'round this office. We hold the law in great respect in these parts despite what you might think down in Virginia of us backward hillbillies."

"You brought my client here with a charge of voluntary manslaughter while all the while you meant to go for murder two?"

"Irrelevant at the moment since we do have him in custody and that being the fact a grand jury can charge him with anything they want once we nol-pros the voluntary charge. It won't, however, be a frivolous move on this office's part."

"There has to be malice. You can't have murder without malice."

"Walt, I'm not giving away my case till the time is nigh, but let me say that there's evidence which don't square with either involuntary or voluntary manslaughter."

"Would you be more specific?" I asked, attempting to appear composed.

"Look in my ear," he said, leaned forward, and again grinned. "You see anybody in there listening?"

"Sam, please, I've had a hard trip," I said. His large ear looked as if it had been battered and did resemble cauliflower.

"I can be more specific but don't feel compelled to at this point, and you'll have the full right of discovery in due course. On the other hand you look like you done been run over by an eighteen-wheeler, and as I said I want to accommodate my fellow officers of the court. Let's see if we can get Sheriff Sawyers to drop by." He thumbed his intercom and tilted sideways to speak into it. "Gail, how about asking

Bruce to pay us a visit." He again faced me. "So you a hunter too?"

"No, I came to Blind Sheep for an outing with friends."

"And more than grouse got bagged, huh? I'm fixing to have myself another mug of coffee. Sure you don't want some?"

I shook my head. He walked out, and I looked through his window to the top of a snow-covered mountain that to a lowlander like me seemed like a white tidal wave about to sweep over and smash the town. Tumbling gray clouds sliding eastward gave the mountain an appearance of falling.

Sam, holding a yellow mug decorated with the blue initials WVU, came back followed by the sheriff, who had taken off his trooper hat and unzipped his leather jacket. Snowflakes melted on the fur-lined collar. Had the two men conferred? Sam sat and drank his coffee. The sheriff appeared freshly shaved, his uniform as before sharply pressed, his red sideburns precisely leveled. He nodded to me.

"Bruce, Walt here wonders why we paying so much attention to his Mr. Dickens. We want to be hospitable 'cause we Virginians too, though not Tidewater born and bred. You been fretted by your findings up on Blind Sheep. Mind telling Walt a thing or two about why without giving away the henhouse?"

"I checked the scene out from all angles and studied my photographs," the sheriff said. His slate-gray eyes fixed me. "First, Mr. Dickens reported that Mr. Ripley lunged to the left just as a grouse flushed. If Mr. Ripley had lunged past Mr. Dickens as Mr. Dickens has stated, he would have been shot in the side or back, not his lower chest and upper stomach. Second, his boot prints don't confirm a move either left or right. Mr. Ripley was downslope and behind Mr. Dickens. Mr. Dickens would've had to fire at an angle of decline, the barrel of his shotgun lowered fifty degrees or more to strike Mr. Ripley in those areas of his body. If a bird flushed, as has been stated by Mr. Dickens, though we found no tracks, it would've flown up, not down. I've diagrammed it."

"The bird could have flushed and flown low," I said.

"Had not Mr. Ripley been there to intercept, the load would've gone into the ground not more than thirty-six inches in front of Mr. Dickens's feet," the sheriff answered. Did he ever blink?

"And Mr. Dickens might have triggered his shotgun involuntarily during the excitement of the moment," I said.

"He stated he swung left on the bird, not down."

"You're basing your conclusions primarily on the reconstructed scene of a shooting that is surely subject to varying interpretations," I said.

"My deputies and I acted it out. What we found doesn't square with what Mr. Dickens has testified to."

"But it's still only what you believe could have happened, not enough for a conviction."

"Well, that just got Bruce started," Sam said and set his mug on his desk. "Roused his interest enough he spent his own time checking things out while down in Virginia on vacation. We can't keep Bruce from working. He talked to people, like those folks out at that place called The Watchers where Mr. Ripley had his domicile till he departed this vale of tears. Mr. Ripley was a deeply religious man, but Bruce here learned things about Mr. Ripley's son, what's his full name, Bruce?"

"Jeremiah Daniel Ripley," the sheriff said.

"Name of Jeremiah and Daniel in the fiery furnace. Bruce learned the youth was a homosexual known to other men of that predilection in the city. Learned Mr. Ripley was mighty upset and despondent about his son's behavior. Learned Mr. Dickens had a photo exhibition that pictured such men showing everything except them doing it to each other. Learned the boy had been Mr. Dickens's student. Began to appear that while Mr. Ripley and Mr. Dickens were up there on Blind Sheep hunting together they had reason to get into a heated disagreement that ended with Mr. Dickens shooting and meaning to kill Mr. Ripley, and that intent supplies the malice. They could have fought but nobody had to die. Malice plain and simple. The fight might have started when Mr. Ripley tried to break up the association his son had with Mr. Dickens or maybe Mr. Dickens feared the truth about him and the boy coming out."

"Too many mights and maybes," I said.

"But enough we could use," Sam said. "That about it, Bruce?"

"About," the sheriff said.

"All theory, not evidence," I said.

"We'll see," Sam said. "Haul it to the grand jury and let them carry the ball."

"And grand juries most often provide what prosecutors request of them," I said. "But it doesn't mean your case will hold up in court."

"Prosecutors don't like to waste their time any more than anybody else," Sam said.

"For the sake of our talking here," I said, "if Wendell Ripley believed he had cause to be angry at Mr. Dickens, any shooting by Mr. Dickens could have been self-defense."

"But your Mr. Dickens never told it that way," Sam said. "He lied. He's been lying all along."

I needed to be careful not to reveal what I did and did not know.

"He has never given a sworn statement on any charge," I said.

"We have his taped account I recorded the day of the shooting," the sheriff said.

"His account claims it was an accident," I said.

"And can be used against him if we present testimony or evidence that contradicts it," Sam said.

"I'd like to suggest to you that if inconsistencies are found, they might well arise from Mr. Dickens trying to save pain and heartache to others. He has friends as well as his professional reputation to protect."

"What I understand, his reputation around Richmond town is he kept company with the limp-wristed and sweet types," Sam said.

"He's an artist. They frequently move in that circle. I've known him all my life, and he's not like that."

"Lord God, you think you know people," Sam said. "You sit in this office, you find you never get down to the final layer of what a person really is. You can peel all the way through to the core and find you grabbed only air in your fingers."

"If there was anger between the two of them, I still maintain it could be self-defense on Mr. Dickens's part."

"I wouldn't advise you to go for self-defense. No sign of a struggle. Neither man had a fight mark on him. Odds are it was hot blood and hate. To justify self-defense Mr. Dickens would need proof his life was endangered."

"Mr. Ripley held a loaded twelve-gauge shotgun," I said. "A threat in and of itself."

As Sam leaned back, he drew his hands from the desk and looked away from me to the sheriff.

"What you think, Bruce?"

"I never believed in ambush," the sheriff said.

"Discovery'd kick it out anyhow. Oh hell, go on and tell him."

"We're holding the guns for evidence," the sheriff said. "The Beretta over-and-under used by Mr. Dickens and belonging to Mr. Wingo as well as the Remington automatic that Mr. Ripley carried. Those were the firearms they hunted with, correct?"

"Correct," I said.

"I wrapped the guns in plastic and drove them to Charleston to undergo a State Police Lab examination. Received a report back that surprised me. While Mr. Dickens's Beretta had a fired shell still in a chamber, Mr. Ripley's Remington was empty."

"He could have shot at the bird a second before he died," I said.

"But he supposedly had lunged past Mr. Dickens, and he would have needed to shoot three times to empty the Remington if fully loaded. He didn't. The Remington hadn't been fired and the bolt was closed instead of locked open."

"Mr. Ripley might've forgotten to load. It happens. To me once in a duck blind. Or maybe he shucked the shells by mistake during the excitement of the flush. That happens too."

"Maybe with a pump gun, not an automatic. As to forgetting, Mr. Dickens's statement made after the killing, and you and Mr. Wingo agreed, you all four had stopped to load at the same time before splitting up to hunt in pairs. Mr. Ripley was bound to notice you other three thumbing in the high brass."

I hesitated, running my mind back to the hunt. Had I seen Wendell loading like the rest of us? I believed so, but I'd been an attorney long enough to know that even the most honest memory could deceive.

"And his safety was still on," Sawyers said. "If he meant to fire, wouldn't he have pushed off his safety?"

"I don't know. Things happen on hunts."

"We found something else," the sheriff said after a glance at Sam, who nodded. "Mr. Ripley had no shells in his hunting vest. It's the reason when the snow melted we backtracked down the mountain from the homicide site. We used a metal detector to find ten twelve-gauge high brass 7 ½s, 1 ¼ ounces of shot, 3 ¾ drams of powder, lying on the ground."

"Mr. Ripley never hunted before," I said. "A case of confusion, fumbling, buck fever."

"He might've fumbled a shell or two but what about the others that fit tight in slots of his shooting vest. He dropped them at approximately fifty-foot intervals, like counting his steps as he climbed. No way they could've just fallen. They had to be pulled out and turned loose of."

I sat silent.

"Sure suggests malice on Mr. Dickens's part," Sam said. "He was facing a man holding an empty shotgun."

"He wouldn't know that."

"Maybe yes, maybe no, but there could be no intent for a man with an unloaded gun to do harm to another individual unless he used it as a club. It don't pan out, Walt. What we got here is a homicidal stew with lots of bad meat. Now you understand why this office just can't let go of this thing?"

"I understand," I said, though still trying to set it straight in my mind. "When's the preliminary hearing?"

"Before the magistrate, ten this morning. Hate to treat a guest in the county poorly but now you know the lay of the land around here."

I walked fast down the steps and to the jail. This time Gilbert let me use a conference room at the far end of the cell block, a space not much larger than a closet furnished with two metal chairs, a wall desk, a telephone, and a directory. He brought Cliff cuffed and locked him in beside me.

Cliff seemed smaller now, shrunken, his eyes a larger part of a tragic face.

"I feel I've been shat upon and stink," he said and rubbed his throat. His palms rasped his beard, and his fingers left his eyebrows ruffled. "Why you looking at me like that?"

"I'm waiting for you to tell the rest of it."

"The rest of what?"

"The game you and Drake have been playing with me."

"There's been no game."

"Listen, now that they have you here, they're thinking of upping the charge to—are you ready for this?—murder in the second degree. There will be no bail. If convicted, you will receive years of hard time."

"Murder?" He paled. "Just a ploy to make me plead to voluntary, right?"

"No ploy, Cliff."

"They can bring me here under one charge and switch it to another?"

"It's their ballpark, and they're able to do pretty much what they want now they hold you. Prosecutors have enormous powers."

"What can you do?"

"At this point not a lot. There will be a hearing, the preliminary before a magistrate during which you'll be able to plead not guilty. While you're held, however, the district attorney can quash the voluntary manslaughter charge and bring in a new indictment of murder two. You'll face trial, I'll need a local associate, and the two of us will defend you. Even if we succeed in clearing you of murder two, a jury might still convict you of the lesser voluntary charge."

"You shouldn't have let them do this to me, Walter. What kind of lawyer are you?"

"Run-of-the-mill variety, and what kind of client do I have that keeps withholding the truth from me?"

"What truth? I told you how it happened on Blind Sheep."

"You told me Wendell threatened you. It's difficult to believe a man using an unloaded shotgun could do that."

"Unloaded? You and I saw him load that Remington."

"The sheriff discovered all of Wendell's shells dropped along the slope up toward Blind Sheep ridge."

"I didn't know his gun wasn't loaded. How could I? I heard him working the bolt and believed he was just checking his load as we all do. Why would he empty the gun?"

"I've been thinking hard about that. My guess is it means Wendell never had any intention of shooting you but maneuvered you into shooting him. True or not, there's little possibility your attorneys will be able to make a plea of self-defense prevail in court."

Cliff again rubbed his face, started to speak, licked his lips.

"Cliff, they're convinced you and Wendell's son Jeremiah had a homosexual relationship, that hostility between you and his father arose from it, and that's the reason you shot him."

"That's not so."

"I'll believe you only if you tell me what you and Drake have been holding back. Otherwise I'm resigning the case."

He turned his face aside, his expression tormented, and again ran fingers along his throat.

"Drake needs to be in on this," he said.

"On what? Tell me or I'm gone."

He inhaled as if he had come up from holding his breath long underwater.

"I thought no charges would be brought if I claimed Wendell's death was accidental. I wanted to avoid a media event and the possibility of a scandal. I had a girl whom I intended to marry. There was a chance I'd lose her along with any career left me in Richmond if what really happened came to light. And there was Drake."

"Drake what?"

"I don't want to tell you."

"Cliff, you tell me or I walk."

"There's got to be another way."

"No, no other way."

He stared at his hands before looking at me.

"Oh Christ, it happened almost three years ago when driving to a New Year's Eve party I passed Grizzly's and spotted his delivery truck and two cars parked in the lot. It was just like him to be working. The lights at the front of the store had been switched off, the ghost grouse floated in darkness, but I knew Drake used a rear entrance when he opened and closed the place. I walked around the building and found that door unlocked."

We heard Gilbert's foot dragging along the cellblock. He paused before the conference room, checked us, and withdrew.

"Go on, " I said.

"I opened the door and stepped into the stockroom," Cliff said. "A ceiling bulb burned, enough light for me to find my way among the shelves and crates. I walked toward the office where the door was partly open. Walter, I hate doing this."

"Don't you stop on me now."

"There's a cot in the office."

"I've seen it."

"They were in his office on the cot."

"They?"

"Drake."

"Drake and who?"

"Another man."

"You have proof?" I asked when I could speak.

"No."

"I thought you always carried a camera."

"I left it in the car but wouldn't have used it if I had."

"The other man was Jeremiah Ripley?"

"I think so but can't swear to it. They were lying in shadows."

"But you're certain you saw Drake."

"He lifted his head and looked at me."

"All this time you've been protecting him?"

"Trying to protect both of us. We thought it would work. Now that you know, what will you do?"

"Shoot myself," I said.

TWENTY-NINE

The hearing at ten charging Cliff with the voluntary manslaughter was only a formality in the small first-floor courtroom that had mingled scents of dust, tobacco, and body odors. The oak benches could have been church pews, and the hanging light fixtures gave off an essence of a distant time, as if the electricity had been wearied by far travel from another age, maybe 1936 when the WPA courthouse had been built according to a plaque screwed to the corridor's wall.

The magistrate, a thin, elderly man whose skin was like white parchment, appeared incongruously dapper in a tattersall vest, a polka-dot bow tie, and a linen handkerchief folded to three peaks sticking from the breast pocket of his tweed jacket.

"How do you plead to the indictment, Mr. Dickens?" he asked Cliff in a fatherly voice.

Cliff answered not guilty. I requested bail.

"Your Honor, the accused was a fugitive, and there's risk he'll flee this jurisdiction," Sam Tuggle countered.

"Your Honor, Mr. Dickens has no criminal record and would have gladly surrendered himself voluntarily to this court."

"I believe we best hold your client a spell while I review the pertaining data," the judge said and tapped his gavel delicately as if it were as infirm as he.

Before a deputy returned Cliff to his cell, I told him I was on my way to see Drake.

"I'm so damn sorry," Cliff said.

I shook his hand, watched the deputy lead him away, and returned to the Mountain View Lodge for my things. The weather had let up, and a faint sun laid a sheen on the snow. I drove cautiously along the slick road between the plowed, sooty banks. A jackknifed trailer truck held up traffic for ninety minutes. It had spilled tomatoes grown in Florida, and many of the people stalled picked them up to carry to their cars.

The snowbanks gave way as I crossed back to Virginia and were gone before I reached Powhatan County. When I stopped at Grizzly's at a few minutes before seven the parking lot was empty except for the Ford delivery truck that on its side panels portrayed an aroused bear rampant above a pair of Kentucky flintlock muskets. The store's doors were locked. The mobile grouse ghosted eerily within the showroom's darkness.

I was not about to confront Drake at his house, where he would be with Deborah and the twins. I had never gone to the expense of installing a cellular phone in my Buick and used the public booth in front of a Winn-Dixie at a Route 60 shopping center to make the call.

"I need to see you immediately," I said when Drake answered.

"Come on to the house, Raff."

"You meet me at Grizzly's."

"Deb and I are just finishing dinner."

"I'll be waiting in the lot."

"Well damn it, Raff."

"Right now," I said and without waiting for him to speak further hung up and drove back to the store. I pulled in beside the truck. The night had become still, and ice of refrozen puddles reflected a gleam from the ghost grouse. The heater running, I left on my gloves. I felt worn, queasy, and a thick, dirty taste coated my mouth.

At twenty minutes after seven the Bronco slowed, the headlights flashing as it turned in, and Drake drew alongside. He stepped out and crossed bareheaded around to the passenger door of my car.

"You in some kind of sweat on a night like this?" he asked as he opened the door and bowed in beside me.

"A cold sweat," I said.

"I don't readily give up nighttime with Deb and the twins."

"They've got Cliff jailed in High Gap. He faces a possible murder charge."

"Sonofabitch," Drake said, turning to me. "How can they do that?"

"They're convinced Wendell's shooting was deliberate and malicious."

"Malicious meaning what exactly?"

"That the force used was not justified by the provocation that arose between Wendell and Cliff."

"It's bullshit."

"They're dead serious."

"Politics then. The sheriff and DA are putting on a show for the voters. Keep their names in the papers."

"They have Cliff for lying and are able to make a connection between him and Jeremiah Ripley."

"What kind of connection?"

"A liaison is the kindest word I can use."

"I been afraid of that," he said and leaned back in the seat.

"Of what?"

"You know how Cliff's changed and become, well, hell, the crowd he runs with these days, plus the Shockoe exhibition."

"I don't like what you're suggesting. He has a girl he wants to marry."

"You ever seen her?"

"I've seen her picture."

"Not the same. Why hasn't he had her around?"

"She lives in Baltimore, and she may be black."

"Damn him, I don't care if she's got red-and-yellow stripes, the fact is she's not been seen in the flesh."

"Why are you so angry at Cliff?"

"I'm angry for what he's done to us, the position he's put us in, not only himself, but me, my family and business, and you think you're going to help your reputation by being associated with him?"

"You believe he and Jeremiah Ripley had that kind of relationship?"

"I believe it's possible. We haven't been close to Cliff of late. He's gone his own way and left you and me behind."

"This thing could ruin his life."

"Cliff hasn't had much life lately, but I'll keep my word and stick by him. Look, maybe it was a onetime thing between him and Jerry, a weak moment. I already told him and you I'd support him financially and otherwise."

"It's the otherwise that interests me."

"Don't follow you, Raff."

"What about you and Jeremiah?"

"Me and Jeremiah what? He sold shoes for me, nothing else."

"Cliff claims there's more."

"Let's hear it."

"Two bodies on your office camp cot New Year's Eve, 1991."

Drake again turned to me. Lights of a passing car slashed across his face, causing him to look bloodless and spectral.

"Poor Cliff's got to be scared shitless to make up a story like that."

"You think he'd do that to you?"

"I think he's reaching out for anything he can grab to save himself. Look, Raff, I'll stand by him. You want to hire another lawyer, F. Lee Bailey, I'll underwrite the expenses and do anything else you ask. How'd Cliff get himself into this fucking mess?"

"It was you who encouraged or persuaded him not to tell the sheriff about what actually happened on Blind Sheep."

"I told you I did that for him as well as myself. It had nothing to do with murder."

"Why was Wendell on the hunt?"

"As I explained before, because I wanted to buy his Blind Sheep land. I never knew anything about a connection between Cliff and Jeremiah."

"Drake, ask yourself why if Wendell believed Cliff had corrupted Jerry and meant to kill him, he never fired his gun."

"How the hell can I answer that? If they had a fight, maybe Cliff got the drop on him. Remember, I was with you, not them."

"I picked up a little piece of information while talking to the sheriff and district attorney in High Gap. Wendell's Remington was empty."

"Say again."

"No shells in the gun."

"Wrong. I saw him loading up."

"And the shells from his vest dropped in the snow along the way. Wendell was a Watcher. They are conscientious objectors and believe in nonviolence. My guess is he never meant to hunt, to shoot, or to kill anything."

"Your guess?"

"I think he tricked Cliff into believing he had to fire in order to save himself. How else do you explain it?"

"I can't 'cause I repeat I wasn't there. Cliff could've had reasons we don't know about."

"Can you think of one?"

"Maybe Wendell told Cliff he meant to expose him. They had an argument, Cliff panicked."

"No shells in Wendell's gun. That's what I keep coming back to. No need to shoot."

"Cliff wouldn't've known that."

"It's the main thing they have on him," I said. "He shot and killed an unarmed man."

"Just tell me what it is you want."

"I want to be convinced you've been completely honest with me."

"How long you been knowing me, Raff? You think I'd go queer and do that with a man?"

"I think either you or Cliff's lying."

"You ever heard me tell a lie?"

"Not before this."

"Take your choice, Cliff or me."

"That's not enough," I said.

"It wasn't me on the cot, but if there was anybody it had to be Boomer and Jeremiah. They volunteered to help take inventory that New Year's Eve, and we worked till after dark but didn't finish. I left early, they offered to keep on, and I paid them double overtime for doing so."

"There were two cars and your delivery truck in the lot according to Cliff."

"Any cars would've belonged to Boomer and Jerry. The delivery truck stays here."

"Where were you that night?"

"I'll pretend you didn't ask that question but give you an answer just the same. I'd taken a young redheaded gal named Rosemary Palmer to a New Year's Eve party."

"Where was the party?"

"The Chesterfield Country Club."

"And Rosemary, where's she now?"

"Last I heard she's married and lives in Atlanta."

"Anyone see you two there?"

"Let me think, sure, Josey. She and her tennis pro sat at the table with us. And I guarantee you if there's any truth to what Cliff claims, Boomer's ass will be out of here faster than shit shat from a goose."

He cocked his finger as if it were the hammer of a revolver, pointed it at the front of the store, and mouthed the word "bang."

THIRTY

I drove to Jessup's Wharf, slept, and when I reached my office sat trying to think how I could check out what Drake had told me. I decided to start with Boomer and at mid-morning called Grizzly's.

"He's left us," a woman's voice told me, I assumed one of the two ladies who worked in billing and accounting.

"Does left us mean he quit or was let go? And I'd like his full name and telephone number."

"I'm sorry, sir, I'm not authorized to give out that information. Would you care to speak to our owner, Mr. Wingo?"

"No," I said and hung up. Whatever Drake told me, rightly or wrongly, would absolve no one but himself.

I had known Boomer only by that name. I called the *Times-Dispatch*, asked for the Sports Desk, and talked to a reporter who identified himself as Bucky Ruff. He remembered Boomer from his glory days at VPI.

"Boomer's in the phone book, listed as Ernest B. Mosely," Bucky said. "The B's for Bartholomew. I looked it up."

I found the listing and drove to Boomer's Oregon Hill, South Pine Street address, a Richmond neighborhood of closely spaced frame houses built during the 1850s and lived in originally by German blue-collar workers. His small, one-story cottage was freshly painted a pale orange, had a crepe myrtle bush in a tiny picket-fenced yard, and was shuttered. Nobody answered the bell.

Next door an elderly hunchbacked woman, her hands gloved, her long black overcoat reaching almost to her ankles, her frizzled white hair wind tossed, stopped sweeping her porch.

"Ernie drove off early," she said and sucked at her toothless mouth as if tasting her pink gums. "Told me he'd be gone a spell."

"Did he say where he was going?"

"Texas. Told me he'd always wanted to see Texas and the Alamo."

"Do you know when he's coming back?"

"Can't tell you that, bud," she said and resumed sweeping. "I'm to feed his cat, and I never seen the first one of them animals I liked."

I drove back to Jessup's Wharf assuming for whatever reason that Drake had sent Boomer packing. I should have tried to reach him earlier. His leaving was inconclusive—either Drake had confronted him and discovered Boomer had been on the cot with Jeremiah or to protect himself had fired Boomer to be rid of him.

I sat at my desk unsure what to do next. Mary Ellen answered the phone and from her chair raised a finger. When I picked up, it was Josey.

"Please come see me," she said. "It's important."

"I'm up to my neck in work, but have I ever been able to refuse you anything?"

"Start the meter running," she said.

I drove to Richmond, no meter running. I hadn't charged Cliff anything yet either, not even expenses. When I entered the trading room at Bunker, Rose & Diggs and started toward Josey's office, the receptionist intercepted me.

"Miss Lynn's occupied," she said.

I asked her to tell Miss Lynn I had arrived. The receptionist fingered her switchboard, spoke into her headset, and listened before motioning me past. Josey's door was closed. She opened it as I lifted my hand to knock.

"Let's get the hell out of here," she said. The skin of her face appeared waxen and tightly drawn. "The goddamn phone's about to drive me out of my skull."

She buttoned on her camel's hair overcoat. The receptionist called after her to ask when she would be back.

"Sometime," Josey answered, and her heels clicked on the lobby's terrazzo floor.

We walked out onto East Main and turned at Ninth Street down toward the James. I liked being seen beside her. She stuck her hands deep into her overcoat pockets as the buildings channeled the wind against us. Her stride was fast and hard.

Past the towering Federal Reserve edifice we crossed the pedestrian bridge over to Brown's Island. The James flowed full from snows in the mountains, the water dirtied by the flotsam and a stirred-up bottom. The river, seemingly wrathful, swirled around bridge piling. She stopped, put her hands on the rail, and looked down at the water coiling viciously beneath us.

"I'm in trouble, Raff," she said. "Prince Jamir's bolted and carried away the ton of money people invested with him."

"Where's he now?"

"The sonofabitch is beyond reach, believed to be in an Arab country, Dubai or elsewhere along the Persian Gulf, but it's no certainty. We discovered only this morning he's gone. Raff, I put hundreds of thousands of my clients' dollars in that investment trust as well as all my own and a big chunk of Drake's. I went on margin to buy shares."

Her eyes closed, and she leaned over the railing. I thought of Charles LeBlanc's escrowed money from the Bellerive transaction that I might have invested with the prince had it been available to me. I felt cold and shivered.

"He's left a mountain of bills unpaid," Josey said. "Most of

Bellerive's construction costs, the furniture, his plane, all rented or leased. I may be sued, investigated by the SEC, even go to jail. Raff, help me."

"I'll do all I can."

She drew away from the railing and looked at me out of those chestnut eyes that made me feel weak and helpless, stepped to me, circled her arms around my waist, and cried against my chest. I felt her body's trembling.

"I'm so frightened," she said.

"Just don't panic and give me time to look into the matter and get back to you. Make no statement to anyone unless you clear it with me."

"You're a good man, Raff."

"And you're the woman I'm stuck with loving."

"Oh, God, don't talk to me like that at this minute when I'm terrified everything in my life's falling apart."

She continued to cry, the first time I had ever seen her tears, even to way back when she was a young girl who could spit as far as Drake, Cliff, and I. I held her, and the water poured under the bridge, causing the sensation that the river stood still and we were moving upstream together.

"All right, enough," she said and touched her eyes.

I walked her back to Bunker, Rose & Diggs. Wind snapped the colorful banners that fluttered over us. I thought of what Drake had told me and stopped her in the building's lobby.

"Josey, I need to ask you something. A New Year's Eve, some three years ago, were you dating a tennis pro and did you sit at a table with Drake and a girl during the party?"

"The shape I'm in, you're asking me about a fucking party three years ago?"

"It's very important. Do your best to remember."

She touched fingers to her forehead, bit her lip, then raised her face to me.

"Let me think," she said. "Oh, God, yeah, the Chesterfield Country Club, and her name was Rosemary. She wore a slinky red dress that was slit almost to her pudendum."

"Thanks, that's what I was after," I said and held her arm as we moved on to the boisterous trading room, where I left her. She breathed deeply, braced her shoulders, and walked toward her office as if ready to fight and take on all comers.

THIRTY-ONE

O bjectively considered, Cliff's situation was more pressing than Josey's, though it was difficult for me to place anyone else's troubles ahead of hers. I couldn't honorably suspend his defense even temporarily to take up hers.

Mary Ellen had left for home, and the day grew late as I sat staring not at lighted St. Luke's and the pigeons but at the office's yet-to-be-decorated back wall in an effort to clear my mind of all distractions and choose how best to proceed.

The phone rang. Wearily I reached for it and recognized the cultured, unhurried voice that belonged to Philip Garrow.

"Concerning Jeremiah Ripley and your problem locating him, I have a ragtag of information," he said. "It is completely unreliable, and I promise nothing. I picked it up from a new employee who claims to have been a friend of a friend sort of thing. If you're still interested."

"Give it to me, please," I said as I drew a pencil from my W&L mug in which Mary Ellen kept half a dozen sharpened and waiting for my use.

"Nirvana Tours, Fort Lauderdale, Florida. I repeat I can't and won't vouch for its accuracy. So many names these days coming and going. We live in a fluid society, nothing permanent."

"The phone number."

"Which I don't have. You might try Information."

"Thank you, Philip."

"Likely a dry well, but the best I can do. Come eat with me soon."

"One day," I said, meant it, and as soon as he hung up phoned Information. I had no difficulty obtaining the number. On reaching Nirvana Tours, I listened to a recorded announcement that the travel agency was open eight to five Monday through Friday and ten till four Saturdays.

At exactly eight o'clock in the morning I called from my apartment and got the recording. I waited five minutes before again trying. The same male voice answered, but this time it was live, and I asked to speak to Jeremiah Ripley.

"Sorry, no one here by that name," he said and hung up.

I called a third time.

"Do you know where Jeremiah Ripley can be found?" I asked.

"No."

"What's your name?"

"Raoul."

"Have you ever heard of Jeremiah Ripley?"

"Sir, this is a travel agency. You want to go somewhere, we'll plan your trip, okay?"

"You haven't answered my question."

"Don't have to," he said and hung up.

A lost cause, I thought. Philip's employee had probably given him information picked up from gossip heard along the Slip. I looked at St. Luke's steeple, where the pigeons gathered on the lee side. But suppose Jeremiah had fled Richmond and was using another name? Raoul had sounded defensive and been rudely abrupt cutting me off.

I considered hiring a private detective to follow through with an investigation. There was no time. Though I had other cases backed up, making a day trip down to Florida to find out for certain would be both faster and less expensive.

USAir was able to provide me a reserved coach seat at 10:51 that morning which after a change at Charlotte would put me into Fort

Lauderdale at 2:43. I booked a return flight at 8:23, again with a change at Charlotte.

I left the office to Mary Ellen, withdrew two hundred dollars from the King County Bank, and drove fast to Byrd Field. A light cold rain rolled across the runway. On the plane I sat next to a man whose nose was almost gone and right hand missing at the wrist, the stump covered by a leather cup. He told me he had been a soldier.

"I saw God's almighty power in the hot pinwheeling blast of a mortar shell," he said. "You can't hide. God searches you out. You hearing me?"

"I'm thinking it over."

"You don't have to think. God'll do your thinking. Mortar taught me that. Mortars speak a universal language that everybody understands—Japs, Chinks, A-rabs, don't make no difference, you know right on the spot. You believe in anything?"

"I believe in yesterday," I said.

"Ha," he said and turned away, hunched in his seat, and slept.

I thought of yesterdays and how Cliff, Drake, and I had grown close during our youthful adventures. The three of us went way back to a Richmond neighborhood called Wellsby Park, an area of houses that sat as snugly comfortable on mowed and tended lawns as hens on their nests.

Up the street rose the stone seminary buildings, and their antiquated, lichen-coated elms dropped a deep shade on uneven brick sidewalks along which theological students strolled, their hands lifted in doctrinal discourses. Drake, Cliff, and I had sneaked onto campus one September night and sewed a jockstrap on the bronze erect figure of John Calvin, who stood gazing upward with arms spread as if conversing with God.

As boys our parents sent us to Wicomico in Westmoreland County, Virginia, a summer camp on the broad tidal river that emptied into the Chesapeake Bay. We learned to shoot with .22-

caliber rifles at bull's-eyes of paper targets and used twenty-gauge shotguns to break clay pigeons flung by a trap out over the lapping water. Oyster spat clung to sunken, shattered pieces and reproduced bountifully.

Sun-blasted, we fished for spot, croaker, and flounder. The black cook and his wife served us so many fried softshell crabs that we complained. The camp's main activity centered around sailing in twenty-foot wooden sloops built by native shipwrights along the river's shore. The sloops were open, no cuddy cabins or lazarettes, no compasses or running lights, and held to course by slablike centerboards located amidship. We bumped our knees on their protruding wells.

Across the Wicomico the girls had a camp named Hiawatha. We spied them at a distance in their bright canoes, the colors reflected in the water. A southern breeze carried their shouts and laughter as paddles dipped up flashing sunlight.

Drake, Cliff, and I got into trouble on a July Fourth because we broke rules by sneaking away a boat at night to intersect with a spit of land near Hiawatha, where the hull ground across sand as we beached her. Hiding under drooping cedars, we spied on the girls dressed like Indians who whooped it up around a campfire, their hunched-and-reared shapes silhouetted against the sparks of the swirling flames. When we returned to the boat, the rising tide had lifted and carried her off. We hiked seven miles to a bridge and worked our way back to Wicomico late that night, where all the cabin lights were switched on and Captain Tom and the counselors waited.

Captain Tom, a craggy man with skin like rawhide from years of boating on the Chesapeake, called our fathers to tell them to come after us. We caught it hot because our parents received no refunds, but passing through tribulation together set Drake, Cliff, and me apart. Mine had been a lesser daring, not really wanting to take the boat and trying to talk Cliff and Drake out of it, yet I had gone along, and to use the military parlance, we had all three shared the action and bonded.

After the change in Charlotte I watched the earth transform itself beneath the plane, a patchy fabric of snow giving way to slowly emerging green, and finally the sun cast the Airbus's shadow onto a sweep across blue water as we made our approach to Fort Lauderdale. The ocean, as if a vast broken mirror, reflected silver shards all the way to the horizon.

At the Fort Lauderdale terminal I stored my overcoat, hat, and umbrella in a locker, used the phone book to find Nirvana Tours' address on South Mahia Boulevard, and hailed a cab. The Hispanic driver drove us along a tropical avenue flanked by royal palms and white houses with red tile roofs, many behind walls overgrown with flowering bougainvillea. Wishing I had brought my sunglasses, I squinted against the glare. In Florida's warmth, my flannel suit felt scratchy and oppressive.

Nirvana Tours turned out to be the first floor of a stucco building in the Mermaid Plaza Mall. Shimmering heat rose from an expanse of dazzling concrete. Atop a fountain a plastic mermaid sat—rouged, her breasts covered by strands of golden hair, her enormous eyes looking astonished at her navel from which water spurted and splashed into a pool at her feet.

The window at Nirvana Tours held a smirking plaster Buddha with raised arms who offered an airline ticket in one hand, a tiger lily in the other. Around him were coconuts, seashells, and colorful brochures offering cruises to the Bahamas, St. John, and Aruba.

I opened the agency's door and stepped into the cooling relief of air conditioning.

"Got a letter here to mail," a young man said. He had a Latino appearance, and when he stepped around me to leave, I smelled aftershave lotion. His voice belonged to Raoul.

I glanced at wall posters of a Hawaiian beach and Gauguin's

Tahitian women. Small clocks displayed the times in Australia, Berlin, London, Buenos Aires, and a ceiling loudspeaker gave out sounds of waves softly splashing a shore.

The door behind the desk opened, and a blonde holding a pencil stepped out. In her hair she had pinned a pink hibiscus which coupled nicely with her white sleeveless blouse.

"Raoul?" she asked.

"I believe he's mailing a letter," I said.

"May I help you?" she asked as she crossed to the counter. Her bare, tanned legs contrasted prettily with her white linen skirt. Before I answered, the yellow desk telephone rang. She reached for it, identified Nirvana Tours, and cocked her head to listen. Her earrings were tiny ceramic pelicans, and around her neck hung a thin gold chain that held a tiny bleached and lacquered starfish.

"I'll send a schedule of events," she said and let her eyes drift upward as if long suffering. They were a greenish-blue turquoise and striking. "Yes, charges include breakfast."

She hung up, penciled a note, and stuck it on the monitor before again facing me.

"Now," she said and smiled.

"I called earlier today and talked to Raoul about locating a man named Jeremiah Ripley who I was told works at Nirvana Tours."

"He doesn't, and to my knowledge never has. Afraid you made your trip for nothing."

"How do you know I made a trip?"

"You're typical of a tourist right off the plane."

"Help me," I said.

"Help you how?"

"By cooperating with me."

"I believe that's exactly what I'm doing at this moment."

A whistling Raoul walked in carrying mail. He stopped to glance at her and me.

"Raoul, how long have you been working here?" she asked.

"You know, Phyllis."

"Tell the man."

"Couple of years," Raoul said.

"Did a Jeremiah Ripley have a job here?"

"Not in my time."

"You've never known a Jeremiah Ripley?" I asked.

Raoul shook his head and gave his attention to the mail.

"Enough cooperation?" Phyllis asked and turned away. Thongs fastened leather sandals to her ankles, and her toenails too were pink. She walked into her office and closed the door.

"Something else?" Raoul asked. He began sorting mail on the counter, slapping down envelopes as if dealing cards to different poker players. He sailed an advertisement into a wastebasket.

"You ever heard of a Jeremiah Ripley?" I asked.

"Only Jeremiah I heard of's in the Bible," he said. "Big-time prophet."

"I've traveled a long way. If you have any information at all about him it could be of great assistance to me."

"Just don't know your guy. Sorry."

Something nagged at my memory. The office door opened, and the woman, Phyllis, looked out.

"I hope you're not becoming a nuisance," she said.

"I don't mean to be, but I have this feeling that things here aren't altogether what they seem."

"Will you leave or do I call mall security?"

"Why won't you talk straight with me?"

"Call them," she ordered Raoul.

Raoul crossed to the desk, lifted the phone, and punched in the numbers with a middle finger that looked meant for me.

"All right, I'm gone," I said.

I walked from coolness into the pain of sunlight flashing and reflecting off this great white city. To have come so far for so little.

A breeze caused fronds of coconut palms to rattle dryly but brought no relief. Children played around the splashing pool on the bottom of which lay pennies. The water, like the blonde's eyes, was turquoise.

Three ancient, white-haired men guiding battery-powered and flagged wheelchairs passed like ducks in a row, the rubber tires making a hiss across the hot concrete. I felt sadness at the plight of the old, the sick, the failing, these chasers of the sun's warmth who could generate little heat of their own. I remembered a line from *Moby Dick*, ". . . tearless Lima the strangest, saddest city thou canst see. For Lima had taken the white veil; and there is a higher horror in this whiteness of her woe."

I had hours to kill before my flight to Richmond. I could eat, perhaps ride a cab to the beach, push off my shoes, and walk at the edge of the surf, allowing it to wash and foam around my pale ankles.

As I stood by the pool and watched the spreading ripples, I thought of the cold rain or worse back in Virginia. I looked upward to the astonished mermaid. Phyllis's striking eyes lodged in my mind. I tried to call up a face briefly seen where and when. While I strolled along South Mahia Boulevard, I passed the incongruity of a Baptist church built after the flamboyant Moroccan style. The marquee read, ARE YOU PREPARED FOR ETERNITY? APPLICATIONS ACCEPTED INSIDE.

I reset my glasses and recalled being at The Watchers and seeing the hillside graveyard that had plots but no markers. A girl wearing a raincoat and slouch hat had been sitting in a rear pew of the church weeping. I couldn't be certain, not in the few seconds I had glimpsed her that day. I might be forcing memory, in effect composing it.

I walked back to Nirvana Tours, where Raoul typed at the computer keyboard. Through the partially opened office door I saw Phyllis seated in a leather-and-chrome swivel chair. She uncrossed her legs and leaned forward to peer at papers on her desk before becoming aware of me.

"Security," Raoul said and again reached to the phone.

"I believe you were in Virginia," I called to her. "At The Watchers' cemetery and church."

"You have lost it, mister. Never heard of anybody named Watchers."

"Ring security," I said to Raoul. "I'll go with the police and ask for their assistance. I'm an attorney and officer of the court. Better for you to talk to me now than later."

She gazed at me, stood, and walked to Raoul's desk where she laid a finger to click off the connection.

"Identification?" she said.

I showed her my Virginia Bar Association membership card. She read it and my driver's license before passing them back.

"Why are you here?" she asked.

"I'd appreciate your allowing me to come in for a talk."

She hesitated before making a listless motion with her hand, a half turn of her palm, and returned to her office. I walked around the counter and entered. She closed the door, sat, and adjusted her skirt across her knees.

On her desk she had set a color photograph of a mustached, bare-chested man holding a fishing rod and standing beside a blue marlin hung by its tail from a dockside pulley, the fish's eyes seemingly widened in shock and astonishment at its situation.

"Talk," she said.

"Wendell Ripley," I said, and looking into her face I pictured a quiet little man in Drake's Blind Sheep cabin whose bleached turquoise eyes had met mine over the pale yellow flame of a kerosene lamp.

"That name means nothing to me."

"You resemble him."

She shrugged. "So?"

"He and his wife had an only child, a son named Jeremiah."

"I know nothing of him or them."

"I believe otherwise," I said, though still unsure. "I intend to pursue it fully with the police."

She delayed speaking.

"There is no Jeremiah Ripley," she said. "He's gone."

"But then it turns out you do know of him."

"Did. He's dead."

"The cause of his death?"

"His was a suicide."

"Can you tell me where he's buried?"

"At sea. His ashes were scattered at high tide from a powerboat off the city."

"You're certain of that fact?"

"Yes, I am, I was there."

"My belief is that you're kin."

"We were. Wendell Ripley was my uncle."

"I've been told Mr. Ripley had no other family."

"You were told wrong."

"Not according to Brother Abram. You remember Brother Abram out at The Watchers?"

"No."

"I'll find out. Believe me, there will be no place you can hide."

She tightened her mouth, ran the fingers of one hand over the back of the other, and looked at the photograph of the man on her desk. He was sandy-haired and clamped a congratulatory cigar in teeth of his grinning, sun-darkened face.

"Did you come to hound me?" she asked.

"I came because a man in jail will go to prison unless I gather evidence that will resolve the charge against him. Now just tell me what you know about Jeremiah Ripley."

She touched the tip of her tongue to her upper lip, removed the hibiscus, and laid it on her desk. The shadowed lids of her eyes heightened their color.

"Jeremiah Ripley's dead. Laid to rest in this world. Phyllis Duke supplanted him."

"Supplanted?"

"Look at me." She lifted and profiled her face. "Look at me good. Am I a woman?"

"Obviously you are."

"Ashes dropped into the sea."

"You're telling me you're—?"

"Say what you're thinking."

"A transsexual?"

"What a loaded word. I'm what I've always been inside."

"Your operation was when?" I asked.

"Two years and four months ago. When I first fled to Florida. I had saved money and borrowed more. The operation cost twenty-seven thousand dollars. God, if you could feel the liberation and freedom I felt. Like a bird released from its cage. All those years at The Watchers, that grim life forced on me. I loved my father but had to break loose. For nineteen years I lived in a prison. I almost died there—like a plant denied sunlight."

There was no lingering male huskiness in her voice, and she was lovely, anguished, and very definitely appealing.

"Jeremiah Ripley's gone," she said. "I changed my name legally and started work at Nirvana as a clerk for the lady who owned it and wanted to retire. She's allowing me to pay for the purchase out of profits."

She glanced at the photograph.

"I'm to be married," she said and held up the diamond on her finger. "I'll answer the question you want to ask. Does the man understand about me? He does. We live together. He thinks I'm wonderful."

"It's your past relationship with Clifford Dickens and Drake Wingo I need to know about."

"Clifford Dickens was my teacher for one English class at

Virginia Commonwealth University, nothing more. Drake Wingo employed me at Grizzly's."

"Why did you leave Grizzly's so abruptly?"

"I saw no future in selling shoes."

The telephone rang. We heard Raoul's voice in the front office. He knocked on the door, stuck in his head, and said, "Allan."

"Tell him I'll call soon as I can," Phyllis said, her every action womanly. Raoul closed the door.

"How did it happen?" I asked.

"What happened?"

"The sex you had with either of them or both."

"What makes you believe I had sex with anybody?"

"You and Drake Wingo were seen on the camp cot in his office," I said, presenting it that way, though not at all certain that's the way it had been. "New Year's Eve three years ago."

She was shaken. Her body softened, and her hands gave way to her lap.

"Do you absolutely need this information? It could cause me great and enduring harm."

"Without it the wrong man will go to prison."

"Goddamn you for doing this to me. I have a new life."

"Believe that I don't like doing it."

"From the first day at Grizzly's I was attracted to Drake. He didn't know. I didn't want it to be that way and hid my feelings. He used to lay his hand on my shoulder as we talked about stock and displays. His touch made me fall apart inside."

She moistened her lips, and her hands continued to lie but had begun to quiver palms upward.

"Drake and I worked late New Year's Eve taking inventory. The others had gone home. When we finished, he brought a bottle of bourbon from his desk and invited me to share a drink. It had been a good year for the store. 'Some way to celebrate,' he said. 'No bands or whistles, just a toast to Grizzly's.'"

She swallowed, raised her face, but averted her eyes.

"We kept drinking. We walked around the store holding insulated glasses taken from camping equipment. While we started switching out lights, he put an arm around my shoulder, a man-to-man gesture. On a drunken impulse, I turned and kissed his mouth."

I didn't speak or move.

"He hit me. He knocked me down, stood above me, cursed and kicked me. I covered my face. He walked off, returned, and knelt to help me stand. I clung to him. He tried to shake me loose, but I wouldn't let go. He stood with me holding to him, my face pressed against him until the fight went out of him and, as the saying goes, one thing led to another."

"That the only time?" I asked. I felt sick and had difficulty steadying my voice.

"Over several weeks we met, but not at the store. He became terribly confused and tormented, yet kept coming back for me. He hated himself for it, and that's why I left. I escaped, no forwarding address. In Miami, Jeremiah gave way to Phyllis."

"Did you dress as a female back in Richmond?" I asked, remembering Phoebe's telling me about shadowing Drake and a young woman to the Shady Spring Motel.

"Whenever I could. I was already considering the change, gathering the money, taking injections."

The phone again rang, and Raoul talked, yet didn't disturb us. Phyllis set both feet on the floor, sat straight in the chair, and ran fingers along the skirt covering her thighs.

"You had no sexual relationship with Clifford Dickens?"

"None. Isn't there any way you can keep me out of this? I've made a new life for myself."

"I don't see how altogether. I'll do my best to hold it to depositions and expose you as little as possible. What about a sailor named Leonard Dawson?"

"There was no such person. I made him up and used him to deflect my father from Drake."

"You won't run?"

"I'm through running. I'm ready to lead a normal life as odd as the word may sound to you."

"I'd like to see your Social Security card."

"So you can track me down?"

"I don't want to have to use it."

"You won't need to," she said and reached to a drawer to lift out a wallet. "I'm through running."

The number and the name Duke were on her driver's license. I copied it and handed the license back. I also asked for her home phone number.

"And I believed I'd become free at last," she said.

THIRTY-TWO

In the airport's sandwich shop, I ate a hot dog at the stand-up counter, smoked, and rubbed my eyes during the flight back to Virginia. I kept shaking my head and received inquiring looks from a stewardess, who passed out pillows.

I let my head fall back against the pillow and remembered how Drake had been our leader the autumn evening we fought three members of the River Rat Gang who accosted us as we sneaked past the twin turrets and arched stone facade of the old King Arthur Hotel. Only a few naked bulbs, one of them red, burned dimly behind begrimed panes beyond which were mysterious and threatening shapes. The hotel's upper windows were as vacant as gouged-out eyes.

We had heard stories that prostitutes paraded around the hotel, and we wanted to see them in their actual painted flesh. We caught only a glimpse of a single dusky woman who wore tight shorts and high heels that cracked against the sidewalk as she diminished into an embracing darkness. As we left disappointed, three River Rats stepped from the reddened alley and mauled us against the hotel's sooty bricks until a blue-and-white cruiser arrived, and two patrolmen broke up the melee and sent us home.

During the fight I had been shocked and sickened by the pain from the fists and mostly just covered my face and ducked around behind Drake and Cliff while they valorously attempted to slug it out. I had shared the glory of conflict and survival but secretly felt they had somehow left me behind and was greatly relieved they still accepted me as their equal and friend. It had been the next night we swore triple oaths of allegiance by candlelight, the words ratified by our shared juvenile blood. *Nunquam trado.*

The plane landed in Richmond at 12:14, too late to go directly to Drake's house and see him without alarming Deborah. That confrontation could wait until morning when I would also begin procedures for releasing Cliff from jail.

I drove to Jessup's Wharf, had a bath, and plopped into the bed. Half a dozen times during the rest of the night I stood to smoke. I finally drifted off listening to the wind and woke startled by the Axapomini Lumber's shrill seven-o'clock whistle. A thick, nasty taste continued to gum my mouth. While still in pajamas, I made the call to Drake.

"He's at his camp," Deborah said. "He never misses the last week of grouse season. He tried to reach you."

I thanked her, thought of conferring with Cliff, but decided to wait till I had it all straight with Drake. My window thermometer read thirty degrees, and I pulled on my hunt britches, Bean boots, and jacket. When I stopped by the office to leave Mary Ellen a note telling her where I'd be, I saw she had logged Drake's call.

I drove west under a scarf of clouds draping a pale cold sky. At New Kent I drove up the ramp to Interstate 64 and four hours later stopped for gas at Monterey before turning north into the Wilderness River Valley. The sides of the road were still flanked by partially melted humps of blackened snow.

Drake would be wary, sure to figure I had not come for the hunting. I couldn't force him to return with me and considered changing plans and detouring to High Gap and a conference first with Sam Tuggle. No, I owed Drake more than that, at least hearing his side of events I didn't yet understand.

At one-thirty I crossed the Seneca County line and twenty minutes later stopped the car at the foot of the logging road that led up Blind Sheep to the cabin. My Buick lacked four-wheel drive and would likely become stuck in the rutted road or bang its oil pan. I locked the car, tightened my belt, and hiked the slope coated with hoarfrost.

Wolf Creek ran full, smashing its way among rocks, the spray misting along the bank. The ground was caught in a partial thaw that caused my boots to lose their grip.

I spotted Drake's mud-caked Bronco beside the cabin. Thin whitish smoke drifted from the chimney. The door's hasp had been swung aside, and the padlock dangled from its chain. I knocked as I stepped inside.

Drake stood lifting his Savage from the gun rack. A plucked and gutted grouse hung from a leather noose attached to a nail pounded in a roof beam. Kraut stood beside Drake, the liver pointer's docked tail wagging, his amber eyes alert and alight.

"I got tonight's meal up Ash House Hollow," Drake said of the grouse. "We'll leave him to ripen. You just in time to join me for the afternoon shoot. Where's your artillery?"

"I'm not here to hunt, Drake."

"Well, I am and mean to," he said and moved around me.

"Stop and talk to me."

"No, man, not now. You too solemn. Only birds on my mind the last week of the season. Everything else is against the rules and off-limits. The last days belong to the grouse."

He fitted shells into his jacket slots, reset his cap, and walked outside.

"If you're staying, I won't lock it," he called back.

"I have serious stuff on my mind, Drake."

"Me too. Brown birds, and I'm hitting the trail."

He circled away around the cabin.

"I'm asking you to wait," I said as I followed.

He ignored me, and I hesitated. Go for the sheriff? Drake moved up the mountain with his determined stride. Kraut stayed at heel, wanting to leap ahead, the restraint stiffening his legs. The small bell attached to his leather collar tinkled.

"Listen to me," I called as I hurried to catch up.

"We'll climb to the ridge and hunt till we reach Sugar Camp and then cut down to Laurel Fork and along Burnt Cabin and back to Slash Lick."

"Don't do this to me, Drake."

"I'm not hearing you," he said and jerked back the bolt to thumb three shells into the Savage. When he pressed the release, the bolt clanged forward.

"And to Cliff," I said.

He hiked on without answering. A swirl of wind caused hemlock branches to stir and waver. Snow still draped shadowed depressions of the mountain, and a damp coldness moved off them.

"I love wind," Drake said. "It wants its meal. Give me something to tear up, the wind says. A spruce, sumac, or ironwood, my belly's never full. Wind's music to the grouse."

"I've heard your talk," I said and climbed behind him.

"Worth repeating. Hold the grouse in your mind, you won't go wrong."

"Is that what you're doing?"

"Got to hie to the mountains to get right," he said and increased his pace.

"Let's stop the performance," I said as I struggled to keep up.

"Raff, you're too grim. Not allowed on Blind Sheep. And the pollution of words can befoul the air. Just listen to the mountain's language, take it in, let it clean your blood."

We reached a stand of laurel, not catalpa, but large-leaf rhododendron, which Drake skirted. He had warned Cliff, Wendell, and me we could become exhausted trying to bully our way through.

The leaves had partially uncurled in the increasing warmth. Our boots dislodged pebbles, maybe former boulders ground down by the relentless creep of glaciers. A dip of land gathered mist like a drifting pool of unearthly water.

Drake's motion of tossing a softball underhanded released Kraut, who bounded forward and coursed ahead along the trail.

"With this wind the birds should stick to the lee side of the mountain," Drake said. "They could be gathering on the beech flats."

"Stop evading me, Drake."

"I'm not hearing you," he answered, and at that instant a grouse burst into flight from laurel and banked left. Drake didn't hurry. He lifted the Savage with seemingly leisurely grace, fired, and the bird dropped in an arc to crash through laurel leaves.

Again the sweep of a hand, and Kraut twisted in for the retrieve. The leaves clacked, the bell sounded, and Kraut emerged holding the grouse. He stood on his hind legs to place his front paws on Drake's chest. Drake patted him and took the bird in hand. Kraut dropped back to the ground, excited, proud, tongue out panting.

"Hen," Drake said, his fingers stroking its feathers, a reverence in his touch. The grouse's dark eyes closed as if entering sleep. Drake slipped the bird gently into his game pouch, where it would cool and stiffen.

"Rockets," he said and reloaded. "Some university pointy head figured they reach a speed of forty-five miles an hour. Maybe that's increasing as the slower birds get shot out. How'd you like to be a grouse, Raff? Live it all to the full? Life not by extent but intensity?"

"Cliff's waiting in jail," I said.

"Grouse don't question the life allowed them. Live hard and die cleanly."

"I know about your relationship with Jeremiah," I said.

Not answering, Drake signaled Kraut forward and moved

upward to eerie thorn apple trees growing in the wild tangled grass that had once been land used by shepherds to feed their flocks. Like sheer, torn rags the mist clung to the bare twisted branches.

"Birds dine on the hard bitter fruit," Drake said as if I'd asked. "Tough and bitter to man but to grouse it tastes of the mountain and freedom."

"I talked to Jeremiah."

"Sure," he said and didn't slow.

Kraut pushed up a bird among the thorn apples. It flew low and canted down the slope. The dog slunk back guiltily. Drake called him in, rubbed his chest, and said, "It's all right, fellow. It spooked long. Hie on."

Kraut resumed coursing ahead of us. A feeble sunlight broke through and glimmered on the wet grass and shiny limbs of the thorn apples.

"No more evasion, Drake," I said.

"Bird," he said and slowed to raise his Savage. With the gun's muzzle he indicated the faint tracks—a dainty stitching across a shadowed patch of snow. "Close. Searching for cover."

He whistled to Kraut, and the bell quieted as the pointer approached softly. His tail signaled interest but not conviction. The Savage held high, Drake stepped forward. No grouse flushed, though Kraut nosed in. Drake squatted to examine the tracks and their abrupt disappearance.

"Didn't get up or we'd heard," he said. "A ghost bird."

He stood to climb on, acting as if I were no longer behind him, then stopped, knelt, and fingered chalky round pellets.

"Droppings but not fresh," he said and smelled them. "Around here we don't call them fresh unless they still rolling."

"Jeremiah told me about the two of you," I said.

"Raff, you're fucking up my hunt."

"Who were you fucking?"

He looked at me hard, then again strode upward toward the ridge at the same time shifting the Savage to the crook of his left arm.

"Not hearing you," he said. "Got brown birds on my mind. The sunshine'll bring them out to feed."

Kraut went on point. The grouse flapped up from under sumac, its wings beating the bush, its neck stretched long, and its gleaming eyes took me in as it curved left away. When Drake fired, the load hit the bird so squarely it went limp, spun into a drooping fall, and bounced against the ground, where it left a sprinkle of blood across snow.

"Poleaxed him," Drake said and stroked the bird before handing it to me. I drew fingers over the beautiful and marvelously complex design of brown and bronze. The black stripe across its tail feathers appeared a masterful touch of creation. I felt the warmth of the bird's breast and the last lingering tremor of departing life.

"That stripe identifies a male," Drake said.

"About Cliff in jail," I said. "This is your chance to explain before I drive to High Gap and tell the authorities what I know."

"I might give up life in the lowlands and stay on the mountain full-time," Drake said, again climbing. "Sometimes I feel I can fly off Blind Sheep to the Ram's Horn. Up to the top of the world with the ravens in the mist. Hunt my own food. Like a bear graze the land. You want to hear some real poetry, Raff, not the crap the arty crowd laps up."

"What I want is for you go back with me."

"Persimmons, papaws, fiddleheads, cattails, mountain rice, ramps, wild hyacinth, Indian cucumber, wild onions, walnuts, sheep sorrel," he recited. "The real poetry."

"Your best chance is to come in with me."

"Here's more: pokeweed, sassafras, beechnuts, shepherd's purse, chokeberries, wild plum, black cherry, Kentucky coffee, sweet cicely, wild parsnips, watercress. You'd grow fat, Raff. No chemicals in the system. All mountain food unspoiled by the human touch. Lowland shit can't reach this high unless you bring it with you."

We heard the batting of wings but saw no bird. Kraut stopped to listen before nosing on before us.

"Kraut knows in his genes that before putting down the bird will flair to one side or the other," Drake said. "Tough scent, the feathers air-washed."

Again he stopped to check droppings.

"J-hooks," he said. "Not grouse, but male turkey. Hens don't have the hook."

"I can bring Jeremiah to High Gap," I said.

He kept on without answering. A bird fluttered from a limb of a shelly bark hickory and barreled directly at us, its head lifted above the plane of its body, seemingly intent on collision. I ducked but Drake stood upright and waited for the bird to pass before turning to shoot him cleanly, causing the grouse to shed feathers and tumble across the trail.

"I love them," he said, taking the retrieve from Kraut. "For me it's spiritual."

"Who else have you loved?"

As he fitted the grouse into the game pouch, he spat and stepped to the top of the ridge. Combers of mountains rolled away westward, a gray, whitecapped sea. Beyond rose the Ram's Horn, the snow-crowned peak dazzled by sunlight that broke through rampaging clouds.

"Indians believed the Great Spirit lived up there," Drake said. "They smarter than us."

"Jeremiah will testify."

"Next Sugar Camp," Drake said and strode fast along the ridge to a cleavage of land where the hollow intersected it. The way down was steep, the footing loose shale, but he didn't slacken his gait.

Under a canopy of hemlocks a creek made up and began its descent to the valley. He stopped, dipped a hand in the water, and drank from his palm.

"Have a swaller," he said. "Tastes of the mountain. The pure stuff that moves down so fast it bashes all the germs. No bacteria can take the beating. Living in cities you forget what real water tastes like."

"Jeremiah will reveal your relationship with him," I said.

Drake didn't respond but jumped the creek to a needle-strewn deer path that wound down among the hemlocks. Again I followed. We walked past the grouse, which flushed to my right. Drake fired, the bird shuddered and fought to keep flying, lost altitude, and drifted into shadows.

"Winged him good," he said. "Kraut'll run him down."

Kraut skirted the side of the hollow, moving fast, his nose low to the ground. He stopped on point as if he'd crashed into an invisible wall. Drake stepped in behind. No bird. Drake circled. Still Kraut didn't break. He trembled, and his eyes bulged. Drake raised a finger. As I looked to the spot he indicated, the bird seemed to materialize and take shape among the moist, leafy mast. Drake reached down and lifted it.

The grouse's eyes were open, watching, seemingly not so much frightened as waiting and accepting whatever the hand would bring.

"Cock in the red phase," Drake said, examining it. He held it close to his eyes. "Just grazed him, one pellet across his skull knocked him silly. He ought to be able to shake it off and fly."

He kissed the top of the bird's head and lifted it on his palms as if presenting an offering to the sky. The grouse dipped almost to the ground before its wings took hold of air and it sped low and away down Sugar Camp.

"Have a good life," Drake called after it before turning to me. "You know anything better than this?"

"I know you're in terrible trouble."

He drew a Winesap from the pocket of his jacket and bit into it. His teeth crunched the bite.

"All right," he said, chewing. "We befoul the high country with words."

THIRTY-THREE

As Drake munched the apple, his blue eyes locked on me. Kraut loped back and stood beside him to wait and watch.

"You're telling me you've been with Jeremiah?"

"Just yesterday," I answered.

"You see, Raff, I don't happen to believe that."

"You'd do well to, Drake."

"What I believe is he's long gone."

"No, I found him."

"Got your proof?"

"He told me about your New Year's Eve celebration at Grizzly's and said among other things that you knocked him down and kicked him."

Drake with one last deep bite finished the apple. He tossed the core down the slope, and Kraut raised his head, alert and ready to retrieve.

"Where is he?" Drake asked.

"Where I can find him."

"So you claim."

"He won't run this time."

"And you won't tell me?"

"Not at the moment."

"I'm not falling for this."

"The best thing you can do is come in with me."

"You told anybody yet?"

"I wanted to talk to you first."

"How can I be sure you got him and he's not lit out somewhere else?"

"I'm looking you straight in the eye and telling you."

Drake spat out seeds, reset his cap, and started down along Sugar Camp Run. He looked at me.

"You think I wanted this?" he asked. "That I meant to hurt Cliff? I'm no fag, Raff. You know it. I been more man than any of you. I just got into a craziness during a moment of liquor and heat. And he was more girl than guy. Had curves on him, ways of moving like a woman. Little bitch knew the buttons to push. I couldn't shake him or live with it."

A plane gleaming like silver flew over high. Through a break in the clouds I looked up among the rustling hemlocks and saw the white contrails it laid behind uncurl and warp slowly in the wind.

"You have to come back," I said.

"Look, Raff, even as things stand now, there's still a chance Cliff won't be convicted and serve jail time. We hire the best lawyers and fight it to the wall."

"And if he's found guilty?"

"I'll set him up, deposit money to his account every month, invest it in his name. He'll be released with deep pockets and can play the artist the rest of his life."

"That won't do."

"You got to see things been going right for me. This shit comes up just when I'm getting all I ever wanted in the world. I'm not turning it loose."

"You'll need counsel," I said.

He took off his cap and wiped it across his face. Crows cawed, fussing and diving at a hawk that flew on unconcerned.

"Your way it can't be kept quiet," he said. "The word'll get out and ruin me. Raff, try to understand I didn't mean for it to turn out how it has. I burned with shame, fired Jerry from the store, but I'd be hit with this call of the wild, and the dirty thing would build up. This last couple of years all that's over. Jerry was gone, I believed dead. I'm a good husband and father. You concede that?"

"I do, Drake."

He set on his cap and shifted the Savage from one hand to the other.

"Wendell was trying to track down Jeremiah," he said. "Biblical name for a slut. Dressed up like a woman, all the intimate paraphernalia. And the sonofabitch could be beautiful, wearing earrings, lipstick, eyeliner, heels. Jerry'd tease you with a nylon thigh that you'd swear belonged to a chorus girl. After he left, Wendell was searching for him and the person he believed seduced his son. Nobody ruined Jerry. He was what he wanted to be."

A shadow slid across broken sunlight on the ground—a buzzard flying over, wings set, wobbling in flight, searching.

"Wendell never suspected you?" I asked.

"He did but Jerry laid a false trail about a man named Dawson, supposedly a sailor from Chicago. Wendell tried to find Dawson, paid a private detective to do it. Wendell considered it wrong to hate, yet hate ate him up. He wanted vengeance, a mortal sin, and at the same time to forgive, and the contradiction tore him apart."

"Why did he suspect Cliff?"

"Wendell received a phone call from a stranger. He began checking, asking questions around. He hated himself for hating."

Drake again started down the mountain, following the stream's flow. Thin, fragile ice along the bank was giving up to warmth and breaking away.

"While hanging out at the store Wendell discovered I knew Cliff," Drake said over his shoulder. "No way I could deny it. He questioned me, and I believed I'd persuaded him Cliff wasn't his man but that it was Dawson."

"Why did you take the risk of having Wendell on the hunt?"

"I didn't consider it a risk. Wendell appeared convinced it was

Dawson. I'd been organizing the hunt for you, Cliff, and me anyhow as well as trying to buy the land. Seemed a time to get two for one. How could I know he'd blame Cliff?"

He lifted a hand and pointed. The shadow within a shadow was a white-flecked doe slipping delicately among hemlocks. She stopped to look at us before bounding off, her flag lifted.

"I never believed Wendell would cause trouble," Drake said, moving on. "Not with his religion. That first evening at the cabin, he and Cliff got along. You were there and saw it."

"Any idea who the stranger was that called and put Wendell on to Cliff?"

"No."

"But Wendell did for a time suspect you?"

"He suspected everybody."

"He grew to trust you."

"As much as he trusted anybody."

Sugar Camp Run had deepened and was flowing faster as we descended. Ice slabs bobbed and broke against rocks.

"It must have been tough for you to face Cliff knowing he'd seen what you and Jeremiah were doing that night at Grizzly's."

Drake stopped, and his eyes searched mine.

"The picture of you Cliff carried in his mind," I said. "Every time you faced him, you'd wonder what he was remembering. He had to be a reminder you couldn't escape, mocking the life you presented to the world."

"You got a smoke?" Drake asked.

We lit up my Winstons. It was the first time for years I had seen Drake with a cigarette. He liked to center them in his teeth, breathe and talk around them.

"Be difficult in such a situation to put up with a person like that, thinking he was recalling memory pictures each time you met," I said.

"So?"

"I'm just trying to put it all together and thinking of Sheriff Sawyers checking Wendell's Remington and finding the safety on, no shells in the gun, slots of his hunting vest empty."

"We been over that."

"My guess is after our talk you got in touch with Josey and asked her to lie for you about your being at the Chesterfield Country Club's New Year's Eve."

"Something like that."

"She believed she was helping Cliff by lying for you."

"She didn't and doesn't know the whole picture. We've always been close. She's also into me for a bunch of my money she invested."

"And you fired Boomer before I could reach him."

Drake shrugged.

"I told you my theory Wendell never meant to kill anybody, that he maneuvered Cliff into thinking he had to shoot to save himself," I said.

As I spoke the words, a sickening option formed in my mind, and for a moment I faltered. Drake's eyes probed, and they saw that I saw.

"Something?" he asked, blowing smoke.

"I'm again wondering how Wendell's religious convictions would have held him in check. He couldn't bring himself to kill, yet still would want retribution for what happened to Jeremiah. What about this—he could resolve the dilemma by compelling Cliff to shoot him, resulting in the end of Wendell's suffering as well as the prosecution and punishment under the law of the person he believed was his son's corrupter?"

"Anything else?" Drake asked. "Come on, Raff, I see it on you."

"All right, another scenario. Picture the situation. A man of standing fears a hideous secret might be revealed. Only one person is left living who shares it, he believes, and our man of standing is haunted by the danger of the secret's ever being revealed and is desperate to be rid of the anguish it causes him. To do so he manipulates a third party full of an obsessive rage into solving his problem."

"Fancy theory," Drake said. "What's the point?"

"Why I guess you're the point, Drake. You said Wendell suspected you. You could have led him on as he grew close by creating false leads. You might have made a telephone call from a stranger. You taught Wendell to shoot and arranged the time and place for it. As I remember, you also cut the cards that paired us for the day's hunt. You had me alongside as a witness to prevent your being implicated in the killing."

Drake drew the cigarette from his teeth, snuffed it with his fingers, and field-stripped it as soldiers learned to do. I dropped mine and ground my heel on it.

"That it?" he asked.

"But Wendell deceived you. He arranged his revenge by bluffing Cliff into protecting himself. You meant for Wendell to kill Cliff and thought he would. How's that so far?"

"Makes a good story."

"A well-constructed plan—Cliff goes to the grave carrying the secret, Wendell is likely to escape prosecution, and you're safe. Except Wendell turns out to be more devious than you considered possible."

"I didn't kill Wendell. There's no way they can put that on me."

"You can be indicted for accessory to murder."

"It's still my word against Cliff's."

"Except for Jeremiah."

"Goddamn you, Raff."

"Is this a confession?"

"You really expect me to turn myself in?"

"Drake, what's happened to you?"

"Survival's what's happened."

"No matter how the law judges you, your affair with Jeremiah will come out. You'll not be able to dodge the media muck."

"You think I haven't considered that? I got the most to lose. Simple, an elementary equation, you do the numbers, like a body count in the military—one casualty lost, Cliff, against another man, his wife, twin daughters, his son about to be born, and 'The Truth of the Grouse.' I can't give those up."

"Come back with me. I'll stand by you and do all I can to negotiate and devise a plea that'll hold publicity to a minimum. There's no alternative."

"Maybe one," he said. "You told me you found Jeremiah. My guess is you're the only one who knows where he is."

"A very bad guess," I said and steadied my eyes.

"You're lying, Raff. You were never a poker player."

"You think I'd come up here alone without telling anybody?"

"Yeah I do."

"I left word and directions with my secretary," I said and started around him down the slope.

"You can't even find the trail back," he said.

"You told us on the hunt if we ever got lost to follow the water, which is what I'm doing now."

"Hey, Raff, I just can't let you go like this."

"What will you do?" I asked. He was following me.

"We'll hike to the cabin and figure out something. Maybe persuade you to go to Cliff with a deal."

"And Jeremiah?"

"No Jeremiah."

"Got to be, Drake."

"Then I advise you to stop right there."

I heard the Savage's safety click off and stopped to face him. Drake held the shotgun at the ready.

"You'd go so far as to kill me?" I asked.

"Have to do what it takes. Just hang around awhile."

"No," I said and continued on down.

"Raff, don't make me do this."

"They'll come after you."

"No sure thing and if so what evidence will they find? I could bury you and your Buick, the car in a certain deep slough I know about. You're leaving me no choice if we can't deal."

"Best to you, Drake," I said, moving on.

He fired the Savage, and I felt the load's heat, tripped, lost my glasses, and for a second believed I'd been hit. The high-brass shot had shattered hemlock boughs, causing them to fall across my shoulders and back.

"No farther," Drake said. "We'll go to the cabin, have us a drink, think up a solution. I mean it, Raff."

I worked out from beneath the branches. I was so damned scared and felt my sphincter release and warmly wet my undershorts and leg. I lifted my broken glasses.

"Last chance," Drake said.

I staggered on.

"I got to admire you, Raff," he called. "'Course you're about to crap your pants, yet with style."

I kept moving and waited for the shot, my eyes half-blinded, my throat choked, my body shaking and giving itself to gravity's pull. But Drake didn't shoot. He allowed me to totter on down beside Sugar Camp Run.

"You did good," he shouted. "You did just fine, Walter."

I looked behind me. He had lowered the Savage, and Kraut stood beside him. Drake waved once before turning to climb back among the hemlocks. I stumbled into a jog only half realizing the last word I had heard from him was not Raff but Walter.

THIRTY-FOUR

Sugar Camp Run fed down into what I recognized to be Slash Lick Hollow. Afraid that Drake might be lying in wait if I tried to circle back to my Buick, I followed Wolf Creek to the paved county road and hiked the shoulder till an International twin-axle loaded with saw logs stopped and the driver offered me a ride.

"Look like you been gnawed on by a bear," he said, a long-faced youth with black hair bound into a ponytail by a thick rubber band. "You lost?"

"I was," I said, feeling weak and light-headed. I smelled my urine and hoped he didn't.

"It happens. Mountains turn people around. Hunting brown birds?"

"Yes," I said, easier to lie than explain.

"Not enough meat on 'em for the cost of ammo you shoot up."

"I need to reach High Gap."

"Where we headed. I figured you was lost. Hard time finding your way out?"

"I followed the water."

"That's the way my old daddy taught me," he said and tapped a palm against the steering wheel as he hummed a tune heard beating only through his head.

I tried to quiet my mind. The sun shone directly into the windshield, and I shaded my eyes. The road seemed to wind on forever until at High Gap the driver stopped at the timber loading yard beside the railroad tracks. I thanked him and walked to the jail.

I wanted to talk to Cliff before I saw Sam Tuggle or Sheriff Sawyers. Bess and Gilbert at their glassed-in control center eyed my clothes. Gilbert unlocked the cell where Cliff sat on the bunk reading a newspaper, his back against the wall.

When Gilbert left us, I explained what had happened between Drake and me. Cliff slowly released the paper, which settled across his lap. He didn't speak till I finished.

"Drake meant for Wendell to kill me?"

"He believed it the only way to protect and save what he has, and he has a lot."

"But Drake," Cliff said, his voice lingering on and sliding off the name.

"You tell the district attorney the whole truth after I talk to him. Jeremiah will need questioning. Once that's done, we move for your release."

"And Drake?"

"That's up to Sam Tuggle, who'll charge him at least with inciting homicide unless Drake can bargain a lesser plea."

"Then what?"

"The worst part. Blood sport in the papers and on TV."

"Poor Drake. What happened, Walter? What's happened to us?"

I had no answer, but I caught the note of genuine sympathy and sorrow that Cliff felt for Drake instead of a justified anger and loathing.

"I'll do some talk-talk," I said and whistled for Gilbert to let me out.

I crossed from the jail to the rear door of the courthouse and climbed the steps to the third floor and Sam Tuggle's office. Gail wiggled her fingers in greeting.

"He's in court," she said, looking at my clothes. She raised her nose slightly. Maybe she too had winded me. "You shoot any-thing?"

I told her I hadn't and sat across the room by the window. The full sunlight melted snow, causing water to collect and run along the street, and the drab houses and buildings appeared as if they had just been released by the earth. Of all things I remembered the long, lazy swims Drake, Cliff, and I had made in the ocean off Virginia Beach during our last summer before college, the languid strokes, the sun drunkenness, our bodies tanned, our hair bleached. We had become denizens of the water—sea creatures.

Sam entered the office, his face flushed and smiling, both signs of victory in legal joustings.

"Sentencing March seven," he told Gail. "Calendar it."

"Don't I always?" she asked.

"You the best, darling," he said and shook my hand. He gestured me into his office, where he closed the door. He thumped his stomach as if he had eaten well.

"A weasel-eyed car dealer selling hot items from Alabama," he said. "He'd changed the serial numbers. There's going to be lots of unhappy buyers around here who believed they got the bargains of their lifetime."

He adjusted his body in the chair, leaned back, and entwined his fingers behind his head.

"Got something for me?" he asked and sniffed.

I began uncovering details on how and why Wendell died. Sam listened, his expression skeptical, but he didn't interrupt until I was through.

"Quite a tale," he said, pursed his lips, and looked at the ceiling. "You, of course, can provide substantiation for any and all of this?"

"I have more than enough for you to drop the charge against Clifford Dickens."

"He's been lying to the law."

"To protect a friend. I expect you understand how to value that quality."

"Some friend," he said, sitting straight and drawing himself to the desk. "And you know the whereabouts of this Jeremiah Ripley who'll give testimony he had a homosexual relationship with Mr. Wingo?"

"I know where and how he can be reached. He's reluctant but has agreed to cooperate."

"Looks like the first thing is to bring in Wingo. He's still at his Blind Sheep camp?"

"He was when I left little more than ninety minutes ago."

"I'll fetch the sheriff," he said and reached to the intercom.

Sawyers arrived holding his trooper hat. In sunlight from the window, his freckles stood out.

"You think Mr. Wingo will resist," he asked me.

"I don't know. It's possible."

"Maybe you could give us help."

"I'd prefer to stay out of it."

"Not a case of prefers. You'd be doing him and the law a favor."

We rode in his Dodge cruiser. A stripped-down Chevy followed carrying two deputies, their names Louis and Belcher. The sheriff kept to the posted 55 mph speed limit. If he detected my urine's odor, he gave no indication.

"I ran these ridges when a boy," he said. "Killed my first buck less than half a mile from here—a seven-pointer. The deer fed with sheep on the sod."

My Buick was still parked at the foot of Blind Sheep. Sawyers stopped beside it and cut the Dodge's engine. The Chevy pulled up behind. Sawyers set on his hat, took the keys, and unlocked the cruiser's truck to lift out a lever-action Winchester. He slipped his walkie-talkie from its holster to report his location to High Gap.

"Wingo at the cabin?" he asked as he picked cartridges from an army-issue ammo box to load the rifle.

"I've no way of knowing," I answered. He saw me looking at the rifle.

"Lock the cars and stay with them," he told Louis. "Belch, you tail us keeping a twenty- or thirty-yard interval. We don't mean to spook him. Mr. Frampton, let's you and me go up together."

The sheriff and I climbed toward the cabin. Drake's Bronco had not been moved. We slowed as we drew closer. The sheriff was watching everything, his moves seemingly casual but his body gathered to react.

"Get you to call out if you will," he said. "Tell him we just want to talk."

I cupped my hands at my mouth and shouted Drake's name twice. There was no reply. The sheriff motioned me to stay back and approached the cabin from its windowless western end. He held the Winchester ready as he worked around the cabin, ducked under the front window, and stepped to the door. He used the rifle's butt to nudge it open. He pulled back and waited before peering inside.

"Mr. Wingo, you in there?"

No answer from Drake. Sawyers looked in my direction before rushing through the doorway. Expecting a shot, I closed my eyes. None came. Sawyers appeared and waved to me to join him. He stood inside looking at the hanging grouse and then Drake's gun rack.

"Any missing?" he asked.

"His Savage."

"Okay, we'll go on up. You stay behind me. Belch will follow. Where you think Wingo might be?"

"There's a trail to the ridge," I said.

"Let's move out."

Sawyers radioed another report while we climbed. He remained cool and observant, holding the Winchester lightly by fingers of his left hand at its balance point as he studied the chain-link treads left by Drake's boots. He stopped to look around him, gazed into laurel and hemlock cover, and licked at the air as if to taste its flavor.

"The dog's stayed with him," Sawyers said. He checked Kraut's paw prints in the softened ground.

When we reached the ridge, we squinted against the sun. Sawyers doubled back twice but had lost Drake's tracks.

"What now?" he asked.

I looked toward the Ram's Horn. Its crown of snow seemed to give off its own shimmering light instead of reflecting the sun's. Drake had said that was where he wanted to live. I told Sawyers, who nodded, radioed in his third report, and looked back to make certain Belcher was in place.

The day warmed as we climbed down from the ridge into what I remembered was named Burnt House Hollow. I felt winded and sweat slicked. Snow ebbed in deep hemlock shade, the melting causing a runoff that trickled. I hoped Sawyers would slow but he kept his steady pace and used the tip of his rifle to indicate Drake's rediscovered boot prints.

"I could use a rest," I told him.

He stopped, and we palmed up water from a pool that had formed beneath a dripping boulder. I patted wetness against my face and neck. Sawyers gave me three minutes. On the go again we reached the foot of the Ram's Horn and began another ascent.

"Sheep laid this trail a long time back," Sawyers said, speaking softly, his slate eyes never still. "Mostly deer and bear use it now."

We climbed until I sucked for air, my calves ached, and my feet felt heavy and clumsy. The pull of the mountain worked stabbing pains into my thighs. Let it end, I thought.

Sawyers stopped and gazed up the slope. I'd heard it too, a dog's bark. The sheriff studied the wooded path before turning to me.

"Hail him," he said.

I collected my breath, shouted Drake's name, and identified myself. Croaking caws answered from on high.

"Ravens," Sawyers said. "The high sod's their country."

We waited as he radioed in a report of our position.

"All right, we'll let Belch come on and you follow us," he said. He signaled the husky deputy, who trudged upward puffing. Belcher wiped the back of his hand across his mouth and drew his .38-caliber revolver.

They climbed ahead of me. The tree cover of oaks, hickories, and spruce thinned. I glimpsed a blue-sky opening in the forest. Sawyers advanced slowly, the rifle now held in both hands, his steps softly exact.

A shot sounded close. I dropped to a knee and thought, Oh Christ, he's going to shoot it out with them. Sawyers and Belcher had crouched. Sawyers pointed at his own mouth and then at mine.

"Drake, don't shoot again," I called, my voice breaking. "Let's talk this out."

No answer.

Sawyers left the path and worked his way aslant the slope. Belcher trailed him, and I followed Belcher. We reached the tree line beyond which lay the sea of grass sod that had once been used for high pasture.

Sawyers shaded his eyes to study the terrain. We might have missed Drake had we not heard another distant bark from Kraut. The sheriff again pointed at his own mouth and mine. I hailed Drake, and my voice caused more barking.

Sawyers stepped back from the tree line and skirted the sod's edge. Belcher and I stayed with him. They stopped, whispered, and motioned for me to wait. I watched them move warily onto the sod and slip out of sight.

Sweat stung my eyes. What the hell were they doing? The ravens fussed. Belcher reappeared and motioned me to come on. He and the sheriff stood at one of those antiquated lengths of fencing shepherds had left. Kraut waited beside Drake's body sprawled among a broken section of rails. The Savage lay just beyond the outstretched fingers of Drake's right hand. The shot had smashed his chest, and blood thickly scarlet under the sun's brightness had found and flowed along channels of his hunting jacket. His blue eyes flecked with gold were opened upward, his face splattered with bits of blood and of flesh. Already the green flies had found feast.

"A sheepfold here once," Sawyers said, the Winchester hanging loose in his fingers as he circled Drake's body. "Locust posts and chestnut rails, they last forever. Funny Mr. Wingo would try to climb the fence when he could've easily slid between the rails."

"It had to be an accident," I said and looked up to the snow-shrouded knob of the Ram's Horn.

"Sure," Sawyers said and patted Kraut, who whined and whose amber eyes beseeched like my own. "Wouldn't you know?"

THIRTY-FIVE

Old Doc Bailey, the coroner from Seneca County's Free Clinic, was too frail to climb the Ram's Horn and examine the body. Sheriff Sawyers radioed High Gap, and a helicopter belonging to Appalachian Power brought the doctor to the sod. The rotating blades caused grass to wave and cower. Two members of the Rescue Squad strapped Drake in a metal basket, loaded him, and the helicopter carried him to High Gap. When I reached the clinic, they had laid him out on the stainless-steel examination table and covered him with a sheet.

From the courthouse I used a phone to notify Deborah. I heard her draw her breath. "Bring him to me," she said, her voice little more than breath itself.

"As soon as I can arrange it," I told her.

After I registered at the Mountain View Lodge, showered, and changed into underwear, shirt, and chinos I bought at High Gap's Dollar General, I sat with Sheriff Sawyers and Sam Tuggle in the district attorney's office. Darkness filled the window. Sam and I smoked as the sheriff remained impassive.

"The fact is you have no case now," I said. My strategy was not only to have all charges dropped against Cliff, but also to protect Deborah and her children from the media by saving Drake's name.

"So you keep telling us," Sam said. He liked to blow smoke rings that coiled lazily from his fleshy mouth and then poke his cigarette through their centers.

"A deposition from Jeremiah Ripley will attest that no intimacy existed between him and Mr. Dickens."

"Attesting's not always the same as truth telling," Sam said. "You got to do better."

"He has nothing to gain by perjuring himself and you'll cause unnecessary pain and suffering to people by pursuing the case farther. I can't believe you want that."

"No deposition," Sam said. "You produce Ripley in this office, where we see for ourselves."

"I request cover for him and that you make no announcements to the press."

"I could law you and make you reveal his location to the court."

"And needlessly create a lack of cooperation and understanding."

"We'll see about that. You bring him in or we go after him. We want him here in person, don't we, Bruce?"

"The best way of nailing it down," the sheriff said.

I advised Cliff where we stood. He paced the cell and held his throat one-handed as if he would choke himself.

"You're certain Jeremiah will appear?"

"I believe so, yes," I said. "I'll keep you informed."

From the Mountain View Lodge I phoned Phyllis's home number and received no answer. I next tried Nirvana Tours, heard Raoul's voice on the recorded message, and Phyllis, screening calls, picked up.

"I've been hoping I'd never hear from you again," she said. "Do you have to do this to me?"

I explained about Drake's death. She was silent on the other end.

"If you won't return voluntarily, the authorities will come after you with a warrant. Our best chance of avoiding the press is for you to appear voluntarily."

"Can anyone ever avoid anything?"

"Make your reservation and I'll pay for the ticket. Bring your birth certificate and the court order authorizing your name change."

"Please no," she said.

"I apologize, Miss Duke, but it has to be," I said.

I met her the next afternoon at the Roanoke airport. Her gray overcoat had dark piping around the lapels and collar. Men eyed her as she rode the escalator up from the passenger gate and tapped across the lobby where I waited. Her blond hair was curled under and bounced slightly with each step.

"I've never liked planes," she said. "They make me feel I'm enclosed in a coffin with dozens of people and we'll all be buried together."

"I know the feeling," I said and carried her leather suitcase to the car. She sat beside me and adjusted her skirt.

"I'm sorry for Drake," she said. "The madness love can cause."

"Atomic power," I said.

"Is less destructive," she said.

I gave her the details of what had happened on Blind Sheep as we drove to High Gap. At the courthouse Gail blinked. She had believed I would be bringing a man to the office. Her expression quizzical, she buzzed us through.

Sam stood and refocused at Phyllis. He was confused, yet recovered his gallantry as he walked around his desk to be introduced. He shook her hand, took her coat, and positioned a chair for her. He also helped himself to a look at her legs as she crossed them.

"I was expecting someone else," he said, giving me a searching glance. "But I'm delighted with Miss Duke."

"And Jeremiah Ripley," I said.

"Is?" Sam asked.

"Here with us."

"The name I used to bear," Phyllis said. She stripped off her thin black leather gloves and flattened them on her lap. Her nails were rose-tinted.

Sam stared at her and at me.

"Jeremiah Ripley was her former name," I said. "After her operation she had it legally changed. We have papers."

"Whoa now," he said and pulled at his porous nose. His bushy brows rose and lowered. "This a first in my office."

Phyllis sat calmly. She returned his gaze, her composure not the least defensive. Sam reset his face to the business at hand.

"Miss Duke, is that what I call you then?"

"Yes."

"The essential question here involves your relationship with Mr. Clifford A. Dickens. Would you care to enlighten me?"

"There was nothing personal between us. He taught a college class I attended. I asked him to sign a magazine, which had published his story."

"You were never alone with him?"

"No."

"Not in his office?"

"He signed the magazine at the campus bookstore."

"He didn't touch you or you him?"

"No."

"It was Mr. Drake Wingo you were intimate with?"

"For a time, yes."

"You're a homosexual?"

"I'm a woman about to be married."

Sam backed off a step with another glance at me.

"Did your father, Mr. Wendell Ripley, know about you and Mr. Wingo?"

"My father was distressed by the life I lived in Richmond. It's one reason I fled."

"What's another reason?"

"I wanted to protect Mr. Wingo from himself."

"You believe Mr. Wingo conspired to manipulate your father in ways that resulted in his death?"

"I do now."

"Mr. Wingo's motive being an attempt to prevent his past relationship with you from being discovered?"

"We can't be sure how much Mr. Ripley was manipulated by Mr. Wingo," I said. "Possibly Mr. Ripley had his own agenda and acted keeping it to himself. Whatever the truth there, Mr. Dickens had no meaningful association with Miss Duke and no reason to kill Mr. Ripley other than acting in what he believed was self-defense."

"I'll study about that one," Sam said. "Miss Duke, we'll need to see your papers and ask you to give a statement affirming what you've told me here. The statement will be taped as well as transcribed and sworn to under oath by you before a notary. It subjects you to a charge of perjury if the law finds any point of truth contradicting it. We will investigate thoroughly, and woe the misery you will suffer if you're playing with the legal processes of Seneca County."

"I'd like to get this over with as quickly as possible," she said.

"I'll have the sheriff join us," Sam said and spoke into the intercom.

Sam introduced Sawyers to Miss Duke. On learning who she had been, the slate eyes took her in without reaction. Sam used a recorder as well as a male stenotypist named Alvin, identified himself, the sheriff, Phyllis, me, and Gail, who was a notary, as being present. Phyllis spoke calmly into the microphone and answered the questions directed at her without flinching.

"You have never as either Jeremiah Ripley or Phyllis Duke had a sexual affiliation with Mr. Clifford Arehart Dickens?"

"None."

Alvin twisted up the telescopic tripod legs of his stenotype machine and left the office to transcribe Phyllis's statement. Sam examined her birth certificate and court-ordered name change adjudicated in Florida. When Alvin returned, Phyllis again took the oath, this time before Gail, who affixed her signature and notary seal.

"Now, about Clifford Dickens?" I asked.

"Hang around for another day or two," Sam said.

"There's sufficient evidence to release him on bail as of this minute."

"Just humor us poor mountain folk. We got to let all this sink in."

"I have a nine-o'clock plane in the morning," Phyllis said.

"We'll do all we can to help you make it," Sam said.

I drove Phyllis to the lodge, where she registered. We ate dinner together, and again she drew eyes. She refused a drink and ate only a small portion of her tossed salad. She remained cold and removed.

"I go to church these days and pray," she said. "The preachers talk of eternal life. I can't really fathom it. Eternal rest is what I ask for. The final, peaceful darkness. Have you ever read the poet Robinson Jeffers? He wrote, 'How shall the dead know the deep treasure they have?' Thanks for helping me as best you could."

She would not allow me to pay for her meal, and I walked her to her room, told her good night, and saw her inside. I heard the click of her door's lock.

My room phone was ringing.

"Man, what a day, and Phyllis is enough to make a man doubt his gonads," Sam Tuggle said. "Well, the circuit judge's going to release your boy on bail pending a final motion. Your client won't be one-hundred-percent sprung but we no longer got any essential reason to hold him. If we find something else, we can come after him with hoe handles and pitchforks."

Deputy Belcher drove Phyllis to the Roanoke airport enabling me during the late afternoon to attend the private hearing held in the judge's musty, badly lit chambers, those present his clerk, Cliff, Sam, and me. Bail was set at ten thousand, Cliff to appear in court on an indeterminate date if so notified. Cliff owned no property except his cameras and Thunderbird, the latter bound by a lien. I paid the bail.

"You think this court ought to accept a Virginian's check?" the judge asked and smiled to show his question a jest.

I drove Cliff to the lodge. He showered fifteen minutes and shaved before we walked down to the bar. We sat at a window that offered a view of High Gap, the lights looking lonely and shattered in a bluish night. He downed two Scotch on the rocks fast.

"I don't believe I'll ever get the smell of jail off me," he said. "And look at my hands."

He raised them to show their tremors.

"You were great to hold out long as you did for Drake," I said.

"Yeah, thanks. What's happened to Kraut?"

"I'll carry him back to Deborah. Right now the sheriff's feeding him."

"Maybe the sea will do it," Cliff said. "Cleanse and make me whole. I want to travel to Italy and might apply for a job on a cruise ship, take photographs, paint portraits."

"Your Baltimore fiancée?"

"Damage repair required. Her father knows about my arrest, so I'm tainted."

He ordered a third Scotch.

"Drake," I said.

"He did the right thing finally, as I believed he would. Walter, I still see him like in the old days, the times we had together, the three of us, the Marauders."

"So do I," I said.

THIRTY-SIX

In the coffee shop of the Mountain View Motel as I ate a Danish and drank my breakfast coffee before leaving High Gap with Cliff, Sheriff Sawyers, trooper hat in hand, entered and crossed to my table.

"Okay to join you?" he asked, adjusting his holster.

"Of course, Sheriff."

He did and shook his head no at the waitress who was on her way to take his order. He eyed me in his intimidating fashion a moment before he spoke further.

"I knew you didn't tell it all," he said and ran fingers through the crease in the crown of his hat.

"I don't know what you mean."

"I smelled your piss in the cruiser when we went after Mr. Wingo. Now, that indicated to me something scared you real bad, something you haven't told. I drove back up to Blind Sheep to revisit the scene, picked up some of yours and Mr. Wingo's tracks. I also found an empty high-brass shotgun shell casing just short of where the hemlocks give way to the slope down into Slash Lick."

"Are you interrogating me, Sheriff?"

"I'll get to that in a second. I picked up the shell casing and noted hemlock branches that had been broken off not by wind or weather but number 7½ shotgun pellets. Under and around the

230

branches I found the boot tracks, yours and Mr. Wingo's. I checked them out. He shot at you, didn't he?"

"Not at me."

"Well, he shot to stop you, but you didn't, at least not for more than a waffling step or two. You kept on down into Slash Lick, and the shot explains the piss. Am I right?"

"I have nothing to say on the matter."

"Look, I've been in combat, and some of the best soldiers I ever knew wet their GI drawers or a hell of a lot worse but also stood and fought. Now, I admit I didn't like my first impression of you, you seemed too fussy, but I've changed my thinking. I figure you're all right, Mr. Frampton. Since I left the service, I haven't come across many brave men. My thinking is you qualify. For what it's worth I wanted you to know that before you left High Gap."

"It's worth a great deal to me, Sheriff, and I thank you."

He stood, shook my hand, and left to drive his Dodge cruiser down toward the courthouse. I thought of Charles LeBlanc. Each of these men should've been a rawboned Texan out west of the Pecos, Winchester cocked in hand, squinting at Apache smoke signals among the scorching buttes. For a moment the sheriff had made me feel I stood among them. Maybe I'd write to invite him down to Jessup's Wharf for a tour of Tidewater Virginia or a day of fishing when the shad were running in the Axapomimi.

A phone call from Sam Tuggle authorized Doc Bailey to release Drake's body for ambulance transport to Richmond. At the eleven-o'clock burial Cliff and I served as pallbearers. The afternoon turned mild, and a light southwest breeze bore scents of ware-housed tobacco as well as the alluvial James. Our hands gripped the casket's hinged steel handles as we carried it from the hearse to the grave, and I felt the weight of Drake's body so close beyond my clenched fingers.

The breeze blew across the cemetery's grass and caused wreaths to stir and the scalloped green canopy to flap softly. Seagulls dipped from thermals, their cries seeming not so much quarrelsome as forlorn. The army's Honor Guard raised their rifles and fired three volleys heavenward.

Hundreds attended the service, both friends and those drawn by Drake's celebrity. A garland of cut flowers shaped like a grouse was laid on the casket, the black roses forming a band across the spread tail. I remembered Drake had told me such markings identified male birds. Deborah stood bravely taut, her moist eyes catching glints from the sun.

Father Everett, the Episcopal priest, quoted Drake's words: "'When I hunt the misty high country of the grouse, God runs the ridges beside me.'"

After the service, Cliff and I drove to the house. Deborah hugged and thanked us for loving her Drake. We looked at the fireplace portrait of him standing in the turret of the sand-colored tank— the wind-and-sun-bronzed warrior.

"It helps to know he died among mountains he loved best," she said.

Josey entered, her black hat, dress, hose, and heels bringing high style to a death gathering. She and I, holding drinks, were able to find a moment alone in the den. I would never reveal to her I knew she had lied for Drake.

"I think you might slip by any charges from the government," I told her. "Since you lost your own money, you can't be accused of fraud. The worst you have to fear is a civil action."

"I'm still hanging on to my job and a few loyal customers," she said and looked at the portrait. "Oh, God, he was the best of us," she cried, and I wondered whether it had been Drake not Cliff to whom in our teens she had given her first love.

The three of us stayed till two o'clock before taking embracing leave of Deborah. On the lawn above the fading yellow winter jasmine we told each other we would get together. Cliff and I walked Josey to her Lexus and watched her pull away under the leafless, overreaching oaks.

"Tears become her," Cliff said.

I drove him to his carriage house and turned down his offer of a drink.

"Maybe I'll visit Greece as well as Italy," he said. "Learn the language, sip the wine, swim in the languid Aegean, revive in the pure white light. I want to thank you, Walter. You're a stout fellow in the breach."

We shook hands, he left my car, and I watched him walk to the walled entrance. I waited till he passed through and closed the studded wooden door before I moved on along the street.

I returned to Jessup's Wharf. At three the yellow school bus stopped in front of my office to let Jason off. He scampered across the street, his book bag strapped to his back, his red billed cap pulled low over his brow. His skinny legs appeared so fragile out there among the stopped cars and panting diesels—a lamb among wolves.

He removed his cap and jacket and sat on his chair. Mary Ellen left for the courthouse to record a deed of trust. Jason slid a book from his bag and opened it across his lap. I recognized *Blood Brothers,* the slim volume I'd bought him that pictured the war-painted Indian brave and buckskinned frontiersman facing each other in friendship. When Jason went to the lavatory, he left it on the chair.

I turned away and looked out the window. A conclave of pigeons moved restlessly on the ledge of St. Luke's steeple. Likely the hawk lurked around. All at once the sorrow I had been holding back welled in me. I thought of Josey, Drake, and Cliff, what life had done to us or we to life. I sagged and felt I lacked the strength to straighten my body or lift my head until I realized that Jason had returned, stood at my side, and for the second time since I'd known him was looking directly at me. I saw the fear surface in his enlarged and anguished brown eyes like a predatory shape from the deep.

I gathered myself, forced a smile, and began my double-jointed clown dance, my legs crisscrossing, my eyes rolling, my tongue lagging out. I soft-shoed across the floor and flung my arms about. I envisioned the gorilla approaching and pulling a giant yellow lollipop from my hand. As we snatched it back and forth, I croaked out a hee-haw.

Mary Ellen entered the office and stopped bewildered. The dance became crazy, like a deranged Indian among tom-toms seeking to invoke the Great Spirit, except this dance was for the past—the good, the love, the loss, and above all the humanity.

Jason's expression didn't change, but his devouring eyes stayed lifted to mine, and the shape sank away beneath them—perhaps a portent, a viewing of promise, and something worth reaching to and drawing forth.

THIRTY-SEVEN

At Miss Mabel's I tossed my clothes aside and attempted to sleep, but mostly I smoked and paced my rooms. The dawn's sunlight worked around edges of the blinds, and for once no frost coated the grass and peonies of Miss Mabel's garden. Her washerwoman named Lucinda came Mondays to pick up laundry, and my plastic bag waited bulging full. I also inserted two suits into the chute of the cleaner's drop-off at the Jessup's Mercantile. All items were carried to Williamsburg for the job.

Miss Mabel tapped on the door that separated her side of the house from mine. I'd never been in her living quarters but had glimpsed tasseled carpets, Victorian furniture, and a grandfather clock whose pendulum no longer swung its arcs. I suspected she had stopped the clock, for she herself seemed stuck in time. I had never seen her when she wasn't wearing hose or bleak unfashionable dresses closed at the throat by a cameo brooch. Her gray hair appeared as stiffly set as stove wire, and she held herself rigidly erect, a soldier on parade. Though small of frame, while a teacher at King County Elementary School she had terrified many a hulking oaf or bully with her stern expression and the swift application of a pussy willow switch to their bared calves. I thought of her as being the essence of brave spinsterhood and the old bygone values.

I'd been about to fix myself a drink and before answering her knock hurried to stick my bottle of George Dickel's Tennessee Sour

Mash Whisky behind the peacock fan that covered the living-room fireplace.

"I heard you walking again last night," she said. She held a paper bag. More beaten biscuits, I thought. She also attempted to peer past me into my pantry. So far I'd still been able to hide my liquor supply from her alert and prying eyes.

"Miss Mabel, I'm sorry if I been disturbing you."

"No ifs about it. You do disturb me. You're not sick?"

"No'm, just fine."

"You need sleep. It's as important as food."

"I know."

"I used to have difficulty sleeping, but I now take a little tonic every night before retiring to the bed."

"Tonic?" I asked.

"In moderation," she said and presented the paper bag to me. I carefully opened it. Inside I uncovered a fifth of Black Jack Daniel's. I stared at her.

"I heard about the death of your friend," she said. "You can keep this bottle along with your others in the fireplace. Remember, the good Lord gave us alcohol to be used wisely. A drink before bedtime is a gift from Him to those of us who have trouble sleeping. I often feel there must be times He has the need of a tonic because of the fret we human beings cause Him."

She turned away abruptly and closed the door before I could thank her. I stood holding the bottle until I placed it alongside my George Dickel behind the peacock fan. I tried to envison her on the other side of the door. She would never be the type who slapped her knees laughing, but a smile yes, maybe even a tightly controlled grin.

At my office I looked over calls Mary Ellen had listed on my legal pad. The first was from Charles LeBlanc's brother Edward at Boone and Massey.

"No one's located Prince Jamir," he said, his voice as toneless and regular as a metronome. He was a man who when walking constantly kept his eyes on the ground for either what might be found of use or missteps that would endanger his footing.

"Thus far we're not hurt and of course still hold his first payment for Bellerive in escrow along with the accumulated and accumulating interest," he continued. "Furthermore, we are receiving inquiries from interested parties, chief among them a Charlotte syndicate with a proposal for converting Bellerive into an English village complete with upscale homes, pools, golf course, marina, stables, and use of the airport, while the mansion itself is to become the clubhouse. Stop by and I'll show you their initial presentation."

I sat brooding how it had come to pass that Bellerive with its centuries-old Huguenot heritage would be transformed into a housing development, a splendid one yes, but instead of family and the grandeur of ancient blood belong to a procession of carted, newly rich golfers hitting balls across grass that had once sustained the hoofbeats of Thoroughbreds.

I called my mother in Venice, who told me she and my father were taking daily walks along the beach bordering the Gulf of Mexico. Occasionally my father picked up seashells and studied their configurations and identities by using a book she had bought him. She had started translating Dante.

"A wonderful way to see the universe," she said. "Everything laid out systematically, no questions unanswered. I'm becoming a Catholic."

"And Dad's fine?"

"He's wearing Bermuda shorts now," she said. "In public."

I finally reached Charles LeBlanc late at night in Chinook, Montana.

"Hope you're not telling me I'm out of dollars," he said.

"No, you have some twenty-six thousand left, but you might

need to put off buying that ranch for a time. You will receive Bellerive money eventually, possibly even more than first calculated."

"Better than dirt in the mouth," was his response. "Just keep taking your cut."

Nothing more, and I again admired and envied his stance in the face of adversity.

Mary Ellen helped me hang my portrait of Marse Robert. I often sat at my desk looking at him instead of working. Mary Ellen had quickly realized I wasn't acting myself. She brought a Jerusalem cherry plant to place on my window's ledge. I remembered when I'd first interviewed her for the job she told me she had once been Miss York County. There were moments when I gazed at her that I could see the phantom beauty of a pretty, bare-shouldered eighteen-year-old girl in a shimmering white gown riding on a parade float covered with full-flowering gardenias.

"Country ham and red-eye gravy you can sop up with my buttermilk biscuits," she said, again inviting me to dinner with her and Jason.

"I'll try to get by," I said.

"We'll wait for you," she said.

I drove out to visit Deborah, the late afternoon warm and sweet with a fleeting scent of the looming spring. I found her in her garden, where she knelt planting tulip bulbs to provide the borders for her box bushes. A straw hat shaded her face, and suppressed grief made her appear beautifully and nobly wounded. She removed her gloves, and we drank tea under the trellis strung with bud-swelling wisteria vines. Following my advice, she had hired movers to drive to Blind Sheep and bring Drake's belongings from his cabin.

"It's empty now," she said. "I have no idea what to do with his guns. Would you care for them?"

"I'm no hunter. Why not let Boomer sell them?"

On my recommendation she had rehired Boomer, and he was temporarily at least running Grizzly's.

"And I don't know what to do about the store. I'll need your continued help there."

"We can always find a buyer if it comes to that."

"The one good thing is 'The Truth of the Grouse' will still be published. I have that assurance from Drake's editor."

When I finished my tea, I stood to leave, and after I kissed her cheek she straightened my tie.

"Please come see me often," she said.

I promised I would and drove not directly back to Jessup's Wharf but in order to have a look at Grizzly's headed westward to Powhatan County and into a blasted red sunset that shattered the horizon. Though the store was closed for the day, the ghost grouse had begun to emerge through a gathering twilight.

I sat in the car watching the ghost grouse's luminous whiteness dawn fully in the converging darkness. As of itself or perhaps because the spirit of Dante Alighieri had taken hold of me, my arm raised, and my hand made the sign of the cross.